DEATH

ON

D'URVILLE

Books by Penelope Haines

The Lost One
Helen Had a Sister
(previously published as Princess of Sparta)
Blood Never Lies

The Claire Hardcastle Series:
Death on D'Urville
Straight and Level
Stall Turns

DEATH

ON

D'URVILLE

A Claire Hardcastle

Mystery

PENELOPE HAINES

For information contact;

www.penelopehaines.com

Published by Ithaca Publications, Wellington, New Zealand

Death on D'Urville/ Penelope Haines. -- 1st ed.

ISBN 978-0-473-36070-2

For Rachel,

my daughter-in law.

A brave and accomplished young woman

who has added so much joy to my life

COURAGE

Courage is the price that Life exacts
for granting peace.
The soul that knows it not
Knows no release from little things:
Knows not the livid loneliness of fear,
Nor mountain heights where bitter
joy can hear
The sound of wings.

How can life grant us boon of living, compensate
For dull grey ugliness and pregnant hate
Unless we dare
The soul's dominion?
Each time we
make a choice, we pay
With courage to behold the resistless day,
And count it fair.

Amelia Earhart

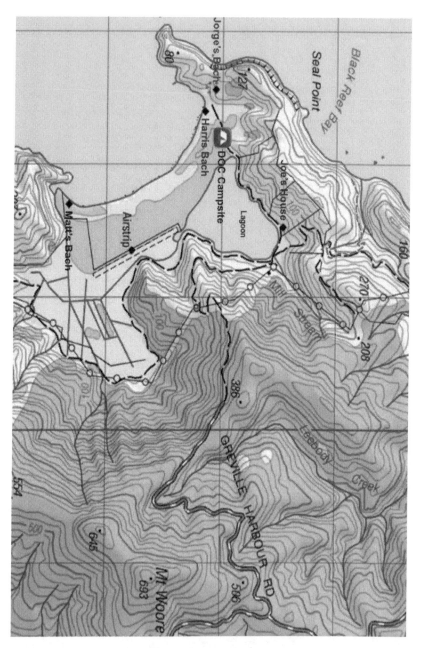

Map of Greville Harbour

PROLOGUE

THE BODY SLUMPED IN THE SAND. An abandoned shell of lifeless flesh, incontrovertibly dead. *Dead, dead, dead.*

The words rang in the head and twined into a chain. A necklace of finality that could be grasped and wound round the fist like a talisman; a rosary of the joyful mysteries; a protection against the evil this man had tried to spread.

But his words weren't dead. He was a writer and they would still live on in his computer.

They must be destroyed.

It was a short step to the house. A quick glance around to see if there were watchers, but the landscape was empty. The house was unlocked. Who locked their home here, when the total population of the bay only grew to around twenty, and that in high summer?

The laptop sat on the table. A tea towel wrapped round the hand to prevent fingerprints. Fumbling to find the keys through the cloth, but it was easy to identify and erase the file.

It would have been useful to have time to search the place, but that would have to wait. For now it was enough to know the man and his words had been wiped out.

CHAPTER ONE

I FELT THE WHEELS TOUCH ON GRAVEL and let the aircraft roll forward down the strip. I gave a sigh of completely unadulterated pleasure. (I was alone and entitled to do so.) God, but I loved my job, and on a day like that when the sky was clear, the wind calm and the surroundings so breathtakingly beautiful, I couldn't believe my good fortune. My office was my plane. It didn't come much closer to heaven than that.

I turned the aircraft and taxied back, pulling off the strip in the space beside the barn. It was the only area wide enough for me to park without obstructing the runway. Another aircraft was already there in the shade of the dunes. I took a look and gave a snort of recognition. I knew that plane, knew it really well. ZK-FOG was registered to Paraparaumu Aviation, and I had watched Roger sign her out to a pair of foreign pilots a week ago. The little Piper Cub was supposed to be miles to the east of us, somewhere in the vicinity of Kaikoura.

How it had ended up on the strip at D'Urville Island I couldn't imagine. I thought Roger would be surprised as well. He had authorised the pilots to fly in New Zealand and accepted their intentions when he leased the aircraft. I wondered whether he had specifically briefed the pair for strip flying. It's one thing to land at a promulgated airport, quite another to fly into the often unpredictable conditions experienced on little country strips. There could be insurance repercussions if the pilots had strayed beyond the limits of their hire.

I parked into the wind and shut the engine down. I clambered out and took a minute or two to stretch my legs before climbing up to dip the wing tanks and check the fuel levels.

Jorge wasn't there waiting for me, which was unusual, nor was there any sign of FOG's two pilots. I looked at my watch. 3.50 pm. I hoped Jorge wasn't going to be late. Sod's Law if he was, of course.

It had been a year since David and I separated, a year of quiet living while I readjusted to singledom. I hadn't seen anyone significant, and hadn't wanted to. Tonight's dinner with Sam would be my first venture into the social world of dating. I wasn't certain it was a good idea. Sam was a nice guy but …

It was the 'but' that worried me. I wasn't sure whether the issue was Sam, or my response to him. I appreciated his sense of humour, and found him a pleasant colleague. We'd met at work where he had a habit of popping in for a visit in his spare time from running the flight information service in the airport tower. I liked him, but he didn't set my world ablaze. Still, at twenty-six, did I really expect a guy to sweep me off my feet? I'd already invested four years of my life in one unsatisfactory relationship.

David had once set me on fire, and there had been a time when we seemed very good together. We'd even talked about getting married. I eventually realised the months I'd waited for him to propose to me were, unfortunately, being replaced by an increasing number of months when such a proposal would be deeply unwelcome.

I'd been shocked two years ago when my mother's death forced me to understand I'd unconsciously fallen into a pattern of behaviour with David modelled on her own unsatisfactory relationship with my father. Luckily I'd recognised it in time.

I took stock of my situation. I wanted more from life than David would ever understand, and our expectations and ambitions were increasingly divergent. Finally, I gathered my courage, confronted him and severed the relationship. David, predictably, had no idea what I was talking about and blamed the whole debacle on mysterious 'women's issues', which rather proved my point.

I looked along the airstrip to the north. Still no sign of Jorge. I decided to follow the other track that led through the sand dunes down to the beach. Greville Harbour's particular geography means the beautiful crescent of the bay is separated from the airstrip by a wide stretch of dunes. The only chance I had of getting cell phone reception was to climb to the top of one and hope I picked up a signal. I plodded down the track, found a likely hill and climbed to its summit.

I phoned Jorge's mobile; it went straight to answerphone. Either he had it switched off, or more likely, he was out of range and already walking towards the plane. I shrugged and called Paraparaumu Aviation.

My boss answered, and I filled him in on FOG's presence on the strip. He sounded surprised at first, then amused.

"Crafty buggers," he commented. "No, I'm not worried about their competence, but they certainly didn't tell me they were planning to end up on D'Urville. I'm surprised they even found the strip. It's not that easy to spot from the air unless you know where it is. Ah well, no harm done, but I'll have a word when they get back."

He confirmed there had been no message from Jorge warning me he would be late. I sighed, hung up and looked round. Off the headland at the southern end of the bay I could see a small boat in the water. Matt and his family out fishing, I guessed.

I began the walk north along the sand towards Jorge's bach. I was in a catch-22 situation. I couldn't see the airstrip from the beach, nor could anyone on the strip see me, but if Jorge arrived he would at least see the plane ready, and realise I had gone searching for him.

If I hadn't felt pressured by the need to be back in Paraparaumu in time for my date with Sam, I would have enjoyed the exercise. Greville is a lovely curve of sand, and I walked its length in solitude, the silence only broken by the calls of the seagulls.

I had reached the northern end of the beach, at the foot of the steps that led to the terrace and Jorge's bach, when I heard the roar of FOG's engine as she took off from the strip. I stood, gazing up, shielding my eyes from the setting sun, as the little Cub climbed out of the harbour and up over the sea. I could see her making the eastward turn which would bring her up over the range towards Cook Strait, and then a direct path back to her home airport.

I grinned. I'd missed seeing the pilots. They must have come back via the landward track.

I climbed the steps. Jorge's bach lay to the left. Ahead was the 'mystery house'. I had been flying into D'Urville for two years or more, and this house was always deserted. I had no idea who owned it.

With a shock, I saw the house was occupied. Windows and the front door were flung wide open, and a young couple were sitting on the deck, legs dangling over the edge into the tussock grass, while the man fed driftwood into their brazier. I reached up to wave.

The man gave a perceptible start when he saw me but replied with a tentative gesture of his own. His companion, whom I saw was very young, registered my presence with a sort of horror, sprang to her feet and bolted inside. She was a little too far away for me to be certain, but I got the impression she had been crying.

I shrugged, nodded again to the man and made my way to Jorge's.

He wasn't at home, which was fine if he was already at the strip waiting for me, but it was soon obvious to me that he hadn't locked the house up. I tried the back door, found it open and went in. The backpack Jorge normally carried was propped against the wall. With insufficient baggage to fill out its interior it had collapsed in its mid-section with a sad, sagging look of a failed fighter about it. The straps were undone and trailed loosely across the floor. I picked it up to check. Jorge had made no attempt to even begin packing.

I looked around. Jorge was a writer, and if what he said was true, he spent his days on D'Urville either wandering the hills or writing his novels. Early on he had discovered I was a reader – in that broad sense of the word that describes a person who reads everything from Victorian novels to the writing on cereal packets.

We had discussed books and explored our mutual interest in words during our flights to and from the island. It had become a game – a challenge between us, for each to bring a new and unusual word to the conversation every time I ferried him to the island. Today I had chosen 'solipsistic'. I was reasonably certain he wouldn't know the word, but sometimes he surprised me. Like many people for whom English is a second language, his vocabulary was considerable and eclectic.

A year or so back he'd shown me the cover design he'd chosen for his latest novel, featuring a man heavily clad in some space-age type of armour with a scantily dressed blonde, bound in chains, at his feet. I gathered the story was set in some dystopian future, was ultraviolent and possibly pornographic.

He had laughed at the expression on my face. "Trust me, Claire, there's a market for my books. They're very popular and sell particularly well in Japan and Germany."

It wasn't the kind of book that appealed to me, but I could see his life at the bach would be congenial for whatever muse inspired his work. With no Wi-Fi, television or phones to distract him, he could, as he said, churn out a couple of thousand words a day, and frequently more.

The sink was full of dishes, and his laptop sat open on his desk, a book beside it. With the automatic habit of a recidivist bibliophile I checked the title. *Horowhenua: its Maori place-names & their topographic & historical background.* I flicked through the pages. It looked interesting but didn't get me any nearer to finding Jorge. He wasn't the tidiest of men, but I had never known him leave the house without cleaning up and packing out the rubbish.

I wondered whether, by some bizarre series of errors, I had come on the wrong day. I pulled out my phone to call Roger, but there was no signal. I cursed, shoved the phone back into my pocket and left the bach.

The man at the mystery house was still tending his fire, which had now caught and was burning merrily in the grate. I waved again as I passed.

Feeling grumpy, I took the inland track back to the airstrip. The path led deeper into the dunes before emerging on the landward side of them, on the shores of the lagoon. This brackish store of swampy water was home to a wide variety of fowl, the most numerous and dramatic being the black swans. Flax, bulrushes and sedge lined the edges. It was an attractive spot, protected by the seaward dunes from any coastal breezes, so the temperature remained warmer than average all year long. This late in the season the Department of Conservation campsite here was empty. It was getting too cold at night to tempt punters in a tent. Even in high summer there were rarely more than two tents pitched on the site.

I strode along, in equal part perturbed and annoyed. Either I had got the wrong date, or something had happened to Jorge. I tried not to worry, but D'Urville is a bush-covered island of steep, mountainous terrain. A lot could go wrong for a middle-aged man, inexperienced in bush craft, who ventured unwisely into territory he couldn't handle.

I had swung past a series of sand dunes before I stopped, realising something in the recurring pattern of marram grass, tussock and sand looked odd. I traced my unease to a huddle of material half-visible in a bowl amongst the dunes and walked over to see the anomaly more clearly.

Jorge was lying sprawled in the hollow at the foot of a dune, just off the track. He was motionless, his head half turned away from me.

CHAPTER TWO

"SWEET JESUS!" I FELL TO MY knees beside him and gently turned his head towards me as plans for loosening clothes and administering CPR jostled in my head. "Jorge, wake up." I tapped his face lightly. There was no response. I sat back on my heels and looked at him carefully. His skin was waxy pale and there was no sign of breathing. I reached forward again to check for a pulse in the neck and caught sight of a wide smear of blood across my forearm.

"Oh, shit." I rolled him over, more urgently this time, and looked at the back of his head. The hair was a mess of clotted blood, sand and other material I preferred not to consider. Whatever had hit him had landed hard.

I laid him gently back down on the sand and considered the situation. Jorge was dead, I had no doubt about that. Not long enough for rigor mortis to have set in yet, so whatever had occurred must be fairly recent. The body still had a faint and rather repellent, residual warmth.

I drew a deep, shuddering breath and tried to curb the nausea that threatened to overpower me. I bent forward so my head rested on my knees, and concentrated on breathing. It wouldn't do for me to faint or vomit.

He may have been a client, but I'd liked Jorge. He was an entertaining passenger and I'd enjoyed our flights together.

Eventually I looked round for whatever had hit him, but there was no obvious object lying nearby. It would have been impossible for him to have hit his head accidentally out here in the sand dunes; there were no low-hanging branches or falling rocks. I glanced round uneasily. I had seen no -one else around, but whatever had happened here was deliberate.

I grabbed my phone and keyed 111. No signal, of course. I muttered some foul words as I stood up. It felt wrong to leave him, but I had to get help.

I clambered up the dunes until my phone registered a network. "Fire, police or ambulance?"

I made my report. "Yes, a body. Yes, I'm sure he's dead. Greville Harbour. Where's that? On D'Urville Island at the top of the Marlborough Sounds. D apostrophe U R V I L L E." I spelt it out slowly.

To do the woman justice, most people wouldn't have heard of the place. She was calm, efficient and thorough as she took down the details. Eventually, after being put on hold several times, I was finally put through to Homicide.

The man on the end of the line was business-like. Would I please stay with the body and guard the site until the police arrived? No, I wasn't to cover the body or touch it.

I wondered about this last instruction. I'd already touched the body, moved it and tromped all around the site. I hated to think how much evidence I had damaged.

"How long will it take for someone to arrive?" I asked. I glanced at the sky. Darkness came early on these autumn evenings, and I needed sufficient light to be able to fly the plane off the strip. There was also a curfew back at Paraparaumu. I didn't fancy being stuck at D'Urville overnight, trying to bed down in a very small aircraft if the police didn't arrive in time.

I explained my problem to the voice on the phone.

"We should have personnel on site within an hour," he said. "We'll be using the Westpac rescue chopper out of Wellington. I'll let them know you need to be released as soon as they arrive."

I sighed, but agreed. It would be a long wait.

I wondered what I was supposed to do if his murderer was still about. There had been no suggestion by the man from Homicide that I might be at risk, and I would probably have pooh-poohed it had he mentioned it. All the same, I felt very alone and exposed out there in the dunes.

To ameliorate the feeling I phoned work. Roger answered again, and I briefed him on what had happened.

"Are you all right?" He sounded horrified. "Are you safe? Is there anyone who can sit with you?"

I was grateful for his reaction. "No, I'm fine," I assured him. "I'll just be late back to base."

"I'll have a wine waiting on the counter for you," he assured me.

I grinned. "I'll need more than one by the time I get back." I felt better after I had spoken to Roger. At least someone who cared about me knew where I was.

I tried to phone Sam, but his number went direct to voicemail. I left a message explaining I would be late and would catch up with him when I got back.

I returned to Jorge and sat down on the dune beside him.

Fifteen minutes later I was getting chilled. No doubt partly due to shock, but the angle of the sun was lower in the sky, so the dune was now half in shadow. Worse, a slight wind had sprung up and seemed to be sucking the warmth out of me. I stuck it out for a while. I didn't have a jacket in the plane – I hadn't needed one on that warm afternoon. My only chance of getting another layer of clothing was from Jorge's bach. I looked down at him. He wasn't going anywhere, and I hadn't seen anyone else I should protect the site from. I apologised mentally to Jorge for leaving him. The bach was a ten-minute walk away. I decided to chance it.

The young couple had moved indoors, the fire burned to ashes. There was no one else around as I made my way to Jorge's house. I wondered about the propriety of entering what I assumed was now a crime scene, then shrugged my shoulders. I had been in here earlier, and my fingerprints were already all over the door handle.

There were a number of jackets and waterproofs hanging up in the porch. I reached for a polar fleece. It was too big for me, but heavy and blessedly windproof. I shrugged it on, grateful for the sudden warmth and returned to keep vigil by the body.

A seagull perched on top of the dune, eyeing Jorge with far too much enthusiasm. I shuddered, waved my arms at it and it rose into the air with a squawk of protest before settling back down again a metre further away. I checked Jorge, but mercifully there was no damage to his body. There were a lot of seagulls at Greville Harbour. I suppose they couldn't be blamed for being opportunistic, but suddenly I hated them. I glared at the bird, which ignored me.

I sat down and played Solitaire on my mobile phone until I heard the beat of the chopper's blades, then got up, climbed the dune and waved to guide them in. They landed on the beach.

I sat back down and waited by the body. It would be the last time I saw this man, and I felt moved to say something while we were still alone. "I suppose this is goodbye, Jorge … I'm sorry we didn't have that last flight home, and … I hope they find who did this to you."

Of course, talking to the dead does leave uncomfortable pauses in the conversation, and I felt slightly silly addressing a dead man, but there was something satisfying about being able to say farewell.

I was relieved to hear the voices of the men coming down the track.

CHAPTER THREE

THE PAIR INTRODUCED THEMSELVES AS DETECTIVE Inspector Trevor Mallet and Detective Sergeant Pete Funnell. I tried to pin the names in my brain. I'm not good with titles, but DI Mallet was clearly the boss. He was a tall, elegant figure with well-groomed hair, stylish casual clothes and, I noticed as he shook my hand, very clean fingernails. I was uneasily aware I was not at my pristine best. I put him in his early fifties, but it was hard to tell. He introduced himself with grave courtesy before turning to look at Jorge.

Detective Sergeant Funnell was a different kettle of fish. He looked to me like the sort of scrapper usually found in a bar on a Saturday night. If I'd met him in a different context I would have put him down as a hard-playing rugby man. He wasn't tall, but he fairly exuded fitness. I could see an admirable muscle structure operating under his shirt and jeans. Close-cropped fair hair, high Slavic cheekbones and a cheeky grin. I was glad to see he was on the side of law and order, otherwise I would have laid good money that he came from a long line of larrikins.

"Claire Hardcastle, isn't it? Thank you for waiting for us."

I summoned what dignity I could, as a steely-eyed commercial pilot, and shook hands, aware my arm was still streaked with

Jorge's blood.

Pete took down my basic details to confirm them. He had obviously received the briefing notes recorded from my phone call.

I gave him the names of the other people around the harbour. "The Johnstones own the bach at the southern end of the bay. The whole family is there at the moment because of the Easter holidays, and they've got a couple of friends staying with them. Roger, my boss, flew them down last week.

"Joe McBeth lives in the house at the head of the lagoon. Up to a few years ago he used to farm this place. Then DOC bought the property from him, and he's stayed on as a sort of caretaker. I don't know a lot about him. We just call up when we want to fly in, so he doesn't have stock on the strip.

"I've never seen the bach beside Jorge's used before, so I don't know the names of the people there. They're a young couple. I waved to them when I was looking for Jorge. She seemed to be crying." I paused to allow time to think. "I don't know how they came in here. We didn't fly them in, so maybe they got a flight out of Wellington, or maybe the water taxi dropped them off."

"OK," said Pete. "I understand you need to leave here while it's still daylight? That's absolutely fine. We'll send a crime squad man to interview you and take your statement when you get back to Paraparaumu Airport. Please don't leave the airport until he does. Is that OK with you? Great."

With that I was dismissed. I felt bereft and unimportant as I made my way back to the aircraft. Still, it was great to be back in the cockpit in 'my world', and there was a reassuring normalcy to the checks and drills before I taxied to the start of the runway, put my foot on the brakes and ran the throttle up to full. I felt the aircraft quiver around me with power before I released the brakes and let her rip down the strip and into the air. As I turned in the climb I looked down to see the chopper on the beach and the two men examining the site around the body.

"Rest in peace, Jorge," I muttered, although I doubted whether either he or his corpse would be getting much rest in the days to come.

I was shattered by the time I pulled up outside the hangar. Sunset had long since passed and it was dark as I taxied in. Roger and Greig, my fellow instructor at Paraparaumu Aviation, came out to meet me and helped me manhandle the aircraft into the hangar. I heaved a sigh of relief as Greig slammed the heavy sliding doors shut.

Roger steered me inside to the waiting room and thrust a large glass of wine into my hand. "Drink that, Hardcastle, then tell us all about it," he commanded.

Roger, my boss, uses surnames rather than first names. This probably dates from time spent in the military early in his life. He's short on height, large on personality and a powerhouse of energy. He's in his sixties but shows no sign of retiring, and rules his small kingdom with a firm hand. Although he's been in New Zealand for the best part of fifty years he still has the lilting accent of an Ulsterman, and all the wayward charm of the Irish.

I accepted the drink gratefully and sank into the old armchair. Roger sat opposite on an upright, and Greig sprawled on the sofa.

I told them all I could, although I couldn't add much to the conversation I'd had earlier with Roger.

"Why would anyone want to murder Jorge?" asked Greig.

"That's probably the first question the police will try and answer," said Roger. "He was a writer, of course, and seemed like a perfectly inoffensive man. Not the sort to invite violence. You're sure it's murder?"

I shrugged. "I can't think of any other way he could have got that whacking great blow to the head. Not unless a super-strong seagull dropped a brick on him from a great height."

I belatedly remembered the blood still on my arm and went to wash up. When I checked my reflection in the mirror I realised I was still wearing the jacket I'd borrowed. I'd forgotten I had it. Crap; I should have mentioned it to Detective Pete, but it was too late now. I'd hand it back when I got the chance. At the moment it was warm, cosy and probably wasn't hindering the murder enquiry. I left it on.

The police down at D'Urville were presumably doing whatever

detectives do in the case of murder. I felt myself relaxing and accepted another drink. It wasn't often that Roger or Greig were prepared to shout me alcohol. I decided to make hay while the sun shone.

*   *   *

He entered quietly, no mean feat as the swing doors to the office were notorious for the squeak of their hinges. Greig noticed him first, and started.

Roger looked up. "Good evening," he said, standing up. "The office is shut for the day, but can I help you?"

"Detective Senior Sergeant Jack Body." He held out his hand as Roger stood. They shook hands formally. "I'm here to speak to Claire Hardcastle."

I gave a sigh. I'd forgotten the statement I was supposed to give the police. I hoped the alcohol hadn't stripped my brain too much.

"That would be me," I said, uncurling myself from the chair.

We shook hands and he presented his ID card to me.

"Is there somewhere we can talk?" he asked.

"I'll use one of the briefing rooms if that's OK?" I asked Roger. He nodded.

I led the way into the room and turned to face Detective Senior Sergeant Body. The gut-impacting effect of his physical presence was startling. If his boss was a silver fox, and his junior colleague a reformed rugby lout, then Jack Body was male model material. Not in the artificially thin, androgynous toy-boy sense, but he was one of the most beautiful men I had ever seen.

I think I may have gaped at him as I took in his dark hair, height, well-proportioned physique and stylishly conservative clothes. I saw a slight flicker of amusement cross his face and pulled myself together. He was a detective, I reminded myself firmly, in the business of extracting information from villains. He would be well aware of the effect he had on women and undoubtedly used his looks as a tool.

I have an unreasonable distrust of excessively good-looking

people. I find their physical perfection intimidating and assume, arbitrarily, they are both vain and vacuous. When I was in standard four we had a classmate called Tiffany, whose assumption of her own privilege and superiority based purely on her prettiness, set me up for a lifetime of prejudice. I reminded myself that David had also been a good-looking man.

It was unlikely that a detective would actually be stupid, but if DSS Body thought to win me over by his looks and charm, he would be mistaken.

"Please sit down." I gestured to a chair on one side of the formica table and sat down opposite him. I pushed aside the little model of a Cessna and the briefing notes we used to teach students to allow him room to open his folder and write.

"What can I help you with?"

He led me through the information I had already given Pete, starting with my name, flying credentials and address. We established the time I had arrived at Greville Harbour and the approximate timings of everything else that had occurred up until I found poor Jorge. Occasionally he stopped to expand on a point. He was admirably thorough. I realised as I spoke that I had forgotten to mention the presence of FOG and her pilots when I had spoken to Pete.

"Would you have details of the men who hired the aircraft?"

"Roger will have all the info. He briefed them and checked their credentials before he leased them the plane."

"What nationality was the murdered man?"

I had to think about that. "I assume a New Zealand national, but I don't know. He had an accent, and Jorge Jorgensen suggests his background was Scandinavian, but he never spoke of being foreign and I never asked."

"The two men who hired this other aircraft – FOG? They were also Scandinavian?"

"Well, yes. I think they were Norwegian. Again, you'd have to ask Roger."

We covered every minute detail I could recall. I found it exhausting – not so much the act of remembering, but trying to transmit those memories into words that exactly conveyed what

I meant; nothing less or more. After an hour or so of having my every word picked over by Jack Body I had revised my opinion. I no longer distrusted him, I detested him. He made the interrogators at Guantanamo Bay look tame. He didn't even have to waterboard his victim. His steady, even-toned questions were enough to wear away stone. On several occasions I noticed he asked the same question twice, but in different words, and wondered if he was trying to catch me out.

I assumed Jack Body viewed me as a suspect. At least I'd been able to wash Jorge's blood off my arm. I wondered how long it took for flesh to cool. Jorge had still been warm when I touched him. If Jorge's time of death was established as before I had flown out from Paraparaumu, then I would be in the clear. Even if he'd died when I was in transit, there must have been someone who'd heard my plane come in and land. I didn't think I was in any danger of being arrested.

Finally he thanked me, let me sign my name to my words, and stood up. "I'll get it typed up. You'll need to go down to the station tomorrow and sign the completed statement."

I nodded, seeing no need to be courteous after the gruelling time he'd given me. I felt stiff with resentment.

I led him back to see Roger. Sam had arrived while I was in with Detective Body and had been sitting chatting. I gave him a smile as Roger confirmed the time I'd left Paraparaumu, and introduced Jack to Sam.

"Sam keeps records of all flights in and out of the airport. He's also got transcripts of any radio calls made. He'll be back on duty tomorrow morning."

Jack nodded. He took copies of all the documents relating to FOG's pilots – which included photos of their passports and foreign pilots' licences – and grunted when he saw that. "They shouldn't be too hard to track down."

He shook hands all round and left. I collapsed back into the armchair feeling as if I had been put through the wringer. The clock on the wall read nine o'clock.

Sam watched Jack walk out the door. "You can always tell a cop, can't you?" he remarked.

"You can?" asked Roger.

"Yeah, even in mufti there's the physical build, the arrogance, the attitude. You know what I mean."

As I'd been the recipient of that attitude over the last hour or so I wasn't inclined to comment. My psyche felt bruised from the interrogation, and I deeply loathed DSS Body and everything about him.

Roger gave a non-committal grunt. "As long as he doesn't arrest Hardcastle, I don't mind. Oh, and Greig said to say goodnight to you before he left," Roger added.

I sat up. "Thanks. I'd better head for home as well; I'm completely knackered."

Roger nodded. "What have you got on tomorrow? Anything important? You can come in an hour later if you want."

I smiled at him. "Nothing that's vital, but I'll be OK. Thanks for the offer, though." It was indeed a kind thought, but I also knew Greig would be in like a ferret, trying to pick up my flights or students if I wasn't there to defend my turf.

I grinned. Pilots are tough, and not just because we fly planes.

CHAPTER FOUR

OBEDIENTLY I TRAILED OFF TO THE local police station the next morning and signed my statement. It was already there, neatly printed, and I wondered what sort of work hours Jack kept. I'd felt exhausted after my interview with him.

Although I'd said I had nothing very vital on for the next couple of days, I had a few students, one of whom was due to sit his private pilot's licence. Tom was a bright guy, who worked, I thought, as a journalist somewhere, although I'd never asked him the details. He'd done well with his lessons, but aviation was a new world for him, and he still struggled to get his head round some basic concepts. His flying was adequate, but his grasp of theory was sketchy so I spent time battling his incomprehension for an hour or two. I refused to put students up for their exam unless I knew they would pass. So far it had panned out, and I'd never had a failure yet. I intended to maintain that record, hence my badgering of poor Tom.

I emerged from the briefing room feeling much as I'd felt after my interview with Jack Body.

I had a scenic flight in the Tiger Moth that afternoon, so I struggled into my flying suit. Naturally my shoe got stuck in the leg of the thing as I tried to pull it on, and Roger grinned as I hopped around the office trying to sort myself out. I scowled at him, grabbed the leather helmet off the hook and went out to prepare the aircraft. The client, who had been given a voucher for Christmas, was very keen, and enthused about the romance of early aviation.

"Marvellous old machines, aren't they?" he said, patting the old Tiger Moth like a horse. "Just imagine the stories this old bird could tell."

I smiled and nodded, although I wasn't a great fan of old aircraft. Canvas wings and wire strings were all too reminiscent of *Puff the Magic Dragon*, and I loathed the chore of spinning the propeller by hand. I much preferred a glass cockpit, ergonomically designed seats, electric ignition and a degree of comfort. Open cockpits get very cold when you're a thousand feet up. Still, it made a certain type of punter very happy to relive Biggles's fantasies, and doing a loop or a barrel roll had an extra dimension when the cockpit was open to the elements.

Ten minutes after I'd got back into the office my phone went.

"What the fuck's that racket?" blurted Roger as he took in its strident ringtone.

"Hey, is that Sheldon from *The Big Bang Theory?*" asked Greig appreciatively. "That's cool."

"Switch the bloody thing off," demanded Roger, "and don't let me hear it again."

I gave him a deprecating look and checked the screen.

Roger subsided with a muttered grumble.

Oh hell, it was Kate. I hadn't got round to phoning her last night.

"Hi," I said.

"Claire, I've just got the *Kapiti Observer* and you're front-page news. I saw your photo first of all, and then there's this frigging great headline: 'Local pilot first on murder scene'. I start reading, and it's all about you. Why didn't you phone me? Christ, Claire, you might have been killed yourself. Who knows what the murderer was after? You could at least have let me know before I had to read about it like this."

I tried to interrupt, but Kate was obviously in for the long haul. Now she was fussing about the hazards of flying, how Dad should never have got me started on such a dangerous career and how her children didn't want to lose their aunt.

I walked outside and onto the apron. If I've got to have someone shouting at me, I prefer not to have the whole office listening in. At last she simmered down sufficiently for me to get a word in. "I'm sorry, Kate, I really am. I meant to phone you last night, but the truth is, when I got home I had a bit of a meltdown. It took a while for me to settle, and by the end I wasn't thinking about anything very much apart from sleep. But I am sorry – I know I should have called you."

There was silence for a bit.

"I know," said Kate. I realised suddenly that she was crying. "It's just that it's you and me against the world, and I couldn't bear something to happen to you." Well, that was a bit of an exaggeration – she had her husband Martin and the girls – but I knew what she meant. When our parents split up, Kate and I had promised to always be there for each other.

"I'm sorry, Kate," I said again. "Don't cry. It all ended safely so there's nothing to fuss about." I heard a sniff at the other end of the phone and felt a pang of guilt.

*　　*　　*

Roger was cheerful when I got back into the office. My student, Tom, had passed his test, so Roger was pleased with me. It irritated him when he had to fail a student and, once the miserable student slunk away with their tail between their legs, Roger usually bailed their instructor up and pointed out their deficiencies as a trainer.

"How long do you give him before he drives in to the CAA to pick his new licence up?" I asked.

It was a standing joke that no new pilot ever waited for their licence to arrive in the mail.

"He said he wants to go flying on the weekend, so I guess he'll be driving down there this arvo to give them the paperwork, and sitting on their doorstep tomorrow to pick it up," Roger grinned.

* * *

Sam phoned, and we arranged to pick up pizza that evening and eat it down at the beach. I was relieved. The casual nature of the picnic eliminated the pressures and expectations of a formal date. We sat at a picnic table and looked out towards the triangular shape of Kapiti Island. The sun was going down and the sky was stained with rich, warm colours. Paraparaumu Beach is a lovely spot on a fine evening.

Sam wanted to know about Jorge's death, so conversation wasn't a problem as I retold the story.

"So what happens next?" he asked eventually.

"As far as we're concerned? Nothing, I should think. Unless they decide to arrest me, I doubt if we'll hear from them again."

He grinned at me. "You don't look an obvious type to commit murder."

"You never know," I said darkly, thinking of the number of times I'd thought of throttling David.

Sam proved to be a relaxed and friendly companion, and it was easy to build on the working camaraderie we'd already established. For a while we talked shop. The aviation industry in New Zealand is a small community, and we inevitably had friends and contacts in common.

"Why are you working for FIS rather than flying?" I asked.

Sam shrugged. "I'd racked up a large student loan and couldn't afford to wait for years before I started to make money as a pilot. A friend had done the training a year before me, and it sounded OK, so I joined up."

"Do you fly anymore?" I asked. I'd never seen Sam taking a plane out, but that didn't mean he wasn't flying out of some other airport.

"No. At first it was because I couldn't afford it, and then I sort of got out of the way of it."

I couldn't imagine anyone voluntarily giving up flying, but horses for courses, I suppose. Not everyone was as passionate about it as I was.

We agreed to go to the movies on Saturday night. Maybe I had been too cautious about Sam. It had been a pleasant interlude, and to my relief Sam made no lover-like advances, just kissed me on the cheek as we parted.

"See you tomorrow," he said casually before turning and walking away.

* * *

Since I'd separated from David I'd been living in a small cottage attached to a farm, in the hills at the back of Paraparaumu. I loved where I lived. The setting was sufficiently rural to ensure I felt permanently on holiday, far away from my workaday life. When I turned down my long drive I felt I'd left civilisation behind me. It was also less than a ten-minute journey to the airport. I was very careful about who I gave my address to, and guarded my privacy fiercely.

My best friend Jen had invited me to join her flat when I left David, but I'd been determined to make a go of living on my own, without the crutch of a flatmate. For four years I'd been part of a couple, and I didn't think I could go back to the girlish world of flatting, fighting for space to hang out undies on the line, and getting plastered every Friday night at a nightclub. I reckoned I needed time to learn to be a grown-up and manage on my own. Most of the time I found I enjoyed my own company. I would love to have had a dog, but the reality of the hours I worked made it impractical, so I made do with the Siamese cat I had kept when David and I split.

* * *

I realised when I got home that I'd forgotten to hand Jorge's jacket in to the police and cursed myself. There was something about the damn thing that seemed to bring on amnesia. I took it off the hanger and began to fold it neatly. I could take it to the police station the next time I had a chance.

I zipped it up and laid it face down on my bed, folding the first side in and straightening the sleeve. I was folding the second side when I felt the faint crackle of paper. I picked the jacket up, turned it over and ran my hands through the pockets. I knew there was nothing in the hip pockets because I'd already used them to keep my hands warm, but the inside breast pocket revealed a used envelope. It was addressed to Jorge. I looked on the reverse. He'd apparently used it as scrap paper. Scrawled on the back was:

40 48 28 84 173 50 02 48 40 48 39 87 173 48 03 21

I studied the numbers but could make no sense or pattern from them. I wondered whether Jorge had copied out a brain-teaser to work on at the bach. I would hand it to the police and let them work it out. But first of all, I went to my printer and photocopied the puzzle to work on later myself.

CHAPTER
FIVE

T HE NEXT EVENING I ARRIVED HOME and flung
open the French doors to the veranda. I sat with my back
jammed against the doorpost, a large glass of wine in my
hand. Nelson, my cat, had commandeered my lap, and both of us
were enjoying the last of the sun when the phone rang.

I was tempted to ignore it, but the caller persisted. "Hello?"

"Is that Claire Hardcastle?"

"Speaking."

"It's PC Roberts here. I believe you were a friend of Jorge
Jorgensen?"

I was caught unawares. "Well," I stammered, "I wouldn't say
we were friends exactly. I used to fly him out to his bach as part
of my job, that's all. Not a real friend."

The voice was impatient. "Yes, but you knew him. You found
his body, didn't you?"

I admitted cautiously that this was so.

"Good." She sounded relieved. "Can you come down to the
funeral directors on Kapiti Road and identify his body for us,
please?"

"Oh," I gasped. "I mean, we weren't close. I'm not family. I
don't think I should be the one. Why me?"

She sounded apologetic. "We haven't been able to find any family, and we need to get the body identified legally."

I looked at the now empty wine glass I was holding. "I don't think I can," I said. "I've been drinking, and I don't think I should drive."

"Well, have you got someone who can drive you down?"

"No, I live alone."

There was silence at the other end.

"I'll call you back in a minute," she said at last.

Two minutes later she rang again.

"Detective Senior Sergeant Jack Body said he'll pick you up in five minutes and run you down there."

I barely had time to clean my teeth (no point in breathing alcohol over an officer on duty) and grab the jacket.

I slid into the seat beside him and handed the coat over.

He looked at it without touching it. "What is it?"

"Jorge's jacket," I said. "I borrowed it when I was on D'Urville because I was cold and then forgot to hand it back."

"You should have mentioned it before," he said curtly as he took it.

"I would've if I'd remembered," I said with some acidity. "There's a piece of paper in one of the pockets."

Yep, my first impression of him had been correct. He was a surly, arrogant dick.

He felt round the jacket, found the envelope and looked at it in silence.

"I couldn't work out what it was," I said helpfully. "Perhaps it's a puzzle?"

He grunted, put the paper away and started the car.

We drove in silence to the funeral parlour.

Here I was taken in hand by a very nice, sympathetic woman. "Have you ever seen a dead body?" she asked.

I shook my head. "Well, only Jorge the other day."

"Ah, you're the one who found him?" Her voice was kind. "It's very peaceful and quite clear the person has moved on and isn't in the shell of their body anymore, so there's nothing to worry about."

She took me through to the room where Jorge was laid out. Jack remained behind.

Jorge's corpse looked more worn than when I had seen it last. I suppose it would. He'd been dead for three days. I was just grateful there was no obvious smell. I formally identified him.

When we came out Jack was hunched over the table, frowning at Jorge's envelope. He pocketed it as I arrived. "All done? OK, just sign here, here and here." He handed me a clipboard. I signed obediently and duly testified to the corpse being the remains of Jorge Jorgensen.

"Thank you," said Jack when I'd finished. He smiled his devastating smile at the other woman, and I watched her melt in its warmth. What a poser, I thought, glaring at him.

"We're all done here?"

She nodded and showed us out.

Jack led the way back to his car.

"What did you make of Jorge's puzzle?" I asked once I was seated.

Jack shrugged. "Don't know. It's probably not important. Just one of those strange bits of evidence that crops up in any investigation."

"How's it going?" I asked. "The investigation, I mean." I wondered if he'd snub me. He hadn't been very chatty until now, but he surprised me.

"It's early days yet. We've finished the preliminary work with the body, of course, but grid work on the site continues. We've got a team examining his house, and we'll have the National Dive Squad coming in to search the seabed. So far we haven't come up with a weapon."

"Quite a performance," I commented. "It must be difficult having to work in such a remote spot. Are you flying everyone in by chopper?"

"Some were brought over on the *Lady Liz* by the maritime police. They've been out investigating any yachts in the area at the time of the murder."

"Has there been any suggestion of a motive yet?" I asked. "That's what's puzzled us. Jorge seemed such an inoffensive character it's hard to see why anyone would want to murder him."

Jack shook his head. "It's too early to tell. We have to consider all possibilities. There could be drugs; some relationship to other crime; neighbourly squabbles. There's all sorts of reasons for murder. The one thing we know is that Jorge will have been killed because of who he was and where he was. If we carry on sifting the evidence, eventually we'll find out 'why'. Then the 'who-dunnit' part usually becomes obvious."

"So it's your job to sort out all the evidence the troops bring back from the front line?" I asked.

He looked at me. "I've been out on the island each day working with the crews. The DI and I have worked together before, so we've got a fairly smooth routine." He smiled at me. "I do the work and he gets the credit."

"Sounds like my job," I said treacherously.

Actually, this was far from the truth. Roger was generous in sharing both credit and blame, but the temptation of seeing whether I could get a smile out of man-model Jack was too much to resist.

* * *

"Fancy a flight out to D'Urville?" Roger asked the next morning. "Matt wants to be picked up this arvo."

I looked outside at the weather. A brisk southerly was blowing. It wouldn't be as smooth a trip as the last time I'd been down.

"Sure," I said. "What time?"

It turned out a no-fly zone had been established by the police over Greville Harbour to protect their investigation. Roger had to negotiate his way through bureaucracy to enable Matt to be picked up. I left him to battle the powers that be, and downloaded the weather information for Cook Strait.

Sam joined us for lunch.

Greig obligingly made space for him on the sofa, and we munched our various meals companionably. Leftover pasta salad for me, sandwiches for Roger, KFC takeaway for Sam and

2 minute noodles for Greig.

When Sam heard I was going back to D'Urville he looked shocked. "Are you sure you'll be OK?" he asked.

I looked out at the weather. It appeared unchanged. "Yes, fine. It's not that windy."

"No, I didn't mean that. I meant the murder. Last time you were there you discovered a dead body."

Roger gave a short laugh. "I doubt she'll find another one, Sam."

Sam looked defensive. "Won't you be upset? You know what I mean. It must have been an awful shock for you, and there's still a murderer on the loose. I'd have thought you'd want to avoid the place. Surely she doesn't have to go back there, Roger?"

Greig began to look interested. In a second I'd have him offering to do the flight for me, purely following his gentlemanly instincts, of course.

Even Roger looked as if he were reconsidering the flight.

"Thank you for your concern," I said firmly, "but I'm not deeply upset or shocked. At least, not as far as flying into D'Urville is concerned. I imagine there's still a large number of police down there, so I'm probably safer there than anywhere else on the planet at the moment. All I'm doing is picking Matt up, so it's not as if I'll be wandering around anyway."

"We thought the same last time," said Greig unhelpfully.

I glared at him. "I'll be fine."

Roger shrugged, but I saw Sam still had a frown. I didn't hold out much hope of our relationship developing if he was going to be overly protective.

"No one wants to murder me," I assured him. "I'm perfectly safe."

I caught the look on Greig's face and wondered if that was strictly true. I grinned at him. After a second he grinned back. We were good friends, if you discounted our fierce rivalry for flight hours. We worked together well, and I respected his innate natural flying ability. In the old days they referred to people like Greig as 'good stick-and-rudder men'. He seemed able to do by instinct what I only achieved by good preparation and hard work.

He was in his early twenties and currently getting the run-around from his cow of a girlfriend. I'd watched her in action a couple of days ago. Greig – tall, thin, dark and a skilled pilot to boot – being bullied by this skinny, uneducated loser of a girl. Her hair was fake blonde as well.

"She's a bit of a witch, that one," I remarked to Roger after she'd left.

"Replace the 'w' with a 'b' and you've about nailed it," he replied.

We were both protective of Greig. He was 'ours', and God help the girl who did him wrong.

*   *   *

Matt was waiting beside the barn when I taxied up the strip.

"Good flight?"

I shrugged. "A few bumps, nothing to disturb you or me. I see the police are still busy."

The southerly approach to the strip meant I'd had a bird's-eye view of the site. The usual peace and quiet of the island had been replaced with an industrial level of activity. There were tents, miles of police tape and what seemed like an enormous number of people milling around doing whatever police people do in these situations.

I had followed the murder enquiry on the TV news. It was called 'Operation Seawind'. I'd seen DI Mallett interviewed a few times, but never his sidekick DSS Body.

I noticed Matt had his camera slung round his neck. "Been taking photographs?" I asked.

Matt looked self-conscious. "I wondered if you would mind flying over the site so I could get a few shots. For posterity, if you know what I mean."

I smiled at him. Matt was a wonderful photographer, but usually his subjects were native bird life or insects that he captured with wonderful light and detail. It would be very different to have him recording 'slice of history' shots.

"No worries. Once we're airborne I'll do a fly-past for you."

Matt snapped away happily as I circled round the site twice. I wondered if the police would file a complaint with Roger, but in the meantime, what the heck. Matt was the customer, and by extension, always right. The police hadn't actually banned us from taking photos. In fact I'd been scanning the airwaves for any calls from other aircraft in the area bent on doing the same thing.

We were halfway back across Cook Strait before Matt put his camera away with a satisfied noise and said, "So what do you think of the murder?"

"Well, I suppose what we all think. I can't imagine anyone wanting to murder Jorge, but whoever it was, I hope they find them soon. I'm not that happy about having a killer strolling around amongst us."

"You found the body, didn't you?" he asked.

I nodded. "But before you ask, no, I didn't see anyone else. I still find it hard to believe he's gone so violently."

"Have you ever read his books?"

I laughed. "No, they didn't sound my cup of tea. Not Rom-Com at all. Why, have you?"

"No," said Matt, "and probably for the same reason. It's just that the night before he was killed he was on fire, talking about a new novel he was working on, which *did* sound interesting."

"Oh?"

"We had a Bay Barbecue. It was an informal party on the beach in front of our place with our lot, Joe and his wife, and Jorge. We had a big bonfire and a couple of guitars for later in the night. Bill and I dug out a hangi pit and Joe supplied half a side of lamb. It was a lovely night. We were determined to make the most of what we thought would be the last such evening before winter sends us all indoors. My kids were playing golf on the beach, and the rest of us were eating and drinking."

I nodded, in between ensuring I stayed clear of Wellington airspace, and reporting to Paraparaumu FIS. It always seemed a little odd to hear Sam on the other end of a radio call.

"Go on."

"Well, the adults put down quite a lot of alcohol. I don't mean anyone was drunk, but we were all relaxed, if you know what I mean. Jorge began talking about this new novel he had just started working on, and for once it sounded like something that would interest me. He was talking about the early inhabitants of Greville Harbour, and he kept saying 'All we've been told about Maori history is wrong and I can prove it'.

"Bill, who is staying with us, took him up on that and asked 'What do you mean?' Bill's part Maori, Ngati Toa I think, and probably related to half the tribes in the Sounds. He didn't seem impressed with Jorge trying to change his tribe's history."

"Fair enough," I commented. "What was Jorge on about? A new Spanish helmet or something?" A Spanish helmet was found years ago in Wellington Harbour and had been the source of endless speculation about whether the first European to discover New Zealand was Abel Tasman, or whether there had been earlier contact with other European explorers.

"No," said Matt. "That's why it caught my attention. He wasn't writing about European explorers, but about Maori, or some pre-Maori culture. He kept on about there being another race of people that settled in New Zealand before the Maori. He called them the Waitaha and said he'd found proof of this up in the bush."

I mulled this over. "Well, he was a novelist," I said. "It's his job to tell stories."

"The way he told it that night, it wasn't a story," said Matt. "He had me half believing it myself, and old Bill was getting really worked up about it. He called Jorge an 'ignorant foreigner and a cultural racist', if I remember rightly. Things got to the point where Ted and I, he's the other friend staying with us, thought we'd have a genuine punch-up on our hands. It got very heated and unpleasant.

"It wasn't clear whether Jorge had actually found something tangible that caused him to go down this track, although it certainly sounded like it when he first started telling us the tale. But he got cagey when Bill asked him outright what this 'proof' was, and he wouldn't say anything more."

"Now you mention it, I noticed he had a book about Maori history on his desk. I saw it when I checked his bach to see why he wasn't at the airstrip. The police must have all his written stuff now," I said. "I suppose eventually they'll pass it on to his heirs, and they can decide whether to pursue the tale or not."

"Well, that's odd as well," said Matt. "I did speak to one of the police people about it, but I gather there was nothing like that found on Jorge's computer. It either didn't exist at all, or it had been wiped."

We were past the southern tip of Kapiti Island now, and I was beginning to focus on the descent into Paraparaumu and joining finals for the runway.

"I think the police have computer forensic types who can tell whether anything's been erased," I said soothingly. "If there's something there, they'll probably find it. Otherwise it will be just another campfire story that never sees the light of day."

"It seems unfair that you're back here working, while the family are still over there on holiday," remarked Roger when we were back in the office.

"Tell me about it," said Matt as he left.

Roger and I waved goodbye to him. Matt planned to fly back to the island in a day or so but couldn't give us a specific time.

Matt worked as a stockbroker, resulting in him being cash wealthy, but time poor, although I had gathered in conversation he actually worked for the adrenalin highs of his job. I suppose that didn't make him any different to the average pilot, although few of us were as wealthy as him.

CHAPTER
SIX

Saturday morning, and Tom, my newly qualified pilot, clutching his shiny Private Pilot Licence, had hired an aircraft for his first flight with a passenger. I looked into the nervous eyes of the volunteering friend. "Tom's an excellent pilot," I assured him. "Take a seat and help yourself to tea or coffee while he does his flight plan."

I followed Tom into the briefing room. "Where are you going?" I asked.

"I thought we'd fly up the coast over Levin. Rob lives up there, and we could fly over his place and then come back. I'm not going far."

"Excellent choice," I said. "Just keep an eye on your passenger. If he's nervous he might vomit. Point out the sick bags, but remember, the symptoms to watch out for are yawning for no good reason, or if he starts salivating and swallowing. It's not likely to happen, though," I said reassuringly. "You'll be fine. It's a lovely day out there."

I checked Tom's plan and signed him out. Tom was a careful sort of man and I knew he would take good care of his passenger.

I waved them off and hoped the guy wouldn't be too nervous. I remembered taking my own first passenger. It's a character building experience to be in charge of both aircraft and passenger, and I'd been lucky with Jen because she was naturally adventurous and brave. She'd laughed like a drain when we hit an air pocket. I smiled nostalgically as I watched Tom taxi out.

I'd been planning a career as an academic when I discovered flying. BA (Hons) are fun to get but don't have much value in the employment market. I'd thought about continuing on to do my master's thesis and then aim for a doctorate. My grades had been good enough throughout my undergraduate studies to give me a reasonable chance of a job within the university, if I stuck to it, and I thought academia might suit me. I liked the musty, dusty atmosphere of university libraries, the impassioned debate over obscure points of theory, and the stimulation of academic discussion with other students.

Dad had, rather unusually, given me some flying lessons as a Christmas present. I turned up at Paraparaumu Aviation for the first lesson, deeply uncertain whether I wanted to learn to fly at all. We taxied out – not such an easy enterprise, I discovered, because steering is done exclusively with the feet – who knew? My feet were clearly dyslexic. We made it to the runway, lined up and Garth, the instructor who took me on that flight, accelerated the aircraft until we were airborne. Ten feet up in the air I knew, without doubt, that I had found my vocation.

I believe, in matters of the heart, this is known as a coup de foudre. The absolute, irrevocable knowledge that this is what you have waited your whole life for – a love beyond rational reason or prosaic understanding.

I didn't drop my academic studies immediately. There were the usual stages of private, commercial and flight instructor licences to be achieved before I could consider making a career out of aviation, and in some things I was inherently cautious. I weighed up the options. I could have a safe career in academia if I carried on working towards it, or I could have a much more volatile career in aviation. I knew already that the big jets held no appeal for me. I was a small aircraft pilot. As I learned more about the possibilities, I fancied myself as a bush pilot in Alaska, flying to remote settlements, or perhaps in central Africa, taking tourists round the game parks. I'd heard exciting things about aviation in New Guinea as well, but the risks seemed unconscionably high.

Academia or aviation? In the end it was an easy choice. Roger allowed me to work on a casual basis, picking up students or charter flights as they came in while I built up my total hours and experience. Eventually he offered me a full-time position, but it had taken a couple of years of serious financial constraint before I achieved this. David, who only valued dollar-based results, had already written me off as a failure.

When the choice became David or flying, it was simple, obvious and completely unexpected by my ex. I wondered then whether he'd ever listened to me or had any insight into what I valued.

A year later I had no doubt at all that leaving David had liberated me in ways I never expected. I might be living a life infinitely less safe than the one I'd originally envisaged, but I was alive each and every day.

Tom and his passenger made it back safely. They walked into the office with smiles on their faces.

"Good flight?" I asked.

Tom indicated his friend. "Let him tell you," he said.

"Magic, just magic," enthused this man who had been scared shitless only an hour or so before.

I smiled at Tom, the recognition of one pilot to another. "You did well, then?"

"It was cool," he said.

I winked at him. I knew full well the stress today's flight would have put on him. It's a massive achievement to take that first step.

Sam came into the office as I was closing up. He waited as I locked the briefing room doors.

"I've checked out what's on at the movies," he said. "How about the new James Bond this evening? It's just been released, and all the reviews are good."

"Yeah, OK," I said. I was bored and restless enough to agree to anything. "Sweet," I added. "Shall I meet you at Coastlands?" I was reluctant to invite Sam to pick me up from my home. Where I lived wasn't exactly a secret, but I wasn't ready to let him invade my territory.

"OK." I saw the quick look of assessment he threw me. Sam's not stupid and could put two and two together. "Fair enough. I'll see you there."

He gave me a cheery wave as he left.

*   *   *

We met in the theatre lobby. Sam was there before me, his head bent as he checked his phone, which allowed me to study him.

He was a compact man, slight and not particularly tall, although well proportioned. He had what they call Irish colouring – dark hair, fairish skin and blue eyes. He looked up and smiled when he saw me walk towards him. "Hi."

I liked James Bond films. Yes, I knew they were formulaic, but they were fun, and Daniel Craig was always worth watching. I was aware of Sam sitting beside me in the dark.

Afterwards we went to the pub. We'd barely walked in the door when we were hailed by Greig. "Over here."

The last thing I wanted was to join Greig and the toxic dwarf he called his girlfriend, but politeness is important I suppose, and I wasn't up to explaining to Sam why I wanted to give her the cold shoulder.

We joined Greig and Jayleen.

Sam went and got us drinks while I discussed the movie.

"I don't like Daniel Craig," said Jayleen. "He's getting too old."

I was surprised, but I forgot she was only eighteen. By extension of course, she was pointing out how old I was. I ignored her.

Chat turned to discussing Jorge's murder.

"You don't think people you've met get topped," said Jayleen. "He came to our school once for a talk. Do they know who killed him?" she asked.

Greig shrugged. "Not yet. Why would anyone kill a writer? He seemed harmless enough."

"Well someone did," said Sam.

"Matt did say one of his guests had quarrelled with Jorge," I said. "Maybe the argument was more serious than anyone realised. Who knows?"

"I thought it was very bad of Roger sending you back down there," said Sam.

"I was fine," I said, suppressing my irritation.

"It might have been dangerous. Someone who's killed once could kill again. We don't know why Jorge was killed. I thought letting you go back there was irresponsible."

I took a deep breath.

Greig looked at my face, read the warning signs and tried to divert Sam. "Claire's tough, and she's back safely, Sam. You don't need to worry about her. How're you finding things now Air New Zealand are cutting back on the provincial flights and have cancelled some of its services? It's not going to affect your job, is it?"

Sam shook his head. "Shouldn't think so." He returned to his theme. "All I'm saying is I care about Claire's safety, and I think Roger made a bad call allowing her to make that flight."

I felt my patience slipping away.

"I'm quite sure Roger cares for me as well, thank you, Sam. But he's not silly enough to try and wrap me up in cotton wool. It's my job, remember? He gave me a choice whether to go or not, and I said yes. If I'd said no, he'd have accepted that as well. If I hadn't done it, Greig would have had to go. Is his safety of less concern than mine?"

"No, but Greig's a man."

Beside me I heard Greig's sharp intake of breath, followed by a small choke of laughter.

I stared at Sam in amazement. "Are you actually saying that because I'm female I can't do what Greig can do?"

Too late Sam saw the hole he'd dug for himself. "No, I don't mean that at all. It's just that, being a woman you're more vulnerable if you were attacked." He turned to Greig, saw no support there and turned back to me. "If someone had threatened you, what would you have done?"

"Well, no one did. I'm fine. It's over, and I think we'd better stop talking about it before we have a major fallout."

Jayleen mercifully provided a diversion by demanding another drink, and the conversation slipped into discussing whether we should participate as a team in the next pub quiz night.

"Jayleen and I are starters," said Greig. "How about you Sam? Are you up for it?"

"Yeah, OK," said Sam. He looked at me uncertainly.

"You'll play, won't you, Claire?" said Greig.

I agreed reluctantly. Usually I enjoyed trivia evenings, but Sam had managed to thoroughly irritate me.

I left soon after. I'd had David telling me what to do for years, and I vowed I'd never put up with it again. I couldn't believe Sam had tried to do the same. Did I have 'pushover' tattooed on my forehead?

CHAPTER SEVEN

IT WAS SUNDAY, AND I HAD two days off. Much as I loved my job, there was something really lovely about being able to stay curled up in bed on a rainy morning. Nelson had joined me, and the two of us lounged around for a couple of hours while I read my book and checked emails on my tablet.

The chief drawback of living alone was having to make my own coffee. I was addicted to the stuff, and it took at least four cups to get me out of bed. I recalled a quaint old machine my nana used to have called a 'teasmade' which dispensed hot drinks at your bedside at a prearranged time. Maybe I'd still be living when someone invented a useful robot to fill the function. As it was, Nelson gave me a disdainful glance each time I disturbed him to pad off to the kitchen in search of another brew.

When I finally left the shelter of my bed, I cleaned the house, chucked out the stale contents of the fridge and, chores completed, went for a walk. The chief attraction of my cottage was that it was part of a farm criss-crossed with trails. I suppose at one time the farmer used them as he went out on his beat on horseback. I loved being out in the fresh air of the country. Occasionally, if I was having a fitness blitz, I would run up the trails, but most often I preferred simply to walk over the hills. I found the rhythm of my steps incredibly soothing and could feel stress fall away under the influence of physical action and the pleasure of being out in the countryside.

Sometimes when I flew with a student we passed over that valley, and I would look down at my home and the geography of the hills surrounding it and give a great sigh of satisfaction.

If I took one of the shorter paths, Nelson often consented to go along for the walk, although he had to be carried if we encountered anything scary like cattle or horses.

Jorge and his murder seemed very far away, and I realised, as I felt the weight lift off my shoulders, just how tense I'd been all week.

*   *   *

On Sunday evenings there was a standing invitation for dinner at my sister's place, and since I broke up with David, I took Kate up on the offer more weekends than not. I cherished my Sunday visits, not least because Kate was an amazing cook and always turned on a great meal.

Kate's noisy, cluttered domesticity was something which both attracted and appalled me. I always came away from her place exhausted, but I loved my two nieces and as they grew older I kept looking for ways to encourage their native self-confidence. Kate was a wonderful wife and mother, but her values were those of our own mother, who valued obedience and order above independence and creativity. I saw my role as encouraging the girls into something other than passive conformity.

Kate's long-suffering husband Martin, who adored his wife, sat serenely in the corner seat watching TV and letting the noise wash over him, a placid smile on his face. I'm not sure whether he had, in some Buddhist sense, achieved detachment, or whether his switch-off mechanism was a Darwinian mutation allowing him to keep his sanity. We got on very well. Or at least, we failed to annoy each other, which was probably as much as anyone could hope for in an in-law.

I hauled out the cryptic series of numbers I had photocopied.

"What do you make of these?"

Martin was an accountant. He liked numbers and did complicated maths games and played Sudoku for recreation. "What's it supposed to be?"

"I found it in the jacket pocket of the man who was murdered. Well, he wasn't actually wearing it at the time. I borrowed the jacket and found the paper later."

"Is that the one down in D'Urville?"

"Well, he's the only murdered person I encountered last week," I said tartly.

Kate had joined the conversation, so I went through the whole story for them. It amused me that Kate, like Sam before her, was horrified that I had flown back to the island.

"But you could have been murdered. No one's been arrested yet."

"I don't think I'm in much danger," I assured her.

She sniffed at that, but went off to check the roast. I cuddled up on the sofa with the girls and read them 'Harry Potter' until dinner.

Martin had been focusing on the numbers. "I can't work out any obvious pattern," he admitted. "Is that how they were originally written out? I mean on the original piece of paper?"

"It's a photocopy of that original," I replied. "I assume it's some sort of code, but if so, I can't see how it can be broken. I gave it to a detective, and he didn't seem to have any more idea than we do."

Martin played with the numbers all evening and let the ruckus of his family ebb and flow round him. I caught Kate looking at him with raised eyebrows.

She realised I was watching and shrugged. "Sometimes I think he lives on another planet," she said.

I smiled and helped her with dinner, the dishes and then the chaos of getting two young children to bed.

By nine o'clock, peace and order had been restored, and I was ready to leave.

"Can I copy this code?" asked Martin before I left.

"Be my guest," I said. "If you can crack it that would be great.

I hate the feeling that it might be important, even if the detective wasn't convinced."

*　　*　　*

I was awoken on Monday morning by my phone. I looked at the number. The office. I sighed. I loved Roger dearly, but he was no respecter of such PC considerations as individual privacy or personal leave.

"Hi," I mumbled.

I heard a choke of laughter from the other end. "Hello, Hardcastle. Are you still in the scratcher?"

I wondered grimly what the employment relationship service would make of my boss. "Mmm," I replied non-committally. "What's up?"

"The aero club had their planes interfered with last night, and Avgas was taken."

I sat up. This was serious. "Any damage done?"

"No, just the fuel drained from a couple of planes parked outside. Nothing else they've been able to discover. The police are here, of course. You haven't seen suspicious types lurking around over the last week or so, have you?"

"None that spring to mind."

Every airport in the land faced this problem. Usually the culprits were young lads seeking some high-octane fuel to power their drag racers. Paraparaumu Airport's security had been upgraded and procedures tightened in the last few years, but a determined teenager could climb a fence, siphon fuel into a can and be safely back over the fence in a matter of minutes.

The problem wasn't so much the loss of fuel, although that was nuisance enough. But there was always the possibility that some bright spark would get creative and interfere with the aircraft itself. We had all heard horror stories of louts tipping sugar into the fuel tanks just for fun. When you trusted your life to a machine's integrity, you didn't want some idiot compromising it.

I didn't envy anyone at work that day. Every aircraft would

have to be checked, even those, like ours, safely locked away in a hangar.

"Oh, and the other thing is – it's Jorge's funeral tomorrow. Eleven o'clock at the funeral parlour. I didn't know whether you'd seen the notice. I'll be going and I assume you'll want to be there?"

"Yes, I'd better be there, I suppose, although I hate funerals. Poor Jorge."

"I'll leave you to it," said Roger. "Don't do anything I wouldn't do," he said as he rang off.

I gave a half smile. Roger was the best employer I'd ever had. Gender equality was never an issue. He assumed I could and would do as much of the dirty work as any of the men. He further assumed they would make cups of coffee and do any paperwork required. No work was designated 'woman's work' and below the male of the species. He gave us all an equal chance to shine, whatever the job. What's more, he didn't just talk the talk; he did as much work as anyone else.

I'd found him usually fair, usually even-tempered and possessing moments of compelling wisdom. Without making an issue of it, he had been quietly supportive when I went through the break-up with David.

I had decided early on that I could be offended by his sexual comments, or ignore them. They were inappropriate, but they didn't embarrass or threaten me and occasionally they amused me. His talk might be riddled with sexual overtones, but he kept his hands to himself, so I disregarded it, seeing his manner as part of his age, culture and personality.

*   *   *

I drove into Wellington. Jen, Lisa and I had been friends since year eight and we tried to meet up every couple of months and 'do lunch'. It was Jen's birthday and the three of us planned to celebrate in style.

When we finished college Jen went straight into drama school and had done very well. She had scooped a major role as one of the bridesmaids in *Mamma Mia*, which was due to open in a few weeks, and was currently in rehearsal. Lisa and I always tried to attend every show she was in to cheer her on.

Lisa was tall, stick-insect thin, highly sophisticated and polished, with long dark hair and dramatically large brown eyes. You could hate her just for the efficiency of her metabolism. Jen and I told her we only loved her because we knew she ate like a horse, and frequently indulged in junk food. If she'd had the faintest interest, I'm sure she would have been the right physical type for modelling. Instead, after she and I had attended Victoria University together, she'd elected to follow a career in accountancy. She was always the brainiest of the three of us, so her choice of working in an industry we thought of as stodgy had come as a shock to Jen and me. She was doing well, working for one of the big multinational firms who were planning to send her overseas. It was through Lisa that I'd met David, although she'd made no secret of her surprise that he and I had got together.

"Chalk and cheese," she'd commented when I first moved in with him.

I resented that judgement at the time. Later I thought it astute.

The three of us had flatted together the first two years after we left college and had supported each other through exams, diets, unreasonable parents, boyfriends, girlfriends, burgeoning sexuality and break-ups. I loved Jen's stories of theatre life, and Lisa's stories from the financial world were surprisingly criminal, funny and entertaining. They both found my flying exotic and thrilling.

We'd agreed to meet at Shed 5, on the wharf. Lisa was already there and we both smiled as we watched Jen walk towards us. I was amused to see new blue streaks in Jen's black hair. Jen was compact, slender, with dark hair bobbed in a pageboy cut. She was extremely eye-catching dressed in her usual black, with a long-sleeved T, very short mini, fish-net tights and chunky boots – a cross between Lisbeth Salander and Mary Quant. Jen had some indefinable 'watch me' quality which manifested in her walk, her gestures and every elegant move of her small body. I've never been able to analyse the appeal, but it poured from her and I was used to seeing heads turn to watch her as she walked by.

We allowed the young waitperson to guide us through the menu. On that autumn day, Wellington was putting on its best for us with a clear blue sky, light winds and a magnificent view of the harbour. We sipped our Sauvignon Blanc (Marlborough, naturally) and worked our way through the seafood assiette (Jen), prawn and crayfish cocktail (Lisa) and the antipasti (me).

"It's a beautiful city," I said as we admired the view from the large windows. Wellington and the smaller towns included in the greater metropolitan area cluster round the harbour. Beyond the flat land adjacent to the water, encircling ranges of hills provide a frame for the city. On a perfect day, such as it was that day, Wellington is a gem, a pearl in the oyster of deep green hills and blue harbour. In winter, the snow-capped hills of the far-off Tararuas provided a stunning backdrop to Wellington and the Hutt Valley. The suburban hills broke up the extent of the city into component parts, so no area was too large or inhuman in scope. I often compared it fondly to the urban sprawl that is Auckland, where no such favourable geography defines or frames the city.

"You know, we can go to other countries and sit in restaurants and admire our surroundings, but I reckon on a good day Wellington rates up there with the best of them," I said.

Jen grinned. "Keep on believing that," she advised. "Me, I'm dreaming of Carnival in Rio."

"You theatrical sorts are all the same," I groaned. "It's all OTT and about the drama."

"So, what about your drama?" she asked. I had told both of them the bare facts of Jorge's murder.

"Do you think Matt Johnstone is a suspect?" asked Lisa.

I was shocked at the thought. Matt was a thoroughly nice person. I'd forgotten that she might know him through her industry connections. It turned out she'd worked for his firm during her Varsity holidays.

"I shouldn't think so," I said. "Mind you, I'm a suspect as well, so any one of us could have done it, I suppose."

Jen snorted. "If you wanted to murder someone, there wouldn't be a mystery about it," she said. "You'd have still been stabbing your victim as they pulled you off the body. There's nothing mysterious about your techniques."

Lisa frowned at Jen. "We all know Claire had nothing to do with it," she said loyally.

"Do you have to be involved with any more of the investigation?" Lisa asked.

"I suspect our part in the affair is over," I said. "It's not nice to be involved in someone's death, however obliquely, but it did make us feel important for a while."

"No more sexy policemen then?" asked Lisa.

"Probably not," I said. "Pity – and talking about men, there won't be a future with Sam either. There's absolutely no chemistry as far as I'm concerned, and if you two had heard him rattle on the other night, you'd understand why I think he's a wasp or two short of a picnic. So. No men. I'm obviously supposed to be a nun."

"Yeah, right," said Lisa. "I've known you for half our lifetimes, and that's not in your future. Trust me."

"Well, how are you doing then?" I asked.

Lisa shrugged. "Nothing important for me either," she reported. "I still want to meet a wealthy woman and be a well-kept wife, but it hasn't happened yet. There aren't enough women in the upper echelons of the financial world."

"Hang in there," urged Jen. "It's only a matter of time for you and Claire. Look on the bright side; at least you don't compete with each other."

Lisa looked at Jen in surprise. "What's that supposed to mean?"

"It means that in the theatre business there are ten straight women for every straight guy. The competition is mega-fierce." Her tone was bitter.

Lisa and I looked at each other. Something was up.

"You should have taken up rugby then," I said lightly. "There'd be much less competition."

Jen pulled a face. "Thanks so much," she said sarcastically.

"So what have you been doing?" Lisa asked Jen.

"Well." She gave us a gamin grin.

We sat back to let Jen tell us about her latest craze.

"Geocaching," she announced. "A group of us got involved, and for the last month or so we've been going out one day a weekend looking for caches."

She explained something of this worldwide phenomenon which works like a grown-up's treasure hunt. Participants track down GPS coordinates, solve clues and are led to a small, hidden token treasure. "I suppose it's the fun of the chase," she said.

Lisa and I glanced at each other again. It wasn't the sort of comment Jen would usually make.

"You're marching round the bush with a compass?" I asked. "This doesn't sound like the girl I know." Jen wasn't, as far as I knew, a proponent of outdoor activities. Very much a metro girl who didn't like to stray outside the city limits. She'd been appalled when she first visited my home in Paraparaumu. 'It's awfully remote,' she'd said. 'Quite creepy. Are you sure you'll be safe?' She'd made it sound as if I lived in the middle of the Appalachians, and rolled her eyes when I pointed out it was only ten minutes from my work. If she could, she'd have been whistling the theme from *Deliverance*.

Now she laughed at the suggestion she'd been tramping the bush. "Hell, no. Most of the ones we look for are local to Wellington city. They're hidden all over the place. Just go to the website, there are millions of caches around the world."

"And would one of the players in this group be a significant male?" For the life of me I couldn't think of any other reason why Jen would suddenly become interested in GPS points.

"Ah," she said, "now you mention it, there is a new someone. But it's early days yet, and who knows where things will go?"

"Well I hope they go in the right direction for you. It's your birthday, you're entitled to a nice present from the fates," said Lisa.

"You can say that again," Jen replied. "Here's to us," she toasted. "And here's to all of us finding sexy partners."

"Amen to that," Lisa and I replied.

By the time we'd finished lunch and I'd driven home, most of the day had gone. Nelson was annoyed at my prolonged absence and refused to greet me until I'd opened a new tin of cat food, after which he graciously consented to scoff the lot, then sat on my lap while he groomed himself.

I got on with re-reading my 'Navigation' notes for the lecture I would give the next evening. A couple of times a year we ran a series of lectures to help our students with their Private Pilot Licence exams. Greig usually taught Principles of Flight; I did Meteorology, and Roger's subject was Navigation. This time, however, Roger had decided not to participate and handed his subject to me. I had groaned and bitched. Navigation was not my best subject, but Roger was unsympathetic.

"You can brush up on it," he'd said with a cheerful grin, and left me to it.

CHAPTER EIGHT

I STOOD ON THE DECK BESIDE MARIA, clutching a cup of coffee to wake me up. It was going to be a long day. In the distance we could see Sam slowly driving the length of the runway checking for any debris dropped or blown onto its surface overnight.

"Any news about the fuel thief?" I asked Maria.

She shook her head. "Not that we've heard. Little scallywags. I hope the police find them soon and deal with it. I can't imagine how they broke through security."

Maria was an exquisitely turned out woman in her late sixties. She'd been Roger's office manager since he started the business, and although she didn't fly herself, she probably knew more about aviation than the rest of us put together.

"You're going to the funeral today?" she asked.

I nodded. "I feel I ought to. What about you?"

She shook her head. "No, I didn't ever really deal with Jorge. Roger's going, so I'll stay behind and man the office. Greig's got a busy day up in the air. It looks as if student numbers are picking up a bit."

"Let's hope so." I gulped down the last of the coffee and went out to help Greig pull planes out of the hangar.

*   *   *

The funeral was a quiet affair. There were few mourners, in spite of the sensational manner of Jorge's death. I saw Matt and waved to him as we went in. The detectives were there in force. I nodded to them and got a smile back from Pete. Otherwise there were few of us to speed Jorge on his way. I felt obscurely embarrassed on his behalf. Although the celebrant did a reasonable job of the ceremony, there was little sense that the congregation had gathered to celebrate Jorge's life. There was no family present to speak on his behalf and I felt I'd said my own goodbyes when I'd knelt beside him in the sand on D'Urville. All in all, it was a sad little business, and I was relieved to see the hearse drive away with the coffin.

Roger and I returned to the airport, where my day got worse as I wrestled my way through updating our manuals. Aviation is a highly regulated industry with a piece of paper for every process or action. In theory CAA could spring a snap audit on us at any time. Keeping paperwork current was an ongoing nightmare. Greig was responsible for the aircraft maintenance records, while I kept the pilots' records, commercial flight plans and the quality manuals up to date.

Greig smiled smugly at me as he ushered yet another student out onto the tarmac. I bared my teeth at him and he chuckled. "And I've got a group to take to Hawera for the day tomorrow as well," he whispered.

Ah well, sometimes you win, sometimes you lose.

"I can rise above petty jealousy," I told him sanctimoniously.

This time he actually snorted.

Lunchtime, and Sam came in.

Shit!

I'd prepared a 'Dear John' speech, but in the end it wasn't needed.

"I fucked up, didn't I?" he asked.

"Hmm. Pretty much, I guess," I replied. "Sam, I like the fact that you're concerned, but no one, and I mean no one, tells me what to do or how to live my life. I make my own judgement calls, right or wrong. You kind of crossed a line."

He nodded. "I guessed that."

We looked at each other.

"We're friends and colleagues, OK? But that's all. I honestly don't think we're compatible."

He nodded. "See you round," he said.

As easily as that, it was all over.

I was relieved. I'd known we weren't right for each other from the beginning, and should have trusted my instincts. I never should have encouraged him.

Late afternoon Roger fielded a call.

"You're taking a couple of people down to D'Urville tomorrow," he called over to me. "Jorge's lawyer has just called. He's organised cleaners to go over and tidy the bach so it can be shut up. There'll be two women here at nine-thirty."

"OK," I nodded.

Five minutes later he called over again. "Matt wants to go down as well. I told him that if he could be here at nine-thirty, he can share the flight."

"You'll be wearing a groove in the airways between here and that island," said Greig.

*　　*　　*

I must have bluffed my way through the navigation lecture adequately, because the students seemed happy and had a basic grasp of the subject by the time they left the lecture. I enjoyed the idea of dividing our ball-shaped planet into orange-like segments that we name longitude, slicing it horizontally into latitude and, by coordinating the two measurements, being able to name and identify positions anywhere on the sphere. The GPS coordinates Jen used for her geocaching being an obvious example.

The problem I had with the subject was not the actual art of navigation. I wasn't going to get lost or forget the basic principles, but I was careless with numbers and inclined to make silly arithmetical mistakes, which I didn't pick up until far too late. In an exam, one silly mistake early in a flight plan could result in a massive discrepancy that compounded through each latter stage. Before I sat either my commercial or instrument flying tests I spent weeks practising basic calculations and honing my accuracy. I passed creditably enough, but the memory of my raised stress levels always haunted me.

We were just packing up when some car headlights shone through the office windows. Mindful of the raid on the aero club's planes, I opened the door to check out the intruder.

"Evening, Claire," a voice called. I stared down the lights and recognised the security van. Their presence on the airfield had been boosted since the Avgas theft.

"Hi, Rick," I said, relieved that I wasn't going to have to tackle marauders.

"We saw your lights on and came to check all was well."

"I've been working late with some students trying to teach them theory. I was just about to let them out. How's it going in the world of security? Have you caught the vandals yet?"

"We haven't even managed to find how they broke into the airport. No sign of any tampering with the perimeter fence, so heaven knows how they did it. Do you want us to let your people out through the gate?"

"That would be great, thanks. Then I can shut the place up and let myself out in a few minutes."

I waved goodbye to the students and started to lock the offices up. I was caught by surprise when a tall figure pushed his way through the swing doors. I had a momentary rush of nerves before I recognised Jack Body.

"I saw you were working late and thought I'd drop in. I hope that's OK?"

"How did you get past security?" I asked before I realised that sounded dumb. Jack was police, therefore he could gain entry anywhere he wanted.

For once he actually smiled at me. "Have you got a moment?"

I hesitated, but only momentarily. "Yes, sure."

Did he really expect an honest member of the public to refuse to help a cop when asked? That's how to get fast-tracked up the suspects list.

"Would you like a drink?" I asked in resignation. I had been heading home to bed, but if this was another interrogation, then I wanted to be primed. "There's tea and coffee if you are on duty, otherwise I'm having a wine. There's beer in the fridge as well."

He followed behind me and pointed out a Steinlager. "I'll have one of those, if I may. Can I shout you that wine?"

I nodded and looked at him with surprise as he dropped some coins in the honesty box. This came pleasantly close to fraternising. I made a mental note that I needed to be particularly wary.

We returned to the waiting room.

"I've got a few more questions, if you don't mind."

I gestured towards my glass. "You've bought a slice of my time. What can I tell you?"

"I want you to go over what you told me the other day, minute by minute if possible. Let's start with what we know." Jack pulled a notebook from his pocket. "You flew from Paraparaumu at one minute past three in the afternoon. You gave me the approximate time, and I was able to confirm it by radio calls and the tower records. Now, go from there. What time did you arrive at the strip?"

"I don't remember looking at my watch, so these are best-guess estimates?"

He nodded.

"OK. I know from experience that it takes forty-five minutes to do that flight, on average. It can take longer on days when I have to divert, or there's a strong headwind. That day the weather was clear and the winds mild, so my best guess is I was on the strip at three forty-five."

"Then what?"

"I waited for maybe five minutes, during which I was checking out the Cub, then I walked towards the beach and climbed a sand dune so I could call Jorge. When his phone went to answerphone I called Roger, and told him about the Cub."

"How long do you reckon all that took?"

"Well, no more than five minutes, tops."

"So it would be fair to say that at three-fifty you walked towards the beach and then along to Jorge's bach?"

I thought back to that afternoon, and let the action replay in my head like a movie. I saw myself walking through the dunes, remembered my impatience with Jorge, and the beauty of the bay in the autumn light.

"That sounds about right. Then the walk along the beach probably took me twenty-five minutes all told. I wasn't hurrying at that point."

Jack scribbled some more notes into his book.

"Before you left that sand dune you are absolutely sure you saw no one around? Not back on the strip, not in the dunes, not on the beach?"

I shook my head. "No one. Well, I saw a dinghy down the southern end of the beach, which I assumed was Matt and his kids, but no one else."

"And you were somewhere along the beach when you heard the other aircraft take off?"

"Yes. I was close to the northern end by then."

"Shall we say five past four then for the plane taking off?"

"I suppose that would be right."

"OK. Then at four-fifteen you were at the bach?"

"Yes. There, or thereabouts. I waved to the couple in the other bach but didn't stop to talk."

"How long were you there?"

"Probably only a couple of minutes. Just long enough to see Jorge wasn't there. I checked his backpack and realised he hadn't started packing up to leave."

"And then?"

"Then I went along the track to the lagoon and found Jorge, and that would have taken maybe another ten minutes, tops."

"Putting it at four twenty-five to four-thirty."

I nodded. "Now, can I ask what this is about? You've already got most of this information."

Jack closed his book and looked at me. "We've managed to find the Norwegian pilots who hired the plane from you. It took us time to track them down, because after they returned the plane here, they went down to Abel Tasman Park and have been sea kayaking around the coast for the last week."

I laughed. "What a busy pair."

Jack grinned. "Well, they're certainly experiencing the best New Zealand has to offer." He indicated his book. "If we compare their statements with yours, and assume both are honest and accurate, then it gives us a very narrow window of time in which Jorge was murdered."

I sipped the wine and thought about it. "What did they say?"

"They arrived at the strip sometime early afternoon – they put it at about two o'clock – and walked down to the beach. They headed northward and met Jorge who was pulling his dinghy in from the water. They gave him a hand, got talking and found they all came from the same area of Norway. Jorge invited them in for a drink, and they sat a while and had a yarn.

"About three o'clock Jorge told them he had to start packing up to catch the flight with you. He walked them down towards the lagoon to show them the route back to the strip. Their best estimate was that the three of them left his bach at about five past three, and the pilots parted from Jorge about ten minutes later, when he turned back. So the last sighting of Jorge alive was at three-fifteen." Jack paused and took a swig of the beer. "Neither of those pilots could recall seeing anyone else around. As far as we can tell, Jorge never made it back to his house. He was hit over the head as he came back through the dunes, which puts the estimated time of death between three-fifteen and three-thirty."

I shifted uncomfortably. So Jorge had died while I was still flying. I'd have been somewhere over the Chetwode Islands I supposed. "It seems horrible that he was being murdered while I was in the air coming to get him," I said.

"That presupposes the statements made by the Norwegian pilots are accurate," said Jack. "If they are, the significant thing is that Jorge's time of death is pinpointed so accurately. Incidentally, the pilots' testimony agrees with the pathologist's opinion. You flew in some fifteen minutes later and report you saw no one about. So our murderer was at the northern end of the dunes at three-fifteen and had disappeared by the time you arrived. There's no sign of him on the beach. You walked down there at three-fifty so, unless he jogged up past your point of access, you would have seen him. He's not walking along the strip either, because you're landing on it. So where did he go?"

I mulled it over, but then a thought occurred to me. "You said the pilots left Jorge to walk back to the plane, but I didn't see them either. They weren't on the strip when I landed."

Jack nodded. "They said that after they parted from Jorge they arrived at the edge of the lagoon. Rather than taking the direct route to the strip, they decided to follow the path that leads around the lagoon. In the half-hour or so it took them to complete the circuit, you had landed and walked down to the beach. By the time they walked down the strip you were walking up the beach in the opposite direction, so you didn't see each other. Incidentally they did hear and see your plane come in and confirmed the time as approximately three forty-five."

"Does that mean I'm not a suspect then?"

I thought he'd laugh, but he was serious when he replied. "As far as we know, so far you're in the clear, unless fresh evidence emerges that alters the timing of Jorge's death."

I quirked an eyebrow at him. "That's not a ringing endorsement. Do you think a woman could have done it?"

He shrugged. "Who knows? It's possible."

He looked at his watch. "It's late. I must be going. There's one other thing I wanted you to know."

You can always tell when people are going to give you bad news and I wondered what was coming. I watched as he gathered himself together. "Our victim, Jorge, wasn't quite the nice guy he appeared. He'd got a record."

"Really?" I stared at Jack. "Whatever for?"

"It seems he liked young girls. He served time for it in 2003."

"Holy crap! You mean child molesting?" I was appalled. I'd liked Jorge. If we hadn't been close friends, we'd certainly enjoyed a relaxed camaraderie on those trips to and from the island. I'd sat beside him in the close proximity of a small Cessna numerous times and been unaware. I'd even bunked down overnight at his bach on one occasion when he'd wanted to be taken off the island first thing in the morning. How could I have been so wrong about him?

Of course, if he liked small children, then I would be well off his radar in regard to my own safety. But even so. I said as much to Jack.

"He liked them around the age of eleven to thirteen, just on the cusp of pubescence. At least they weren't any younger," said Jack soberly. "There may be other incidents we don't know about, of course. You have to wonder what he's been doing since he came out of clink, but there's nothing the police have a record of. Anyway, I thought you should know. It will be all over the media tomorrow."

"Thanks. Roger will be devastated." I shook my head. "That's horrible. It changes the way I feel about his murder, which may not be rational. One less kiddie-fiddler seems like a good thing, however wrong murder is."

"Fortunately police don't have to deal with moral judgements," said Jack. "We just nab the baddies."

I was still trying to absorb the information, a process harder than I could imagine, given I now felt distinctly nauseous. I knew I shouldn't have had that Sav.

"Matt," I said suddenly. "Matt's got small children. Oh shit, please don't tell me Jorge was after them?"

Jack shook his head. "We haven't found evidence of that so far," he said firmly.

I shook my head to free it from those horrible images. "So who killed Jorge?"

"Well, if we knew that, we could save ourselves hours of work!" Jack sighed. "And talking about work, both you and I are on duty tomorrow?"

I nodded. "I'm flying a cleaning crew down to sort out Jorge's place. Matt's flying with us."

Jack smiled. "That's all good then. Make sure you get enough sleep tonight, and fly safely tomorrow."

I smiled slightly. "Well, of course."

CHAPTER
NINE

I GOT TO WORK EARLY TO GET the aircraft fuelled and complete the paperwork for the trip to D'Urville. CAA had strict requirements for commercial flights, so I had to gather weather information and clip it, with the weight and balance form, to the flight plan and set it aside to record the passenger names when they arrived at the office.

There was low cloud out in the strait so we wouldn't be climbing very high. I just hoped when we got to the island we'd be able to get over the saddle above Catherine Cove and not have to divert round the northern tip of D'Urville, which added appreciatively to our flight-time.

In spite of being tired the night before, I'd slept badly, my mind a seething mass of child molesters, navigation notes, geocaching and Jack Body. Somewhere between dreams and awake, a thought had taken root in my brain and I wanted to explore it. I spread a chart of the Sounds out on the desk and took out the photocopy I had made of Jorge's envelope.

It was the recurrence of the number 40 in the puzzle that I'd remembered. When I was explaining latitude and longitude to the students, we had naturally looked at New Zealand's position on the globe and talked about the 'Roaring Forties'. I examined

Jorge's numbers. There were no degrees, minutes or seconds separating the figures, as you'd expect with properly written coordinates, but if I remedied that, the figures now read:

$$40^\circ\,48'\,28.84''\,S \quad 173^\circ\,50'\,02.48''\,E$$
$$40^\circ\,48'\,39.87''\,S \quad 173^\circ\,48'\,03.21''\,E$$

I studied the chart. Had Jorge tried to notate two different locations? Grabbing a ruler and pencil I painstakingly plotted the first of the coordinates and, bingo, it landed right on the edge of Greville Harbour.

I was working out the second location when Greig came in.

"Morning," he yawned. "What are you doing?"

"Working out where this location is," I said.

He opened his can of Red Bull, leaned against the whiteboard and watched me measuring out the coordinates.

"You realise you can do that in a fraction of the time using your mobile phone and Google Earth?" he stated politely.

I'd just put my cross on the chart marking the location of the coordinates. "Basic navigation," I said piously. "I'm keeping my skills current."

Greig wasn't buying it. "You didn't think of it, did you?"

I laughed. "Well, no. I was so focused on the class last night that I forgot about modern methods."

He gave an amused grunt and went off to get his own paperwork sorted. I looked at the position of the second location on the chart. If I was right, it was high in the hills behind Greville Harbour. I wondered what it signified, and whether Jorge had been up to the spot. The bush was pretty dense over the island, and the topography on the chart looked rugged up there. I knew hunters went out after pig and deer in those hills but I couldn't quite see Jorge bush-bashing his way through. Still, what did I know?

Maybe there were other secrets to discover about his life.

*   *   *

Matt arrived just after nine. Jorge's conviction for child molestation had been on the news, and he couldn't wait to discuss it with us. "It definitely gives someone a motive for murder," he said.

"Yes," I interjected, "but the only one on the island with young children was you, Matt."

"Wonderful," he replied. "Now even you think I'm a suspect. Mind you, Jane made the same point. She's devastated we allowed our children to run free when there was a paedophile in residence. I still can't believe that inoffensive man was a pervert."

"I imagine everyone on the island at the time of his death is a suspect," said Roger.

"At least I'm probably in the clear," I said.

"How do you know that?" asked Roger.

I had to explain that Jack had come in the previous night to ask more questions.

"Do they have an idea who did it, do you think?" asked Matt.

"If they do, he didn't tell me. But they're obviously being very thorough checking through everyone's story," I said. "They've got Jorge's final moments pegged out almost on a minute-by-minute basis."

*   *   *

The women from the cleaning firm arrived. They'd brought rolls of heavy-duty bin liners and flat-packed cardboard boxes that were unwieldy and weighed a ton. I looked at them in dismay as I amended the paperwork to allow for the extra freight. There's not a lot of space in a small aircraft, and the boxes were awkward to stow. Eventually, with Roger's help, we managed to force them into the luggage area and piled the liners and cleaning supplies on top.

"God knows how you're going to unpack that at the other end," said Roger, "let alone get it all across to the house."

"You can borrow the quad," offered Matt. "I can give you a hand to unload and get it on the bike."

"That would be magic," I said gratefully. "We've also got to get all the rubbish off at the end of the day, and the quad would be really helpful."

I got the passengers loaded up. They were a cheerful mother-and-daughter team. No, they'd never been in a small plane, but they were looking forward to it.

I put Martha, the mother, in the passenger seat beside me. She was a generously built Pasifika woman and I hoped her weight would counterbalance the boxes. Matt and her daughter Lucy climbed into the back seats.

The cloud ceiling kept us fairly low over the water, but I was pleased to see the ridge was clear for us, and we made good time across Cook Strait. I dropped the women at the northern end of the strip, with their cleaning products, and pointed out the track round the lagoon.

"If you just stick to the trail you'll come out close to the baches," I explained. "You can't miss them, and the one you want is the furthest one along."

I taxied to the other end of the strip, parked up and began unloading while Matt went to get the quad. I needed his help to get the boxes out of the plane and tied on to the bike.

"You'd better not drive too fast," Matt cautioned. "They're not tied on that securely."

I grinned. "If I go too fast they'll act as an aerofoil and I'll be parasailing down the beach."

Matt smiled. "See you later then. You know we're all flying back out tomorrow? I've only come back to help with the packing out and cleaning." Matt looked sheepish. "Jane reckons the only reason I slip away from here for a day or two is to avoid the chores."

I smiled. "I think I saw Roger and Greig booked out for the flights tomorrow," I said. "I'll see you when I drop the quad back."

*   *   *

Jorge's house was open by the time I got there and the women hard at work emptying the fridge and freezer. I turned my nose up at the smell of rotten milk getting tipped down the sink.

"Can I help?" I asked.

The women looked at each other, then at me and laughed.

"No, thank you," said Martha. "We're a team and we're used to working together."

"And I'd get in the way? OK." I smiled and, after I'd unloaded the boxes for them, left them to it.

I stood outside the house and looked down at the grey water in the harbour. It was barely over a week since I'd stood in the same spot looking for Jorge. Even in that short time you could feel the change in the season. It was still warmish, but the long Indian summer we'd enjoyed was over, and I was grateful enough for the warm jacket I wore. Daylight saving finished next weekend, and I knew from experience just how fast the days closed in after that.

I took Greig's advice and hauled my mobile phone out of my pocket. I knew, from my work with the chart this morning that the location of the closest site was up behind the houses, away from the bay. I kept an eye on the phone and watched the GPS tick over as I climbed. I followed an old sheep track winding up the valley. Up ahead I could see a water tank set among a cluster of flax bushes on the side of the hill. There was no other object to focus on in the valley, so I made my way towards it.

Once beside the tank, the GPS confirmed I had found the correct location. I looked around. The tank was clearly in current use. A trickle of water leaked from a small crack in the concrete, and I saw the line of black piping which ran, partly hidden in grass, down the hill along the fence line. I looked back down the valley, the way I had come, to a fine view out to sea. Unless Jorge had been recording the position of water tanks on the island, there didn't seem to be anything useful or significant about the site.

I walked round the tank, rifled amongst the flax in case something was concealed there, and eventually, disappointed and bored by the pointlessness of the exercise, sat down on the concrete slab on which the tank rested. The few remaining black

Angus cattle on the island, a reminder of Joe McBeth's farming past, grazed peacefully along the sides of the valley.

I thought about Jorge. Now that Jack's information had had enough time to penetrate, I'd had to accept I'd never really known Jorge at all. Given his criminal history, who knew what other secrets he'd been concealing? Even so, it was odd that he would have written down the GPS location of this isolated water tank.

I'd hoped I was on a treasure hunt. Fired up with notions of geocaching, I had decided the coordinates on the envelope were a clue, and I'd solve Jorge's murder if only I could discover the secret of the cipher. I was evidently wrong.

I kicked moodily at the grass in front of me. Honesty forced me to acknowledge the charm of that notion had lain in returning triumphant with the solution to the murder and laying it all at Jack's feet like an enthusiastic gun dog. I had to ask what I had thought I was doing. Did the sight of an attractive man turn me into such a nerdy, needy person? Which led me to ask a further question – was this what I'd done with David? Had I given away my common sense as an offering at the beginning of our affair, and then resented it later when it was too late to go back?

The concrete was crumbling. I picked up a small fragment and pinged it at a nearby clump of tussock. I missed – typical of my throwing skills.

I swore, and reached for another fragment. My nails scrabbled against the old slab. This time, a lump of concrete came away that was far too large to throw. I looked in dismay at the mess I'd made. The chunk I had pulled out was large enough to expose the dirt below the slab. The damage approached vandalism.

"Shit." I started trying to replace the chunk. Maybe if I could shove it back into position the damage would be negligible. There was a lip on the concrete which stopped me easily inserting it. I got to my feet, turned and concentrated on fitting the concrete back together.

Some snag prevented the lump from sliding in. Hoping I didn't encounter any spiders, I slid my hand gingerly into the space beneath the concrete, to free whatever rubble blocked the wedge, and felt the unmistakable smoothness of plastic.

Intrigued, I lowered myself onto my tummy in the grass so I could reach deep into the cavity, and my fingers folded round the object. I pulled it towards me, and with a bit of manoeuvring wrangled it out of the hole. I was holding a PVC pipe, sealed top and bottom with that thick silver tape plumbers use.

I was about to rip into it to examine whatever was inside when some guardian angel tapped me on the shoulder and advised discretion.

Jorge had been murdered, and we didn't yet know why. He had hidden this canister and kept the code obscure. Maybe the two were connected.

My jacket had an inside pocket, and although I had to twist the container to make it fit, once snug in place it was hard to tell from the outside that I was anything but a plump, generously busted woman. I defied anyone to challenge me on that one!

I repaired the mess I had made. Without the container blocking it, the concrete chunk fitted neatly back into place. A few handfuls of sandy earth over the corner, and you would be hard pressed to know there had ever been a disturbance.

I sat back and rested my head against the tank. This time I really was relaxed. Whatever I had found surely had to be significant. Jorge, if he was the one who had buried it, had gone to some effort to hide the object. I'd been on a treasure hunt after all. I couldn't wait to tell Jen all about it. I imagined she'd be very smug and lord it over me and Lisa. I smiled, leaned back and very nearly snoozed off.

In the end it was the tugging at my shoelaces that stirred me. I opened my eyes to find an opportunistic weka experimentally searching my feet for food, pulling at the laces and testing the quality of those odd-looking worms. I'd seen a few of the large, flightless birds on previous visits to D'Urville. In this environment they saw few humans so were fearless. Matt had told me of one so confident it would walk into his bach every morning in search of food.

I watched it as it pecked round me. Eventually, when I shifted my feet, it ran away. It had been a lovely sight. I rose to my feet and made my way back down to the bach.

CHAPTER TEN

I'D ONLY BEEN GONE AN HOUR or so, but the women had already cleaned out the kitchen, stripped beds, cleaned the bathroom and were now packing Jorge's possessions into boxes. The place looked cleaner than I'd ever seen it. I carried the rubbish bags out to the quad bike and stacked them on the carrier. The boxes of personal possessions were to stay and would be picked up by the water taxi and shipped back to Wellington. I wondered who would buy the house, or whether it would be leased out. It was in a wonderful location, and having a previous owner murdered there might add a certain cachet for a new occupant, if they weren't superstitious. At least Jorge hadn't actually been murdered in the house.

The rubbish bags were heavy.

"Shit, what's in them?" I called back to the women.

I heard Lucy giggle. "Half packets of porridge, Weet-Bix, macaroni. You name it. It's all got to go."

I pushed another bag onto the pile and we heard a clank of bottles. "Did you find the wine cellar as well?" I asked.

"Tomato sauce, olive oil, lots of glassware."

"I just hope it doesn't smash and leak all through the plane," I muttered.

I was busy strapping the bags on to the bike when I realised, with a start of surprise, that I had company. The man standing across the other side of the quad was a stranger. I straightened up. "You gave me a bit of a turn. Can I help you?"

"Sorry," he said. "I didn't mean to startle you. I'm Bill Travers. I'm staying at Matt's place."

So this was the guy who had been so upset by Jorge's theory about Maori settlement.

"Oh, hi," I said. "Yes, Matt mentioned he had guests."

I looked him over. He was short for a man – not much taller than me – and thickset. Something about him seemed familiar. I had a feeling I'd seen him somewhere before and tried to place it.

"Matt said people had come in to clean this place up, and I wondered if you needed a hand."

As he was speaking he was peering over my shoulder at the open doorway behind me.

"Well, that's a kind thought," I said, "but I think the team in there have it all in hand. They made it clear to me when I offered to help that I'd only get in their way."

"I thought I could make myself useful lifting heavy stuff," said Bill.

"No, we're fine, truly," I said.

"Please let me help. It's the least I can do for Jorge's memory," insisted Bill. "We quarrelled the day before he died, and I've been feeling bad ever since."

I'd given no thought to security but suddenly realised I probably should protect Jorge's property from scrutiny by anyone unauthorised. I was uncomfortably aware of the hard PVC pipe pushing into my ribs under the cover of my jacket. "Matt said you'd argued with Jorge. Something about Maori settlement?"

"Jorge was a typical, uninformed foreigner who thought he knew more about being Maori than we do ourselves," said Bill scornfully. "He had some fancy idea about a tribe of people who came to New Zealand before the great Maori migration. He kept insisting he'd found something which proved his theory but wouldn't say what it was or how he found it. I was afraid he'd stumbled on an old gravesite and desecrated it. His story was a load of cobblers, of course, but he was insistent and I got angry."

I nodded. "Every now and again a new theory pops up." I suddenly realised where I'd seen him before. "Aren't you the guy who did the karakia a few years back, at the beginning of Victoria University's graduation day?" I asked. "You seem familiar."

"Probably," he said. "They call on me from time to time. About five years ago?"

I nodded. "That would be about right." It also explained why Bill had been so upset with Jorge. "If you're involved in Maori ceremony and protocol, I imagine you must have taken Jorge's assertions very seriously," I said.

"I could only imagine what would happen if he wrote a book about it," he said. "We'd have every racist crackpot in the land telling us that Maori aren't the real tangata whenua and trying to rewrite history. The only reason I regret the quarrel now is because he died. It was completely bloody irresponsible of him to try and spread rumours." Bill was getting heated. His face was flushed and with his short, stocky body he'd begun to look like an enraged turkey.

"Well, he's dead now, and I understand from Matt there was no sign of any book he might have written among his papers," I said in an attempt to calm him down. "So all's well that ends well."

He shrugged. "It's over anyway. We may never know if he really found anything. Which brings me back to saying, I'm happy to help you with lifting and carrying and doing the heavy stuff. That way your team can concentrate on the cleaning."

His intensity worried me. Bill looked as if he was still going to try and push the issue.

"Thanks again for the offer, but I can't let anyone unauthorised handle Jorge's stuff. I'm sure you understand," I said firmly.

"Oh, of course. I understand." He hesitated, but I looked steadily at him, making it clear he'd no choice but to leave. I saw his shoulders drop as he accepted defeat.

"Enjoy your day," he said as he turned to make his way back

down to the sea.

I waved to him once he had made it to the beach and wondered why he had come round. I might have been reading too much into it, and Bill might just have been trying to be helpful, but I'd got a creepy vibe off him. Was he interested in whatever it was Jorge claimed to have found? I gave a mental shrug. Once everything was packed up it would be a problem Jorge's lawyer could deal with. I wondered again whether they'd managed to find some next of kin.

I got the plane loaded with the bags and took the bike back to Matt's place. He was sitting out on the deck with Bill and another man I'd never met. I assumed this was the Ted that Matt had mentioned. I nodded at Bill who waved back.

"All done?" asked Matt.

"Yes, we're out of here. The boat will come in a couple of days and take off all the stuff that's still in the house boxed up. Otherwise it's all done and dusted."

"Apart from the murderer," said Matt.

"Apart from," I echoed. It was a nasty feeling that the murderer could conceivably be one of the men sitting here on the deck. I wondered about their alibis. Jack had given me a detailed description of Jorge's movements that afternoon, but he hadn't been forthcoming about anyone else. It was easy to become paranoid. I put the thought away and said my farewells.

"We're just taking a break from our own packing up," said Matt. "See you back in Paraparaumu tomorrow."

I thanked Matt and left them to it. I couldn't help but wonder how Bill had managed the time off to cross the bay and offer me help with Jorge's stuff, when he was clearly needed here to pack and clean up.

I got the women into the plane then finally took my jacket off, rolled it up and shoved it under the seat. The object in its pocket was heavy, and I had been getting increasingly overheated.

"Ready to rumble?" I asked my passengers as we taxied out.

*   *   *

I waved the women away. They went laughing. I had rarely met happier passengers.

"They loved it all," I said to Roger. "They thought the flying was exciting. They thought the island was great. I think they found the work fun. I don't know what they eat for breakfast, but the world needs more of it."

"That's Pasifika for you," said Maria. "Lovely people."

Fortunately none of the bottles had broken. I unloaded the sacks into the back of my car and took them to the rubbish tip. The fee could be added to the lawyer's bill for the flight.

I pulled out my jacket and went back into the office. "I've got a story to tell you," I said to Roger and Maria.

I went through the tale of finding Jorge's envelope, cracking the code (I didn't mention that was pure luck) and searching the site by the water tank. I prised the pipe out of my jacket. "And this is what I found. Shall we open it?"

"I think you'd better call the police first," said Maria. "Heaven knows what's in there, but you can't help but suspect it's drugs. After all, why else would the man hide it anywhere but at his house?"

Roger nodded. "Call that detective you were talking to."

I phoned Jack and explained. I wondered whether he'd think I was stalking him. Unexpectedly he didn't sound at all pleased with my news.

"What do you mean you went exploring and found this thing? Didn't you think you should let me know first before you went charging in? I'll be right down." He hung up and left me glaring at the phone. Well, really!

I stomped off to let Roger know that an arrogant, jumped-up git of a policeman was about to visit us.

Sam wandered in for a cup of coffee and caught the tail end of my pique. He looked at Roger who rolled his eyes. Sometimes I could swear if he weren't my boss I'd throw something at him.

I went outside and worked off my temper by pushing the plane back into the hangar for the night. Nothing like a bit of physical work to take the edge off a tantrum. As I got the aircraft put away the first drops of rain began falling. I looked up at the sky, then glanced out at Kapiti Island. The cloud level had lowered so that half the island was obscured.

"Let's hope that cloud doesn't get too low," I said as I went back inside, "otherwise Greig will be in for an overnighter up in Hawera. What time is he due back?"

"Fiveish," said Maria. "There's still time for it to clear."

Jack had the good sense not to have brought his snide remarks with him. It was all business as he took his notes.

"So just to confirm. You only discovered this morning that the numbers were GPS coordinates?"

"Yes," I said. "It came to me when I was lying awake in bed last night that the sequence looked familiar. I'd been teaching navigation yesterday evening. It just clicked into place."

"And you identified one of the sites as close to Jorge's bach?"

"Yes," I said breezily. "It's quite easy with a mobile phone."

Jack frowned as if he read something in my tone, but let the comment go. "I suppose we'd better look at it then," he said, picking up the cylinder and inspecting its sealing tape.

"Here." Roger handed over his penknife and Jack sliced along the tape.

The object inside was protected by bubble wrap. Jack put gloves on before removing the wrap.

"Well, it doesn't look like drugs," said Maria.

"No, it doesn't," said Jack, sliding it out onto the table.

"What is it?" asked Roger.

"A pendant, I would think," replied Jack. He studied it closely, turning it gently in his hands. The greenstone was an elongated triangular shape about eleven centimetres long. At the broad end were two small holes. Jack poked a careful finger at them. "I assume that was how it was suspended round the neck," he said. We stared at the opaque dark green artefact. The light from the windows brought out the dull gloss of its polished finish.

"Look at the carving," marvelled Maria.

On either side of the pendant a line of chevron ornamentation ran down the edge while the centre held a thin, raised carving.

Jack turned the piece onto its side. In relief, the creature looked a bit like a lizard. "I don't know much about such things," he said, "but I think it might be an amulet."

"It's unusual, don't you think?" said Maria. "I've never seen anything like that before. Most Maori carving is curvy, even sinuous, if you know what I mean, like the koru motif. This is very geometric and angular."

"It looks old, not something bright and shiny and newly purchased in Hokitika," said Roger. "It's a very simple design. It almost looks like a museum piece."

We stared at it in silence.

"Why was it hidden in such an odd place?" asked Maria eventually.

Jack lifted his head and smiled at her. "That is the million-dollar question. We have to assume it was Jorge who buried it, because he had the coordinates. We'll get the envelope checked, but I'm certain we'll find it was his writing. Why hide something you would normally expect him to have in his house as a piece of art?"

"Because it wasn't his," I said slowly. "He must have stolen it, or got it illicitly, and didn't want to leave it where it could be found if someone searched his house."

"That's probably the reason," agreed Jack. "There's something significant about this pendant and we're going to have to find out what it is and where it came from. Whether it relates to Jorge's murder is a different issue."

"I don't understand why it was hidden on the island at all," said Roger. "Surely it would be easier to hide something like this here on the mainland? None of us would have noticed if he'd put it into his backpack. He must have taken it out to the island like that."

"It's not easy for most people to get out to D'Urville. Maybe he thought it would be more secure out there. Alternatively, perhaps it actually came from somewhere on the island," said Jack.

"When I flew Matt back last week, he said Jorge had found something that would change our understanding of Maori history," I said. "It annoyed Matt's other guest Bill, who is

Maori. Bill came round to Jorge's bach today when we were there and started talking about it to me. He was still fired up over whatever it was Jorge said."

"Yeah, Matt told me about it. Well, maybe this is what he was talking about, although, I can't quite see why a greenstone pendant should be expected to change our understanding of history," said Jack doubtfully. "This'll be one for the experts, I should think. We'll have to find out if someone has reported a missing pendant, either stolen or otherwise lost. If that doesn't help, we'll need the staff at the museum to look at it and give us an opinion on its provenance."

He carefully repackaged the parcel and I showed him out. He stopped in the doorway. "I got the impression you were a bit pissed off with me back there."

"When I phoned to let you know about the package, you sounded annoyed I hadn't told you about the coordinates before I went searching. I don't like being snarled at."

He gave a rueful grin. "I thought you'd been holding out on me last night, not telling me that you'd cracked the significance of those numbers."

"And now you know I wasn't?"

"I'm not snarling anymore."

We looked at each other. His eyes were laughing, daring me to continue being angry with him.

"I don't like arrogant cops who make assumptions," I said at last.

"And I don't like stroppy pilots with attitude problems," he replied, "so it's just as well that doesn't describe either of us." He was openly grinning now.

His eyes held mine. I tried to think of something clever and acidic to say, but in spite of myself I smiled. Bugger, he'd managed to get through to me.

"Have you got the hots for the detective then?" Roger of course, with his usual elegance of mind.

"I'm assisting him with his enquiries," I said tartly.

"I'll just bet you are," was Roger's reply. I suppose it stopped just short of being a leer, but not by much.

My eyes met Maria's and we exchanged a glance of female solidarity. She smiled as she looked away.

CHAPTER
ELEVEN

THE RADIO CRACKLED INTO LIFE ANNOUNCING that Greig was joining on long finals. I looked outside. The light was going; it was gusty and pouring with rain. We watched as he touched down.

"He'll be happy to be back," remarked Roger.

The passengers climbed out of the aircraft and rushed across the apron to the warmth of the waiting room. I grabbed a coat and went outside to help Greig put the plane away. "How was the flight?"

"A bit bumpy. One of the passengers wasn't too happy. He doesn't like flying even on a good day."

"It was a good landing," I remarked.

Greig laughed. "It's so windy, I had to bring her in at full speed. The second I pulled the throttle back, we landed. There's no gliding along the runway in this weather."

By the time the aircraft was tucked neatly into the hangar I had filled him in on the day's events.

"Wow." Greig was impressed. "So we're thinking this item is 'hot' in some way?"

"Why else would Jorge have hidden it in such an odd spot? I still don't see why he didn't take it off the island. The package was well hidden, but even so, the concrete was chipped and broken. Water could have got in, or a cow or rabbit might have disturbed it."

"Maybe he was planning to take it. He might have been going back for it when he was murdered that afternoon. It's only our assumption that he was going back to the bach to grab his luggage. From what you've said, it wouldn't have taken him very long to walk up the valley, retrieve the cylinder, go back to the house for his stuff and then get down to the airstrip."

"It's possible, I suppose." I shrugged.

The doors to the office slammed and Greig's girlfriend stomped in.

"Here comes trouble," murmured Greig from behind me. "I'm late. I said we'd go to the movies."

I left him to deal with her. For Greig's sake I tried to be polite to the girl, but I deeply disliked both her attitude, and the way she treated him. Every time I looked at her I saw trailer-trash material. It was inevitable her name was Jayleen.

I'd made such a comment to Roger, who I knew disliked her as much as I did and was surprised when he said, "That's a little harsh, don't you think? Your prejudices are showing, Hardcastle."

Well, they were of course, but I still thought she was a waste of space and oxygen. "Her name sounds like a toilet cleaner," I replied.

Roger gave a small, appreciative grin. "Maybe so, but it's still not a very gracious comment."

He pretended not to hear my muttered, "Pot calling kettle black."

Greig must have succeeded in pacifying Jayleen because they joined us in the waiting room.

I liked our ritual, a couple of times a week, of an after-work drink to wrap up the day. It was an opportunity for a social chat and a catch-up.

Jayleen leaned over towards me. "You knew I'd met the pervert who got murdered?" she asked. "The one the police said was a paedophile?" She gave a bit of a leer, as if his salacious reputation excited her.

"Yes, you told me the other day."

"He gave a talk at our school when we were in year seven."

I had a sudden image of Jorge in a classroom of pubescent children, and shuddered. "I hope he didn't spend too much time with the kids," I said.

Jayleen shrugged. "There was talk back then that he was a dirty old man. I think some of the girls knew him better than I did, so there was gossip. It didn't bother me; I wasn't interested in books so I didn't pay much attention to him."

A genuine case where ignorance was bliss, I thought. Jack had said there was a possibility Jorge had continued to offend after his release from prison. I wondered whether to tell him about Jayleen's comment.

*　　*　　*

I picked up the phone and dialled Jen. "I've been geocaching," I said when she answered.

"You have?" She sounded surprised. "Which one did you look for?"

I chuckled and told her the story of the coordinates. "So you see, it was you telling me about geocaching that got me started. I owe you one, and so do the police."

"That's really exciting." Jen sounded pleased. "I've been instrumental in solving a murder."

"Well, not quite," I cautioned. "The pendant may or may not be relevant to the murder. Still, it's interesting, isn't it?"

We chatted some more. Rehearsals were going well.

"How's the love life?"

"No progress," she said, sounding disappointed. "This one might take a while to hook."

"Good luck," I said.

"How're things going with Sam? Did you sort out your differences?"

I shrugged. "We've agreed we're incompatible, so it's back to the drawing board."

My mind flicked involuntarily to Jack. I might be wary of his physical presence, but he had definite magnetism. I suppressed the thought. For all I knew he was married with four kids.

CHAPTER TWELVE

ROGER AND GREIG SPENT MOST OF Friday ferrying Matt, his family and guests home from D'Urville. It took three trips to get them all back. The tarmac was covered with a clutter of baggage, young children and their family pet, an Irish terrier puppy, which frisked around and got in everybody's way. It was chaos while we unloaded the aircraft.

"School holidays are finished," remarked Maria once the group had left the office.

Roger nodded. "That'll be the last of the flights out to the island for a while. Just as well. The weather is on the turn."

I looked at the rain that had begun falling and sighed. More paperwork.

Roger looked at my face and grinned. "I've good news for you. A young chap is coming in next week who wants to do his instructor's rating. He's yours if you want him."

"For his C Cat? That's great," I said enthusiastically. Taking a student through an instructor's course was one of the best parts of a flying instructor's job. It was intensive, demanding, a lot of fun and kept everyone on their toes. It also guaranteed flying hours for Paraparaumu Aviation as the student built up the hours they needed to qualify. No wonder Roger looked as if he'd won

Lotto.

Paraparaumu Aviation punched well above its weight when it came to attracting students, and I'd been part of training a few instructors now. Roger, besides being a great pilot, was a very savvy businessman. He was good at selling the benefits of training with us to prospective punters. They came to train at Paraparumu in equal parts because of his charm – because he convinced them of the advantages of flying from a small airfield so close to the capital with the aviation challenges that posed – and his final trump card was the opportunity for young pilots to do their first commercial flying with us, taking scenic flights and charters. A young pilot who met Roger's high standards and played their cards right could get a strong grounding in a wide aspect of aviation. Roger was a respected presence throughout the industry.

"He's moved up from Christchurch," he said. "When he left Canterbury they advised him to come to us."

"Even better," I replied. "If you want quality, come to the best," and I went off happily to make everyone a cup of coffee.

The clocks were going back that weekend, which meant it would be slightly easier to get up in the mornings, but the evenings were closing in early and I missed my walks. I was getting a little stir-crazy.

We'd heard no more about how the investigation into Jorge's murder was going. The media had lost interest in the story, and it had faded from the news. I wondered whether the police had followed up on the second lot of coordinates, but there had been no mention about the Maori pendant on the news, so I supposed they were playing their cards close to their chests.

* * *

My mobile showed a message from Kate asking if I could babysit for her and Martin. I could, and texted back to confirm the time. My Friday nights were rarely booked up.

The two girls were looking suspiciously angelic when I arrived. They'd been fed, bathed and were, I was told, ready for an early night. I smiled reassuringly at Kate, who worries, and waved her and Martin out the door. Martin gave me a wink as he left. I suspect he knew exactly the sort of shenanigans his daughters got up to when left in the charge of their aunt.

I was expecting to be cajoled into letting the girls watch videos. *Frozen* is a wonderful film for little girls, and I'd have been happy enough to see it again, and sing my way through the choruses as required. To my surprise, the girls were more interested in hearing the story of the body I'd discovered.

I sighed. Kate and Martin had probably tried to keep the tale hidden from them, failed (of course) and now the girls wanted details. Preferably the gory details.

I had no licence to scare small children with ghoulish stories, the elements of which were too horrible for me to willingly recall. I knew I trod a very narrow line on this and gave them a bowdlerised version of events, focusing less on what had happened to Jorge than on the police work and detection that such an incident occasioned. They were caught by the story of the hidden envelope, its code and the hidden treasure.

"Did the treasure belong to the dead man?" asked Sophie.

"We don't know that yet, darling," I replied. I felt like Robert Louis Stevenson doing a public reading of *Treasure Island*.

By the time I managed to satisfy their questions, calm them down, get their teeth brushed and finally tuck them into bed, I felt I deserved the large glass of wine I poured from the bottle Kate had obligingly left on their bench.

Kate and Martin were home before midnight.

"I remember babysitting for you two when the earliest you were home was two o'clock," I teased.

"Mm," said my sister tiredly. "Well, Sophie's up at six, so it's not really an option. Charlotte at least stays in bed until seven. Old married people go to bed by ten."

"This is living on the wild side," said Martin, joining me with a wine. "You wait until you get to this point. How were the girls?"

"Fiendish and angelic as always," I said cheerfully. "They wanted stories about Jorge, and I gave them a sort of *Treasure Island* version. They seemed happy."

Kat gave a 'hmph' noise.

"Now you sound like Mum," I smiled. I stood up and stretched. "I'll leave you to it. I'm working tomorrow myself."

I'd left no house lights on, so everything was pitch black as I made my way up the drive, but I knew the place so well I could manoeuvre through it in the dark.

I parked and went to unlock the front door. As I leant against it, fumbling for my key, the door moved open. I took a step back in surprise.

I was absolutely certain I'd shut and locked it before I went out. My heart beating fast, I shoved the door hard open and switched on the inside lights.

He had been waiting just inside the door. The sudden light blinded him. For a brief moment he paused, before launching his attack.

I had no time to be afraid. His full weight landed on me in a tackle, throwing me sideways towards the floor. It was too fast for a planned defence.

All I could do was grab onto his shoulders and pull, so he fell with me. In that movement, my bent leg wedged between his thighs, and his weight and momentum forced his crotch onto the hard surface of my patella.

I felt him flinch, and his breath went out of him in a high, girlish shriek. He rolled sideways away from me.

I rubbed my bruised hip as I struggled to my feet.

My would-be assailant was in a moaning huddle on the floor. Luck had been on my side, but I wasn't about to chance it running out.

I looked round for some means to secure him.

Lacking any handy lengths of rope, I pulled the charging cord for my mobile from its socket and tied it tightly round his feet. Once certain they were secure, and working to a theme, I grabbed the cord from my tablet and used that to tie his hands.

I had to drag at his arms to pry his hands away from his

genitals. He moaned then, not, I think, from the awkwardness of my bondage methods, but because he wanted his hands cradling his crotch.

CHAPTER THIRTEEN

IT HAD ALL HAPPENED TOO QUICKLY for fear, nerves or any other normal shock response. I realised this happy state wouldn't last long. Reaction would set in quickly now the situation was controlled.

I phoned 111 and went through the now-familiar process.

Yes, I wanted the police. Yes. I meant now. The offender was still here and immobilised.

The dispatcher was calm, professional and prosaic. The police would be with me when they could get there. I resisted the urge to question how long it would take them if I executed this intruder myself and rang off.

Taking frustrations out on a functionary shows a lack of class, I reminded myself.

I took the opportunity to kick the man at my feet in the kneecap. My hip was sore from the fall, and his moaning was getting on my nerves.

"You bastard. Look at all the trouble you've caused."

I walked backwards across the room to the log fire and took the poker from the fire stand. If this idiot tried anything funny I had every intention of knocking him over the head. Now armed, I felt safer, and approached him again.

"Who are you?" I asked. "What do you want?"

I got no reply. I hadn't expected one.

His head was turned away from me, his face masked with nylon hose. Very 1980s TV cop show reruns, I thought. Surely he realised that modern thieves wore Joker masks?

I reached down and tried to yank it off. It was tight and got caught around his chin as I pulled. At last I realised it was quicker to roll the thing up from his neck. I knelt beside him and finally managed to work it free from his face.

I studied him for a moment.

He kept his head turned away but I'd seen enough to know who it was. "It's Bill, isn't it? As in Bill, Matt's friend and last seen by me on D'Urville? Perhaps you'd like to tell me what the hell you think you're doing in my house trying to be a bogeyman?"

It was irrational, of course, but for some reason I felt much safer now I knew who it was.

The lights of a vehicle went past the window and I heard the sound of car tyres squealing on the driveway outside.

"I think we've got company," I told Bill and went to see who it was.

It was Jack. He rushed up the step, grabbed me by the shoulders and gave me a quick, assessing, once-over look.

"I heard your call come over the radio," he said and turned to the man on the ground.

"It's Bill," I said helpfully.

"So I see," said Jack. He looked at the trussed man, gave a grin as he realised Bill's degree of incapacity, and looked at me. "What have you got to say for yourself?"

"Me?" I asked in surprise.

"You," said Jack. "Would you care to explain how this man comes to be tied up on the floor? You aren't hurt, I take it?"

I was starting to get annoyed. If he was going to be arrogant he could just turn around and leave. "He must have broken in and been waiting for me. When I turned the lights on, he tried to jump me."

"Which you duly dealt with," said Jack.

"Yes," I said curtly.

"Well done," he said softly, for only me to hear. I was surprised to hear the smile in his voice.

"I called 111. God knows when the police will come."

"Just as well I heard the call go out on the radio then." His eyes were amused when they looked at me. "What were you planning to do with that?"

"What?" I asked stupidly.

"The poker," he said, gently taking it from me and putting it back in its place by the fire.

He knelt down beside Bill and checked his bindings. He undid the one round his ankles and handed it back to me.

"You may need that," he said. I replaced the cord in the wall plug, connected my phone to charge, and by the time I'd turned, Jack had rolled Bill onto his back and lifted him up by the front of his shirt so he sat with his back against the wall. Bill showed a marked disinclination to cooperate. Presumably the damage to his genitals was seriously painful if his hunched posture was anything to go by.

"You sit down," Jack instructed me, "and I'll pour you a drink, then we can ask your house guest what he's doing here."

He settled me on the couch, which was just as well, as my knees were getting wavery and my hands starting to shake. He poured a generous slug of wine into a glass and put it in my hands.

"I'll put the jug on, but get that down you while the water boils." He turned back to Bill. "You've got a good deal of explaining to do. We can take a statement when the police get here. In the meantime you'd better start talking to me."

"Why did you attack me?" I asked. "What have I done to you?"

"I didn't come for you," said Bill. I thought he sounded downright sulky.

"Well, what did you want?" asked Jack. He looked round the house. "What were you searching for?"

I lifted my head. I had been too busy to notice, but it was clear Bill had been ransacking my home. Some of the drawers were not pushed in properly, and I could see books in the case were out of order. I'm not anal, nor a fanatically house-proud woman, but I live alone and prefer to keep my surroundings neat and tidy. I got up and walked to my bedroom. It was even clearer there that an intruder had been through. The pillows were untidy on the bed, the sheets rumpled and, worse, no Nelson.

"What have you done with my cat?" I asked angrily. "He's always here to greet me. What did you did to him?"

"I haven't seen a cat," said Bill in alarm. He could probably read the murderous intent on my face.

"If you've hurt a single whisker, I swear I'll kick you in the balls again," I said. I was furious. Breaking and entering was one thing; disturbing my cat brought the crime to a whole new level.

I saw Jack wince slightly as I moved past him to the door. "Nelson," I called out into the night. "Nelson, come on."

"I haven't seen your bloody cat," Bill said again, sounding rather desperate.

"Why are you here?" Jack repeated.

"I was looking for the pendant she found," Bill replied.

I turned and looked at him in surprise. "You were looking for the pendant?"

"Matt said you'd found one at Jorge's place. I needed to see it."

"Well it's not here," I said crossly. "If you'd asked me, I could have told you the police have it and saved us all a lot of trouble."

"Does the amulet belong to you?" queried Jack. I recognised his quiet tone of voice. It was the one he used on me when he interviewed me about the murder. From personal experience I knew it could wear away stone.

Bill looked flustered. "No, it's not mine."

"Then what made you think you could break in here and take it?"

Bill took a deep breath, gave the shadow of a shrug and recovered his confidence. "I want my lawyer here before I answer any questions."

Jack looked at him as if he was some particularly unpleasant insect. "Is that so?" he asked. "Let's see now. You were over on the island at the time of the homicide. You were the only person that we know of who'd quarrelled with the deceased – and I've heard it was quite a nasty quarrel."

"No," Bill blustered. "You've got it wrong."

Jack ignored him and ploughed on. "You admitted that you had no alibi the afternoon of the murder. Now you've owned up to breaking into Miss Hardcastle's house with the intent of committing theft. Who knows what else you had in mind?"

Jack turned to me. "And he won't cooperate with the police and answer questions either. It's not looking too flash for Bill, is it?"

I'd suspected there was a core of steel within DSS Body and now I was seeing it. I doubted he would actually beat Bill up, but the intensity of his gaze held unmistakable menace. Bill squirmed.

I stared at Bill and said nothing.

"By the time we've charged you with murder you're certainly going to need that lawyer," said Jack, smirking at him. "It looks like this has been a nice, easy homicide for us to solve."

"I didn't have anything to do with the murder," said Bill. He was starting to look desperate. If he hadn't just tried to attack me I might have felt some sympathy.

"Soon the rest of the team will be here to take care of you," said Jack. "They just love crims with attitude problems."

"You can't charge me with Jorge's killing," said Bill, who was floundering now. "I didn't do it."

Jack looked down his nose at that.

"OK, I'll answer your questions," said Bill, abruptly caving in. "What do you want to know?"

"I want to know why you broke in here to steal the pendant. You've already admitted it isn't yours."

"I think Jorge raided an ancient grave and found the pendant there, which means it would belong to the ancestors. If that's the case, the taonga needs to be returned to my iwi."

I saw Jack considering this. "What makes you think that?"

"Jorge told us. We were at a barbecue, and he was talking about a great find he'd made. He wouldn't say where he found the item, but he implied it was from up in the bush. I know he'd been up there the previous week. He said it would blow the socks off archaeology in this country. He was gloating about it, even though he knew I was Maori and he was being offensive. He said he could prove Maori weren't the first settlers in New Zealand. The Waitaha people had arrived centuries earlier. When I asked him to be specific and tell us what he'd found he laughed at me and told me not to be nosey. I'd learn all about it when he wrote his new novel."

"The new novel that we found no trace of on his computer," remarked Jack thoughtfully. "We didn't even find any notes when we searched Jorge's papers." I saw he was watching Bill closely.

Bill squirmed a little on the floor. I don't imagine he was comfortable.

I called again for Nelson, and this time heard his cry.

"Nelson," I called again, and he emerged from the bushes and walked towards me. I scooped him up and hugged him, which he tolerated for a minute before indicating he'd prefer to be on the floor.

He sidled up to Bill and sniffed him cautiously. His tail was rigidly upright, and I thought he gave a little quiver of disdain as he caught Bill's scent. I went to open a tin of cat food. Nelson turned his back on Bill, sat down and ostentatiously began to lick himself clean. Every line of his being indicated that he had never been scared of this low creature beside him on the floor. He had come in late because he had chosen to do so.

I smiled, filled his food and water bowls and returned to sit beside Jack.

"Did you ever read any of Jorge's novels?" Jack asked Bill.

Bill grunted. "I tried once, but it was like reading Mad Max: motorbikes and desolation and women getting beaten up. I couldn't finish it. When I heard Jorge was a pervert I could well believe it. There was something nasty about his writing."

Jack nodded. "But I think Jorge said this new novel was going to be about something very different?"

"That's what he said that night," agreed Bill.

"So the next day you went in search of the grave you thought

Jorge had desecrated?"

"No, not really," he said. He registered the expression on Jack's face. "Well yes, maybe. OK, I went for a walk in the hills." Bill began to look less confident and his face had lost colour.

"A walk that you hoped would take you to a grave?"

"I didn't know that one existed really, and if there was one, I didn't know where it was." I could see Bill was beginning to get flustered and remembered how Jack had managed to get me on the run with his questions.

Bill continued, "But yes, OK, I thought it was worth a hike in case I stumbled upon it. It couldn't have been too difficult to get to, else Jorge wouldn't have found it. He tramped in the bush a bit, but he was no bushman, if you know what I mean."

"And at the end of it, you were unsuccessful?"

Bill nodded. "The country is very dense. A grave could be hidden anywhere, and maybe Jorge just got lucky."

"So then you went back to Greville Harbour," said Jack. "What time did you get there, do you think?"

"Maybe about four o'clock; I can't be too precise," said Bill. I could see he'd begun to sweat.

"And you said in your statement that you came down the ridge at the southern end of the bay, so you'd have headed down towards Matt's bach? I think that route brings you out of the bush fairly high up on the ridge, doesn't it? The last part of your descent would have been through grassland."

Bill nodded cautiously.

"It must have been a lovely view down over the harbour; it was a sunny afternoon. Did you see the rest of your party on the beach and out in the dinghy?"

Bill nodded. "Yeah, that's right." He was watching Jack now with all the intensity of a hypnotised snake.

Jack nodded. "I see. So whereabouts were you when the Cub took off?"

Bill stared blankly. "What?"

"The white, single-engine, high-winged, tail-dragger aircraft," I added helpfully.

"I don't know." Bill was looking rattled.

"OK," said Jack. "Then where were you when Claire here flew in? You know her plane, you've seen it before."

"Um … yeah, I heard a plane. Must have been when I was on the ridge. I didn't take any notice of the time."

"It would be pretty hard to miss, I'd have thought. It would have been noisy, and the aircraft must have come quite close to where you were on the ridge as she made her turn down towards the strip." Jack shook his head. "I'm afraid I'm not believing much of what you're saying, Bill," he said.

"It's true …" Bill tried to cut in.

Jack put his hand up. "Yes, I'll accept that you went up into the hills looking for a grave, but I don't accept you came back down the southern ridge. I think you came down the northern ridge and went to Jorge's bach."

"No, that's not true!"

Jack ignored him. "We were able to get a clear print of your tramping boot from the dirt around Jorge's place."

There was complete silence for a few minutes, during which I watched Bill crumple. I could see beads of sweat form on his forehead. "I didn't do anything," he pleaded.

"And while you were in his house, on your own, you took it upon yourself to steal his notes and delete the file on his computer. Just like this evening you took it upon yourself to search Claire's home for the pendant. I have to hand it to you, Bill; you've got an independent mind. You think outside the box."

"I didn't touch him," Bill said at last. "I swear I never hurt him. Yes, I had wanted to ask him about the grave, but he wasn't in the bach." There was silence for a few minutes. I could hear Bill's harsh breathing. "I didn't kill him."

"Let's say the jury is still out on whether you actually killed him," said Jack. "But you certainly knew he was dead. Otherwise, what would be the point in trying to destroy his files and notes if he could just rewrite them again?"

I gave a gasp and stared at Bill, horrified. I'd had a murderer in my house trying to attack me? It didn't bear thinking about.

Bill opened his mouth and shut it again. I saw him swallow.

"OK," said Jack patiently. "Let's have it again, but this time the true version."

"I did what I said," Bill started again. "I went up into the hills but didn't find anything useful. I came down the ridge." He saw Jack about to interrupt and said, "Yes, OK, the northern ridge."

"What time were you back on the flats?"

"I don't know, I didn't have a watch, but I would think it would be about three-thirty, or a bit after. I walked the northern side of the lagoon to Jorge's place, and I found his body in the dunes, just where the path turns towards the beach." He turned to me. "Where you found him."

"Then what?"

"I thought if I went to Jorge's house I could find anything he'd written about a grave. If I could stop people knowing about it, then maybe the site would be safe. I found the notes on his desk then checked his computer. He had a file called D'Urville. I had a quick look and it seemed what I was looking for, so I deleted it. That's all I did, I swear."

"And you took his notes? You realise our forensic people can retrieve files on a computer?" asked Jack. "They found the file you deleted."

Bill looked even paler. "I didn't know. Well, I didn't think," he whispered.

"How did you get back to Matt's place?"

"I walked back round the lagoon the way I'd come. That's when I heard a plane take off, but I was well round the lagoon by then."

"What about the young couple in the house next to Jorge's?"

Bill looked confused. "I didn't see anyone."

"They were sitting on the deck with a fire going when Claire went past. Surely you must have seen them, and they must have seen you?"

For a moment Bill looked hopeful, and then shook his head sadly. "I saw no one. And as I hadn't actually done anything wrong, I thought I was safe and it would be OK."

"You'd failed to give a stricken man help, and you then burgled his house and thought it would be 'OK'?" Jack's voice rose. "I think, mate, you need to redefine your ideas of right and wrong."

"I couldn't help him. He was dead," protested Bill.

On cue, another set of car lights swept up the drive. I went to let the cops in, thinking they were only half an hour too late if Bill had tried to murder me.

They entered and didn't look too impressed with my set up, until one of them saw Jack.

"Hello, Jack," she said. "What brings you here?"

"Hi, Tina. I'm working on a case for which Ms Hardcastle is a witness. I heard she had a problem with a break-in, and came round to lend a hand. As it happens, she had already competently dealt with the situation."

The PC went through the processes of charges, statements and paperwork while her partner hauled Bill outside to the cop car. I wasn't sorry to see him go. Murderer or not, he had caused enough mayhem.

Finally they left, and Jack and I were alone. I looked at the clock; it was past two in the morning. I was exhausted and gave a great, inelegant yawn. Tomorrow was already today, and I was due at work in far too few hours.

Jack stood up. "Are you OK now?"

I nodded. "OK, yes. Tired, and shattered by what Bill told us tonight, but OK. I didn't realise you already knew he had been at the bach."

Jack looked at me sideways. "I didn't know. I knew Jorge's computer had been tampered with, but we didn't know who by. I thought Bill was a probable suspect because he had reacted to talk about Maori artefacts, that's all."

"But you said you had found his footprint," I said, confused.

"Did I? Perhaps that was just a serendipitous mistake I made. I probably meant I had found his footprints around Matt's place. Still, it would have been hard to prove Bill had been at Jorge's place if he hadn't admitted it. He's not the sharpest tool in the shed. He didn't know that although he deleted the D'Urville file, he'd left it sitting in the Recycle Bin."

I looked at him sharply, but he smiled serenely.

"Go to sleep, Claire. It's been a long night, and you did very well. Now you need to let it go and get some rest."

"Thanks for coming round," I said, sincerely. His presence had been immensely reassuring, and I'd felt safe with him, which had mitigated the shock of Bill's attack.

"It was the least I could do," he said, "although you had it all in hand by the time I'd arrived. Not bad for a mere pilot."

I rolled my eyes at him and opened the door.

"One more question?" he asked.

I looked at him.

"Are any of those rings you wear a wedding ring, or something like it?"

I gasped slightly and looked down at my fingers. I liked rings. Unfortunately we don't come with enough fingers to wear as many as I would have liked, but I always wore my mother's engagement ring and my auntie's eternity ring. It made me feel they were still with me in spirit, even though my mum had been dead two years. Then there was the gold ring my parents gave me when I graduated, and … You get the picture. As I say, I liked rings.

"No," I assured Jack. "No wedding rings, or significant others."

"That's a relief," he said seriously. "Then would you like to have dinner with me tomorrow night?"

Wow, I hadn't seen that coming. I shut my mouth, which had fallen open unattractively, and smiled at him. "That sounds good to me."

He grinned back at me. "I'll phone you."

I think my smile could have won an award. There was no way I could politely suppress it. I didn't want to gush, so I shut my mouth and said nothing, but I'm guessing my face gave the rest away.

Jack grinned again. "Make sure you lock your doors behind me."

He gave me a quick peck on the cheek and was gone.

I watched his car back up and swing round in the turn that took him down the drive. I waved as he left, locked the door and turned out the lights. I just managed to make it to bed before I collapsed into an exhausted sleep that lasted through until the ugly noise of the alarm broke into my dreams.

Usually I'm an early waker, but that morning I struggled to get out of bed. Nelson, who had slept the night curled beside me, yawned, stretched and jumped off to investigate breakfast. It was his yowl of protest when I didn't appear in the kitchen to feed him that finally drove me from my warm mattress.

* * *

Saturdays and Sundays were always the busiest and most social days for flying organisations. Pilots who'd spent the week at work, earning the money to feed their flying habit, now wanted their fix and there was usually a steady stream of enthusiastic flyers taking off to master turns, stalls and the other aviation exercises. On fine days, there would be one or two who simply wanted the pleasure of a scenic flight over Paraparaumu and Kapiti. If they lived in the area, they probably wanted to fly over their property and take pictures.

Invariably they came with extras who hung around our waiting room drinking coffee and enjoying being around the glamour of aviation. Roger had his own little band of groupies who turned up regularly because they 'loved flying'. He managed to impart basic flying skills to some of them, and he'd even managed to send a couple solo, but the truth was these ladies wanted to spend time with their hero and would prefer to admire him without the risks involved in actually flying the plane. It irritated the hell out of Roger and amused the rest of us.

I felt a certain leaden heaviness after all the excitement of the night before and found the social interaction more trying than usual. Even Greig noticed.

"Got out of the wrong side of bed this morning?" he asked after he'd heard me swear when I ripped a fingernail while unscrewing an aircraft's oil cap.

"Heavy night last night," I replied.

His eyebrows went up. "Really? Should I hear the details? Remember I'm still young and impressionable."

"Idiot," I smiled. "No, I had a break-in." I told him the details.

Roger came across to find out why we were leaning on a fuselage rather than working. I included him in the tale. "That's not good," he commented at the end. "Maybe Bill's the murderer, maybe he's not, but the sooner they find the culprit, the better. Are you all right?"

"It all happened too quickly last night for me to worry about it, but I'm feeling a bit rattled today," I confessed. "Probably because I'm tired. And I've got a massive bruise on my hip from when we hit the ground."

"Clever, the way Jack got Bill to talk, though, wasn't it?" said Greig.

"They're obviously privy to a lot of information they haven't yet released to the media," said Roger. "It does make you wonder whether they already know who the murderer is. Did you get the impression it was Bill?"

"Well at first, after I heard he'd found Jorge's body and done nothing to help, I was certain. But Jack didn't seem to be making a big deal out of it, so I don't know. Anyway, at least the police took Bill away, and now he knows I don't have his precious pendant, I should be safe."

"Back to work then," said Roger, marching back to the office to run the gauntlet of his groupies.

Jack phoned mid-morning. "How are you today?"

"Tired and crotchety," I said, "but otherwise fine. How about yourself?"

"Much the same," he laughed, "but all the better for speaking to you. Are you still up for a meal this evening?"

"Sounds good."

"I'll pick you up from your place at six," he said. "We'll go into Wellington."

"That's the first bit of civilisation I've been offered so far today. See you later." I was smiling as I hung up.

On the way home I popped in to the library. I wanted to have another look at the book I'd seen on Jorge's desk. I had a hunch the coordinates were an important part of the case, even if Jack would prefer to discount them. Bill had already proved they represented something serious, if only to a nutter like himself. Unfortunately, I could remember neither title nor author. Beyond recalling that it had been an older book and the title had mentioned the Horowhenua, I had little to go on. After some minutes of fruitless search through the New Zealand section of the shelves and then the computer system, I sought out a librarian. "It's about the early Maori history of the Horowhenua," I said hopefully.

I love librarians. Why they don't recruit them into the CIA, I'll never know – or perhaps they do. Given the opportunity for some research and detective work, they stop at nothing to achieve their goal. Within quarter of an hour she had tracked down a copy of *Horowhenua: its Maori place-names & their topographic & historical background.*

"Thank you so much," I said as she ordered a stack copy.

"My pleasure," she said with every sign of complete sincerity. "It'll be here in a couple of days."

CHAPTER
FOURTEEN

JEN CALLED WHILE I WAS GETTING ready to go out.
"I'm going on a date," I said proudly.

"Really?" Jen sounded enthusiastic, her own problems forgotten. "Not with Sam?"

"No. That's so yesterday," I said. "Keep up!" I smiled. "This is with a police person, name of Jack, who, incidentally, is the most stunning example of manhood I think I've ever seen."

"I've got to hand it to you, Claire. You do nothing with your love life for a year or more, but when you come back, it's with a hiss and a roar. Go girl."

"Actually, I'm terrified," I admitted. "I've been out of the loop so long I don't know what to do."

"It'll be like riding a bicycle. It'll all come back to you."

Jack picked me up. He looked good. I realised that although he wore civvies for work, and wore them well, they were still a form of uniform. Their quiet understatement was there for a purpose. Let's keep the public onside and confident in their police force.

Now he was in a casual open-necked shirt, well-cut jeans and a leather jacket. A very nice jacket, made with good leather and smartly styled. The effect was sexy and understated.

I had put hours of thought into what I should wear. Jack had mentioned dinner, but we hadn't discussed anything else, which meant the possibilities were endless, and the potential of my being inappropriately dressed was high. Would he want to go nightclubbing, take a romantic walk along the beach, go to a late-night movie? Really, men have it so easy. The same clothes and shoes see them through every social occasion. It's much harder being a girl.

I'd settled on a favourite white silk shirt because it was flatteringly cut, teamed with a matching white camisole so I could wear the shirt open. The shirt fell to the hip, and I added black leggings and my favourite maroon ankle boots. These were high-heeled, but not so cripplingly high that I wouldn't be able to walk if the need arose. I felt I needed all the height I could muster as Jack was so tall. I didn't want him looking down at me in any sense of the phrase.

I checked myself over in the mirror. The shirt did its usual slimming trick, and the leggings and boots made my legs look longer. Not bad, if I did say so myself.

Then of course came the worry about what to do with my hair. Mine is dark and shoulder length. Should I put it up, or leave it loose, which looked more casual. I opted for the loose look, added some gold hoop earrings and I was done.

Jack greeted me with a big smile. "You're looking great. Not that you don't look good in your pilot's uniform, but it doesn't do you justice."

"Thank you," I said. "You scrub up nicely yourself."

Jack drove well. After years of teaching students to fly in small aircraft with dual controls I had a tendency to be hypercritical of handling skills, which carried through when I was a car passenger. David, a poor driver, had hated my occasional comments, and I in turn had disliked being driven by him. I preferred not to die because my driver wasn't concentrating on the road. That concern tended to override my tactfulness or desire to stroke the male ego.

Jack was relaxed in his control of the car, and neat and tidy in any manoeuvre he made. I allowed myself to sink back into my seat and trust him.

"Do you like Italian food?"

"Absolutely," I replied.

We went to Scopa, the restaurant bar in Cuba Street. A perfect choice. The food and vibes were relaxed and friendly. We chatted easily and shared a rich Montepulciano. I chose the open lasagne and wrapped up the meal with an affogato; Jack opted for spaghetti with clams and selected the fig and almond tart for dessert.

"What made you want to be a pilot?" he asked as we waited for our meal.

"Freedom, I suppose. I like feeling free to move. When I got my first driver's licence, which was for a motorbike, I knew that being able to go where I wanted, when I wanted, was important." I smiled at him. "What about you. What made you want to be a detective?"

"Partly family reasons. My grandfather was a prison warden and my father's a lawyer, so there is a sort of family tradition that we're on the side of the good guys. And I like that my job is solving puzzles, which I find intellectually satisfying. It's like a jigsaw – scrambled until you have all the right pieces and put them in the right order. I like that."

"Is the Jorge case typical?" I asked.

"Well, yes and no. Your discovery of the pendant was an unexpected piece in the puzzle, and it may or may not be relevant to his murder. It does explain some of his emails. He'd been in contact with antique dealers in the US and UK, sounding out their interest in New Zealand artefacts. There are also a couple, written in what we assume is Norwegian, that we haven't had translated yet. It looks as if he was trying to find a market for the pendant, which of course would be illegal unless he owned and had provenance for the item." He took a sip of wine.

"We already knew that Jorge wasn't the upright citizen everyone assured us he was at the beginning of the investigation. Now we have to discover why he was hiding Maori taonga. The emails indicate he was interested in antiquities. Was that pendant important enough to provide a motive? Who knows? Until you found it, the child molestation history was providing a point of focus. Now, your pendant adds an extra dimension. The process will be the same – plenty of methodical investigation to reach a conclusion."

"Do you always get your man?" I was amused. There were enough reports in the media about police cock-ups to make me sceptical.

"For us it's not so much getting the man, it's being able to put up a sound body of evidence to the courts to help a jury to make up its mind. That's our role in all of this." He smiled at me. "What about you? Do you want to be an airline pilot when you grow up?" he teased.

I shook my head. "No. I love what I'm doing right now. I like teaching students and sharing something I love. I like the hands-on immediacy and freedom of the flying I do. I've never had any ambition to drive a big commercial jet on a promulgated route for hours. I'd be hopelessly tempted to do a barrel roll just for fun, to alleviate the monotony."

Jack grinned.

This point had been a big bone of contention with David. "If you want to fly, then why don't you do it properly?" he'd ask in frustration. Useless telling him that I *was* 'doing it properly' and there was more to life than international airports.

"This is perfect," I said when I felt I couldn't possibly manage another mouthful. The shot of Baileys I'd had with my affogato was curling through my blood stream.

"They do a great job," Jack said appreciatively. "Would you remember the old Il Casino? When I was a kid and we visited Wellington, my folks would take us there for lunch sometimes as a treat. I loved the place, it was all nooks and crannies and different rooms. It was a right maze."

That led to a long discussion about our respective childhoods. Jack's had obviously been a happy one. He was one of several children.

"Roman Catholic?" I hazarded.

"No, part Maori, and very family orientated. Dad was an only child, and he didn't want the same for his children. Fortunately Mum wanted a large family as well, so it worked out for them."

"You're close to your parents?"

Jack nodded. "I don't get to see them as much as I'd like because they live in the Waikato and my job can be pretty intense, but yes, we're a close-knit family. How about you?"

"Mum died of cancer two years ago. She and Dad divorced years before, when I was just entering my teens. Dad's remarried and I've got one sister and two half-sisters."

"Do you see much of your father?"

"Not really. I adored him when I was a small kid, but that ended when he walked out on Mum, so we don't have much to do with each other these days. I'm very close to my sister, although we're like chalk and cheese."

We dropped in to the Matterhorn for a while, and danced and drank a little. Later Jack drove me home. I was sufficiently relaxed and drowsy to nearly doze off in the car.

He dropped me off at my cottage. I wondered whether he expected to be invited in, but like him as much as I did, I didn't feel ready for the next step yet.

He opened the door for me and helped me out. "Thank you for a great night," he said, and bent his head for a gentle kiss. "I'll give you a call next week. Enjoy your day off."

Then he was gone. I remembered Jen telling me the trick to entertainment is to keep your audience wanting more. If so, Jack had the trick down pat.

Later I lay in bed wondering why I had let Jack leave without inviting him in. He was almost perfect, and the evening had been more than enjoyable. But there had been that moment beside the water tank on D'Urville when I'd realised I needed to be more intelligent in my dealings with men. Part of me knew I wasn't yet ready to go to bed with Jack.

CHAPTER
FIFTEEN

ROGER CALLED ME OVER TO TELL me he'd had a phone call from Jorge's lawyer.

"Apparently he's managed to track the family down and establish the next-of-kin is a nephew. He arrived in New Zealand yesterday and is keen to meet the person who found his uncle. He also wants to go out to the island and see the bach. He needs to make a decision whether to sell it or lease it out. He's planning on taking photos of the place for his family and pick up a keepsake or two."

"I thought everything had already been transported back to the mainland," I objected. "There's only the empty bach left at D'Urville."

"Yes, well he wants to see it. Can you phone the lawyer and organise a time with him?"

Jorge's nephew was nothing at all like his late uncle. He looked the stereotypical image of a Viking. Tall, scruffy blond hair and green-eyed. All that was missing was the helmet and battle axe. He introduced himself as Sven Knutsen. I shook hands with him and was relieved to discover he spoke fluent English. I saw he had brought a bunch of flowers.

"To lay on the place where he died," Sven said when he saw me looking at them.

"I'm sorry about your uncle," I said.

"Well, it's sad of course, but I'd never met him." He smiled slightly. "He left Norway long before I was born. I don't think he and my mother were very close at all. From what she told me, in his teens he was a wild boy with a track record of juvenile crime: petty theft, receiving, that sort of thing. Although he avoided getting caught and convicted, the family had enough and packed him off overseas to start somewhere afresh. Mum washed her hands of him when she heard he'd got a criminal conviction in New Zealand. She rarely spoke of him. When she died I sent him a letter, but he never replied."

Well, at least that meant I wasn't going to have to pack a box of tissues for the flight. I'd wondered whether I'd be spending the day with a grief-stricken mourner.

I introduced him to Roger and left them while I got the plane ready. When I returned it was clear Roger had briefed him fairly thoroughly about what little we knew.

"So the police have made no progress yet?" Sven sounded surprised. "It's been, what, two weeks now since Jorge died?"

I shrugged. "Nothing they've told us about or that's been reported in the news." I had a feeling Jack might have an opinion about the culprit, but I hadn't liked to push him for information he hadn't volunteered.

"Surely there were very few people on the island at the time? It must have been one of them."

"If so, we haven't been told, and no arrest has been made."

After a week of horrible wintry weather, the day was one of those lovely autumn days that start out bitterly cold but turn into a gloriously sunny day.

"You're going to see the island at its best," I commented as we turned towards the west.

Sven exclaimed at the beauty of the Sounds with its many coves and bays. I took the opportunity to give him a bit of a tourist spiel, pointing out some of the more interesting features. "That's where the wreck of the *Mikhail Lermontov* went down,"

I said as we flew past Cape Jackson. "It was a miracle only one person lost their life."

Greville Harbour was at its immaculate best. We walked along the strip and followed the track around the lagoon.

"This is where I found him," I said, pointing out the hollow. There was nothing now to indicate that a violent crime had occurred here, or that squads of policemen had walked all over the site.

Sven laid the bunch of flowers reverently on the spot, and we both observed a moment's silence.

"That's really all I can do for the poor man," he said. "I feel bad that he had to be buried with no family in attendance," he continued, "and it's ugly that he was murdered here in the first place. What a sad way to end up – all alone in life and in death."

I agreed with Sven, and shivered, although the sun was fully out.

Sven pulled his camera out and took a few photos of the bouquet lying in the sand, then a few more of the lagoon and the dark, bush-covered hills. He insisted that I be in some of the shots.

"I need to show my children," he said simply when I declined. "They will want to know what you were like." I gave up my protests and let him snap away.

We walked up to the house.

"How beautiful, so beautiful," Sven kept saying as he took in the sweep of the bay. "I can see why he came here."

He had the key to the place and unlocked the door. The women had done a thorough job, and the place was now as impersonal as a motel room. It seemed rather forlorn in its stripped and anonymous state.

"Do you know what you want to do with the house?" I asked.

"It would be wonderful to keep it as a holiday house," he said. "My kids would love it here. But it's not practical. Norway and New Zealand are just too far apart. It takes too long and costs too much to cross the distance."

I nodded.

"Maybe if I retain ownership of the place and lease it out we will one day be able to come out and visit. I don't know. At least then the place will be maintained, and I won't have given up something this lovely. It's why I wanted to see it for myself. To see whether it was worth keeping with all the problems long-distance management would involve."

I left him to it and went outside to sit in the sun on the edge of the deck. At least I didn't need to have any qualms about letting him poke around the place.

At last he came outside and joined me. We sat in peaceful contentment, looking out over the bay.

"I stayed here one night," I explained. "Jorge wanted to leave the island very early in the morning. Too early for me to be able to fly across to collect him, so I came over the evening before. It was a beautiful night, and there was a yacht moored in the harbour which was lit up. We sat out here and watched the stars. It was so beautiful."

"I heard that you found an artefact somewhere?"

"Oh, did Roger tell you about that? Yes, I found a parcel that contained a pendant. Jorge had left a series of numbers that I worked out were coordinates. I'd some spare time while the women were cleaning the bach, and went for a look. He'd hidden it at the water tank further up the valley. I don't know what he was doing with it, or why he hid it. There'll be a story there, that's for sure."

"Is it valuable?"

"Don't ask me. It looked like greenstone, which is reasonably valuable, but I would think its main value would be if it's a historical piece. The police were going to investigate and see if they could identify where it came from."

"So who will it belong to now?"

I heard a sharpness in his tone that surprised me.

"I don't know. I guess it depends on how Jorge obtained it. If he bought it legitimately in a souvenir shop, then it will all be part of his estate. If it was stolen, then I suppose it belongs to the original owners. I don't know its legal status. If it's part of a historical treasure, there could well be a tapu on it."

"Tapu?"

"Sort of like a curse. Bad things happen to you if you break a tapu. Maybe that's what happened to Jorge," I said lightly and stood up.

We walked back towards the strip, past the other empty bach. There was no one there and it looked as deserted as ever. I wondered again about the identity of the couple I'd seen, and what had brought them to D'Urville that day.

We made our way back via the beach. I think neither of us wanted to go past the spot where Jorge died and see the sad little bouquet lying in the sand.

Back at the barn we encountered Joe on his quad with his dogs milling around him. I didn't know him particularly well. Most of our conversations were conducted by phone when I called to let him know I was flying in.

I introduced him to Sven.

"Sorry thing," said Joe, shaking his head. "The most disturbing thing that's ever happened in our quiet bay."

"Well, I doubt that," I said. I didn't want the conversation veering off into the maudlin. "When Matt was building his house here, he researched the history of the bay and told me a bit about it. Maori used to live here in pre-European times, and I bet there were plenty of battles and fights. Then Te Rauparaha's lot came this way in the 1800s when he was rampaging through the country and conquering every tribe he could. I seem to remember Matt telling me about a cannibal feast they had here after he'd won a battle on D'Urville."

Joe laughed. "You might have a point. Anyway, it's been quiet here as long as I've known it. You should have seen the place while the police were working here. You couldn't move without falling over them, and of course, half the bay was taped off so we couldn't cross it. It made getting round a bit tricky."

"It must have been very disturbing," said Sven gravely.

"Well, I think the wife liked the activity. She used to bring morning tea down to the cops. Put in a good word for me as well, I've no doubt."

"Did you need a good word?" I asked lightly. I couldn't remember if anyone had told me where Joe was at the time of the murder.

"Probably," Joe said seriously. "I'd been up in the bush laying possum traps. I told the cops I didn't see anyone. I was too far round in the hills from where the murder took place, and the bush is too thick to see anything anyway. The only problem was that no one could see me either to confirm my story. Fortunately, when the detectives climbed up they saw the traps, but it might be hard to prove at what time I'd laid them."

"It must put a lot of strain on everyone, wondering who killed Jorge," said Sven.

"It's an uneasy feeling," I said. "I think they thought I might have done it at first, until they worked out that he probably died before I landed on the strip. I've never been a suspect before and I didn't enjoy it." I suddenly remembered that Joe could probably answer a question for me. "Hey, Joe, who were the young couple in the other bach? I'd never seen them before."

"Oh, that's the Harris boy and his girlfriend. The family used to come down regularly some ten years ago or so but they don't visit much now. They only use the place about once a year. There were three kids. Jason, the one you saw, would be the oldest. I think he and his girlfriend had come over for a long weekend. They'd only arrived the morning of the day Jorge was killed, poor things, so they didn't get much peace and quiet, as it panned out. By the time the police had interrogated us all and put us through the wringer they were probably grateful to be allowed to leave."

"How did they get on and off the island?" I asked.

"Ted, that is Harris senior, owns a fishing trawler out of Nelson. They dropped the couple off, and picked them up again when the police were through with them. I think they live in Wellington somewhere."

"Ah, I wondered about that," I said. "Professional curiosity, you know. Sounds like a useful sort of dad to have."

"Did you think someone else was encroaching on your patch?" grinned Joe.

"Just checking." I smiled.

Sven was quiet on the flight back. I left him to his thoughts and wondered how disconcerting the whole experience must be for him. We said our goodbyes back at Paraparaumu, and he expressed his deep gratitude for the day.

"How was it?" asked Greig.

"He seemed a nice enough guy," I replied. "It must be odd to be related to a murder victim when you hardly even knew he was part of your family. And then inherit his estate in a foreign country. It must be unsettling."

"It sounds good to me," said Greig with a grin. "I can think of a few rellies I'd happily sacrifice."

I smiled.

"Don't forget it's think and drink night," he reminded me, referencing quiz night at the pub.

"I'll see you down there," I agreed.

CHAPTER
SIXTEEN

I ARRIVED LATE, BY WHICH TIME THE pub was noisy and crowded. Greig had used his elbows to good effect and scored us a table. I smiled at his brutal efficiency and sorted out a round of drinks before I joined the team.

I'd been worried that socialising with Sam might be awkward, but he seemed friendly and unconcerned. I realised he'd had no more personal feelings invested in our relationship than I had, and relaxed.

We'd competed as a team in pub quizzes a few times and between us we covered a surprisingly wide spectrum of general knowledge. My academic past meant I fielded any questions to do with books or history. Greig had a surprisingly encyclopaedic knowledge of current affairs. I doubt if there was a single newscast he missed.

Sam's strength was sport, a subject in which, rather alarmingly, he could quote the team members of the 1964 tiddlywinks championship in Bombay. I was always impressed by the range of his sporting knowledge.

Jayleen, bizarrely, was very good on everything left, which included modern music and crappy TV shows.

It was a closely fought match that evening. Other teams fell, leaving us facing 'Wordsmiths', as our opponents in the final round. They were experienced, with wide ranging knowledge and we'd crossed swords with them before. We called ourselves 'Fliers' and jostled for points throughout the competition. As we went into the round we were tied equal.

"How many times has Dr Chris Warner, from Shortland Street, been married?"

I'd have had more chance if you'd asked me the circumference of Uranus. Greig and I stared at each other in despair. Sam, when consulted, had no idea.

Jayleen laconically sculled another alcopop, took the pad from Greig and entered the winning answer: four times.

The pub cheered, and we sent Jayleen up to collect the certificate. Greig and I looked at each other sheepishly.

"Fuck me," he said. "Well, I knew the currency of Latvia."

I choked out a laugh. "And I knew the bloodiest of Shakespeare's plays."

"I knew who won Wimbledon in 1964," added Sam sadly.

"And Jayleen goes and wins the title for us!" Greig tipped back his drink. "There's a lesson for us there, Hardcastle."

I nodded. "To the victor the spoils."

I made a mental note to eat humble pie. Maybe knowledge was universal and not simply a game for elitists. "Well done, Jayleen."

We toasted her when she made it back to the table.

Greig got another round of drinks. "Sure you don't want one, Claire?"

I shook my head and yawned. "Not for me, thanks. I'm headed for bed."

I congratulated Jayleen again, said my goodbyes and started to ease my way through the crowded bar area. A man in front of me turned and I found myself looking up at Jack. "Hi," I said.

He cracked a wide smile. "Hi, yourself. I didn't see you were here."

"Ditto. I didn't see you either. We've just won the trivia quiz," I said.

"Was that your lot?" He glanced over at our table then turned to introduce me to his companions.

"Tina I think you've already met?"

I smiled at the woman who had responded the night of Bill's attack and nodded at them both as he introduced the other two.

"No more break-ins?" asked Tina.

"No. It's all been quiet since then."

We exchanged a few more pleasantries.

Jack turned to me. "Do you want another drink?"

"No thanks. I must be on my way. After all the excitement of a trivia quiz I need an early night."

"I'll walk with you to your car,"

"I'd better say goodbye again to my lot." I turned back to our table.

I saw with a shock Sam had been watching Jack and me and his look wasn't friendly.

I stared back at him and he looked away.

"Jack, I think you've already met Sam from the tower – and Greig? May I introduce you to Greig's girlfriend, Jayleen?"

I realised how comfortable I'd become around Jack's magnificent physical presence when I saw Jayleen's reaction.

Poor kid, she could hardly have been more obvious. Of course, the alcopops wouldn't have helped. I saw Greig wince as Jayleen turned on a bravura performance of 'available tart'. Her neckline and vocal range dropped in one rapid adjustment.

"Are you the cop that's following up on the pervert's death?" she asked.

I saw Jack take a step backwards as he took in her vibes. "I'm part of the investigative team," he agreed.

"I knew him, you know," said Jayleen. "That's Jorge, of course," she simpered.

Jack didn't give much away, but I saw him focus on her for the first time. "Oh? In what way? Did you know him well?"

"Nah, not well. He was just a guest speaker at our school. Still, I can say I knew him, can't I?"

Jack smiled and agreed that she could. I watched her melt. I thought I'd better get Jack away before she combusted.

"See you both tomorrow," I said to Sam and Greig, "and

congratulations once again, Jayleen."

We made it as far as the doors of the pub. Jack opened them for me, stepped back and smiled down at me as I passed him. In that moment I understood just how far gone I was. His smile lifted the workaday week from me and made it all fresh and special again. I felt a terrible impatience to be alone with him.

I couldn't wait to tell him what I'd done; I couldn't wait for him to tell me what he had been doing. More tellingly, I couldn't remember when David had ever made me feel like that.

I turned to wave a final goodbye to the people at our table. Sam was once again staring at Jack, and I was startled by the malevolence in his glare. His eyes flicked to mine before looking away. I gave a mental shrug and decided to ignore his hostility. Not my circus, not my monkeys.

Jack and I walked slowly down the road. It was a beautiful night. We stopped when we reached my car. He kissed me lightly on the cheek. It was such a small, socially acceptable gesture and yet its effect was intimate, sensual and a promise of so much more. I smiled at him, wondering how to convey my pleasure at seeing him, without sounding gushy and girlish. He beat me to it.

"You've taken a bad week and turned it into something heavenly just by being here," he said, smiling at me.

I'm a mixture of Irish peasant and Anglo-Saxon stock, so I swing emotionally between stiff-upper-lipped staunchness and wild exuberance. The Anglo-Saxon part of my persona kicked in. "Thank you," I said, like an automated idiot. "What was so bad about your week?" My sub text was more along the lines of: 'You're the best thing that's ever happened to me. Let's go away and celebrate. A few orgies would be good.'

Jack looked at the moonlit sky. "Shall we walk on the beach?"

I nodded.

The tide was out so we had a wide area of firm sand to walk on. The soft sound of the surf was a soothing backdrop as we headed south, the island of Kapiti visible as a dark shark's-fin shadow out to the west.

"We've been working on Jorge's backstory. The fact he's

done time, particularly for something like underage sex, is a massive potential area to explore. It's the obvious motivation for someone wanting to do him in. We've been trying to trace anyone who ever laid a complaint with the police about him. Then try and crossmatch them with the suspects on D'Urville that afternoon. It's been huge."

"I was over at the island today," I told him. "I spoke to Joe, who said he'd been up in the hills laying possum traps. He didn't see anyone, but then again no one saw him. He thought he was a suspect."

Jack sighed. "There are always people who don't have alibis. If they'd known there would be a murder, they'd have arranged things better. But there you are. How would it be if I told you that not only does Joe not have an alibi, neither does his wife? She says she was at the farmhouse doing the garden, which is round the back of the house. She didn't see the Norwegian pilots, and they didn't see her. The pilots have given each other alibis. On the face of it there's no evidence to link them to the homicide, but they could be in cahoots. Maybe there's something in the shared Norwegian background.

"As you know, Bill said he was walking in the hills, which turned out to be a load of bollocks. So far, he's the most obvious suspect.

"Matt and his family were on the beach or out in the dinghy with the kids, but there was a lot of coming and going to his bach. For some of that time they were even out of sight around the headland. I've discounted him because even if he'd got to shore he'd never have left his kids like that." I nodded.

"Then there's Jason Harris and his girlfriend in the house next to Jorge. Like the pilots, their only alibi is each other. They claim they were having a massive quarrel in the half-hour or so before Jorge's death and had only arrived out on their deck just before you said you'd seen them there. Incidentally they reported seeing you."

"I asked Joe about them," I said. "I'd never seen them down on the island before, but Joe said the man used to come there as a kid, with his family."

"Yes, so he told us. He was OK, but the girl was a wreck and caused us endless hassles. She wanted to get off the island immediately if people were going to be murdered there, and didn't take kindly to being told she would have to stay. I'd call her high maintenance. Fortunately we had a female PC with us who ended up coping with the hysterics. I felt almost sorry for Jason. He didn't look happy."

I grinned. "So where does that leave you?"

"Still putting the pieces together," he said.

"Have you had a chance to identify the other site Jack's coordinates indicated?"

"Not yet, that's on the schedule for next week if I can get approval for it. It's a very long shot that it relates to anything pertinent to the murder. The only substantive aspect are the emails Jorge sent to art houses seeking a market for the pendant. He implied in them that he could supply more than just the pendant, and makes mention of an ancient skull."

"Ugh," I said. "That's unnecessarily gruesome. Was he going to rip a skeleton's head off?"

"Dunno," replied Jack. "If we go, we'll take a helicopter in. That's one of the reasons we haven't released any details about that pendant in the media. We don't want to start a rush of treasure seekers into D'Urville's hills unnecessarily. We've also run checks but no one has reported a pendant missing."

I'd been certain it must have been stolen, otherwise why try and hide it? I said as much to Jack, who nodded.

"It would be logical to think there was something suspect about its provenance. I'm taking it down to Te Papa next Monday to see if they can shed any light on it. I wondered if you'd like to come with me?"

"Me?" I was surprised. "I'd love to." I grinned. "I feel slightly proprietorial about the thing, so I'd be really interested in what they have to say. Sven asked me today who the pendant would belong to and I said I didn't know."

"Sven? Ah yes, the nephew. He's coming in for a meeting tomorrow to get briefed on progress. What's he like?"

"Seems OK. A bit overwhelmed by the situation, and weighing

up what to do with the house on the island. But he was interested in the story of the cache."

"He won't get any answer from us until we know more about it."

I tripped slightly over some object and Jack held my arm to steady me. It was natural for that to evolve into him holding my hand. We walked for a while in silence, enjoying the night and each other. I was incredibly aware of his physicality. Every hair on my arms had lifted in response to his electricity.

I became aware our steps had automatically synchronised – left, right, left – as our bodies adjusted our rhythms. We walked unhurriedly along the edge of the water. I listened to the rhythmic sound of small waves rolling in and out.

"We will be lovers?" He made it a question to be answered.

I drew in a breath. "Yes. Soon," I said softly.

His grip on my fingers tightened a little as he swung me round to face him. I realised again how tall he was. I'm not small, but I barely reached his shoulder. He ran his finger gently down the curve of my cheek. I closed my eyes and leant in to the caress. A strand of hair blew across my face and he gently tucked it back behind my ear. I was very aware of his scent. Something spicy, I thought, but deep. The kiss was gentle and searching before it gradually deepened into something more erotic and demanding which took my breath away.

"That would be very good," he said at last.

I heard the smile in his voice.

* * *

The trainee 'C' Cat Roger had promised me turned up for his interview.

Nick Burrows turned out to be a self-effacing young man in his late teens with a nice smile. Part of my job would be to turn that shyness into assertiveness. Students don't need a diffident flying instructor. I thought he looked promising, and we agreed he would start the course the following Tuesday. I gave him the usual warnings about just how much work was involved, and how few employment opportunities there were for newly qualified instructors.

"I know," he said. "They told me all that back in Christchurch. But I want to be a pilot. It's all I've ever wanted to be."

"And becoming an instructor is one of the quickest and cheapest ways of building up your hours? Yes, I know. Well, as long as you understand it's a vocation rather than a normal job, you'll be fine."

"You've probably scared the poor chap off and we won't see him again," remarked Roger as we watched Nick walk away.

"I don't think so," I replied. "I think he's tougher than he looks. Anyway, if he does run away, it's better he does it now rather than later."

"She's hard," Roger said to Maria.

"You can talk," I grinned. "When you interviewed me you warned me that I'd be going to the funerals of lots of colleagues if I chose to be a light-aircraft pilot. If that didn't put me off, nothing could."

"Well, I was right," said Roger. "You have been to some funerals."

I shrugged. "And I'm right too. The sooner Nick learns that flying is a vocation, and it's all about poverty, chastity and obedience, the better," I retorted. "Well, perhaps not chastity precisely, but certainly poverty and obedience during the early years."

"Definitely not chastity," murmured Maria. "Not if he's a pilot."

CHAPTER
SEVENTEEN

S ATURDAY NIGHT, AND I ACTUALLY HAD a
date. Jack had phoned earlier to ask if I had plans for the
evening, and would I like a quick meal out. I grinned as I
accepted. Jen and Lisa would be impressed if I was now getting
dated every weekend. I phoned Jen to skite. "It's a second date
tonight," I said.

She chuckled lecherously. "The *second* date, huh? Does this
one look like a keeper?"

"Too early to tell," I replied, "but so far so good."

"What's he like?" I could hear female curiosity for details in
her tone.

"Nothing's happened yet," I said soothingly. "It's only a
second date, remember?"

She snorted at that. "I've been allocated seats for the dress
rehearsal next Thursday. Do you want to come?" she asked.
"I've already asked Lisa, but she's going to be in Auckland."

"Do you think you could stretch to two tickets? I'll see
whether Jack can come with me."

"So I get to meet him? OK. I'll sort you out your tickets. Can
you confirm tomorrow?"

"Yes, I'll call you. Even if he doesn't come with me, I'll

certainly come and see the show. Make sure you break a leg, and all that stuff."

I was a foodie fan, but if there's one nation's cuisine I rated higher than any other, it was Thailand's. I loved the freshness of the vegetables, the simplicity of the preparation and the capacity they have to infuse more flavour into each gram of ingredient than any other nation on the planet.

We exchanged small talk while we ate. "How is the case progressing?" I asked. "Were you able to get any more information out of Bill?"

"No. Apparently he didn't see anyone else either the afternoon of the murder. It's beginning to look as if everyone on that island wanders around with their eyes shut. We know now that you, Jorge, your foreign pilots and Bill were all within the same area at the time and yet none of you saw each other."

"Be fair," I said. "I was coming in to land. At that point I'm focused on the touchdown point on the strip. There's not a lot of spare capacity for sightseeing."

Jack grinned. "I'm very pleased to hear it. It wasn't a criticism, just a general observation about the case. The biggest issue is the geography of Greville Harbour. People can be in close proximity yet not see each other because of the dunes, the ridge of the hill or tree cover. What we needed was an intelligent eight-year-old to have been out and about. They tend to notice things."

"If what you found out about Jorge's predilections is right, then it's just as well the only children around were out on the water with their father," I pointed out. "Matt and Jane are sufficiently freaked out as it is about the times their kids ran around free, and Jorge could have had access to them." I hadn't managed yet to reconcile the inoffensive passenger I used to ferry across Cook Strait with my vision of a child molester.

"Hmm," he said non-committally.

"Is there anything significant in the fact that the two pilots came from the same part of Norway as Jorge?" I asked. "It seems a bit of a coincidence."

Jack shrugged. "It's one of the areas we're exploring,

particularly as he'd been emailing Norway with promises of Maori artefacts for sale."

Our plates were cleared, and I was sipping green tea when Jack's phone rang.

"Bugger," he said. "Sorry, I'll have to take it."

He stood up and went out onto the pavement. I could see him walking to and fro, talking into the phone. In a few minutes he was back. "I'm really sorry, but that was work. Something's come up and I'm going to have to go into Wellington. I don't know how long I'll be or I'd suggest you come with me, but as it is, I'd better just take you home."

"That's OK," I said. "I understand."

We looked at each other. We'd both known we'd been going to end up in bed that night. I could see the rueful amusement in his eyes.

I tried to avoid a childish whine. "Has something significant happened?" I asked.

Jack hesitated. "It's too early to say. I won't know until I've interviewed the person they've brought in." He smiled. "I promise I'll let you know what I can, when I can."

I shrugged. "Of course," I said lightly.

He pulled me towards him as we walked to the car. His arm was round my shoulder and my hip bumped against his thigh. I let my head fall against his shoulder and it felt right.

"Mañana," he said and kissed me goodbye.

"As long as you don't say 'laters, baby,' you're forgiven," I said.

He chuckled. "I wouldn't dare. I'll see you tomorrow."

"If you've got exciting news, and it's not too late, you could drop in when you get back from town," I offered.

He hesitated. "If it's not too late," he repeated. He kissed me again, and was gone.

At least Nelson was pleased to see me back at home. The colder nights had curtailed his wandering, and his preference was now to spend the evening with me.

I poured myself a glass of wine and sat on the sofa patting him. "We've been abandoned," I said.

Nelson indicated that he couldn't care less, and this was in fact his preferred option. His purr soothed and consoled me. All was right in at least one creature's life.

I wondered what had been so important as to drag Jack back to work on a Saturday night. Had they found the culprit? He'd been referencing the need to interview someone, and I assumed that meant someone important to the case. I ran my mind over the suspects I now considered probable, namely Bill (my first choice), the pilots (they had provided alibis for each other), Joe (whom I rather liked) and person or persons unknown.

I rather hoped it was the last case. The thought of a murder trial involving someone I knew was disturbing.

To soothe myself I poured a deep, hot bath, lit candles around the edge of the tub and poured in the foam Kate's girls had given me for my last birthday. Once it was full, bubbling and scented I climbed in, taking my glass of wine and my latest Deanna Raybourn novel with me. An hour later, I had shed my tensions and rose from the bath a new woman. Why didn't I pamper myself more often? My skin felt silky and smelt sweet. I was sure the washerwoman's fingers would plump out again soon, and Deanna had proved to be just as much good therapy as any woman could hope for. I'm a sucker for happy endings, and her heroines were agreeably intelligent and resourceful.

It was still early, but I couldn't muster the necessary energy to light the fire, even though I'd laid it. I took myself off, having recharged my glass, and sat in my nice warm bed while I read a few more chapters. Nelson considered his options and joined me. I wondered whether Jack would, or could, take me up on my offer and decided that in all probability the answer was no.

I was starting to doze off when I heard a car come up the drive. Under any circumstances that would be unusual at this time of night. Bill's incursion had made me wary, so I was instantly alert. I looked at the cat. Nelson's ears were pricked. He'd heard it too.

The night had got colder, and it was with some reluctance I climbed out of my warm bed and padded my way through to the living room, grabbing the handy poker on the way. I looked out of the window. It was too dark to recognise the car, but I knew the shape of the man silhouetted beside it, looking at the house. I smiled as I put the poker down. I thought I would have recognised him anywhere.

I opened the door. "Hello, stranger," I vamped. Belatedly I realised I was in my PJs, with no makeup or other feminine wiles to assist me. David had despised women who 'let themselves go'. I decided retrospectively that I despised David, and gave Jack my widest smile.

"I didn't know if you'd still be awake."

"Only just," I said. "But you're very welcome to come in and have a late-night beverage with me. How did the interview go?"

"Inconclusive," he said tersely. "It's been a frustrating night, in more senses than one, but if you're awake enough to invite me in, there's still time for the evening to improve."

I poured him a rich red wine, put a match to the fire and curled up beside him on the sofa. "Tell me about it," I said.

Jack sighed, took a long swig of the wine and leaned back. "One of the areas we've been looking into has been Jorge's history of sexual offending. He was convicted and imprisoned, of course, but there has always been the possibility that he had reoffended after his release. We've checked official records, and nothing has shown up, but tonight a young woman came forward to claim Jorge had interfered with her when she was thirteen."

"Poor girl," I said. "Why didn't she report it at the time?"

Jack shrugged. "You'd be surprised how few cases get reported. She comes from a rough family, and if Jorge hadn't got to her, then she seemed to take it for granted that one of her uncles or cousins would have been at her themselves. She never told her mother or reported it to the police. She left home at fifteen and has been living on the streets picking up tricks wherever she can."

I shuddered.

"She heard Jorge had been murdered but didn't think to come forward until a couple of days ago when the Sallies gave her a bed for the night. A counsellor there got talking to her, and when she heard her story, insisted that she must tell the police. It's taken her this long to pluck up courage."

"Jesus," I said. "That's sickening. Can anything be done for her? I mean to rehabilitate her?"

"The Sally Army counsellor seemed keen to support her, so maybe they can help. Unfortunately she's well beyond any help Child Youth and Family can give her, and she's the sort who won't want the state interfering."

I got up from the warmth of Jack's arm and poured myself a drink. A million miles away from this warm room with its creature comforts, other young women slept rough on the streets at night. Except they weren't a million miles away. They were in my city, Wellington, which was not very far away at all, as the crow flies.

"The complaint she laid against Jorge was bad enough," said Jack, "but she told us she knew of other young women he abused. She said he kept a photograph album of them all. He'd taken photos of her as well." Jack swirled his wine round the bottom of the glass. "So now we have to find that album if we can. Unfortunately she wasn't able to give us names or other details, although she said she knew a couple of other victims from her school. Jorge was keen on a threesome. I don't think he achieved it, well not with this girl anyway, but she was in contact with some of the others for a while."

I went back to sit beside him. He put his arm round my shoulder and pulled me to him. We sat quietly together for some time, allowing the fire's warmth and the rich wine to work its magic.

I put my hand on his arm. "How do you cope with it?" I asked.

"I don't think I do cope with it at all," Jack said seriously. "I have such a deep hatred for those who abuse the innocent, the young and the vulnerable. I've got younger sisters. Thank god, they're all now above the age of consent, but the potential for abuse is always there. How would I feel if a forty year old latched on to any one of them? Abuse can be so many things. Age and power inappropriateness, coercion, foul acts. . . . I think about Jorge and my blood boils. I can't imagine what I would be moved to do if someone hurt them. If we find Jorge was murdered because of his criminal activities, I'll find it hard not to sympathise with the killer."

I nodded, trying to imagine Kate's children being abused. My rage would be overwhelming. Kate's would be at the level of ancient Greek tragedy. I could imagine the furies pushing her to action.

Eventually Jack put his glass down and turned to me. The kiss was slow and sweet. I closed my eyes and let the moment take me. I was bathing in a warm bath of hormonal excitement when hearing returned and I realised Jack was talking to me.

"Sorry, pardon?" I asked, feeling out of breath.

"Shall we move to your bed?" he asked again. "It's warm and lovely here, but this couch is a bit short and a bit narrow for what I have in mind."

I nodded. Jack stood up, bent and picked me up in his arms. I gave a startled squeak. I'm not fat, but even so, I'm not a small woman. He lifted me effortlessly.

I remembered David lifting me once, then dropping me a few seconds later. "Gosh, you're a lump," he had said.

Jack carried me through to my bedroom, laid me on the bed beside Nelson and sat down.

I looked at Nelson. Nelson looked at Jack. I wondered how Jack would handle this situation. I'd known David pick Nelson up by the scruff of the neck and sling him out the door.

Jack looked at the cat and smiled. "Good evening," he said, before ignoring Nelson and focusing on me. He bent his head and kissed my lips, gently at first, and then more demandingly. I linked my arms behind his head. His hand slipped inside the pyjama top and began to rove.

I squirmed with pleasure and desire. The hand came to rest on a nipple, squeezed it gently and then withdrew.

I gasped and squirmed at the slight pressure. I could feel my nipples crinkle with desire, sending a direct message through my body to between my legs.

Jack sat up. "What do you like?" he asked.

I've always hated that question. I never know what to say. I didn't know what I wanted – all of it; maybe not that; gently! More to the left; no, higher; harder. How do you explain something that varies from moment to moment? From person to person? I was shy about articulating desire. But I accepted Jack had asked the question because he wanted an answer. And I'm a woman, I reminded myself. Get over inhibition.

I looked at his face, at the classic beauty of the straight nose, strong cheekbones and chin. "I want to see you," I said.

His eyebrow quirked at that, but he stood up slowly and unbuttoned his shirt. He peeled it off and stood for a moment letting me look. His muscles were well defined under the smooth, olive skin. There wasn't a surplus ounce of fat on him anywhere.

He bent, pulled off his shoes and socks and stood again.

His gaze latched on to mine. He smiled a little, shy but proud, as he unzipped his trousers, let his pants fall, and kicked free of them.

I've seen classic statues and been to plenty of art museums. David had liked 'culture', as he referred to it. I don't believe any artist had a model as purely beautiful as Jack to work with. It wasn't so much the components – long, well-shaped legs and buttocks, slim hips, well-muscled arms and torso, beautiful olive skin – but the living, breathing man was more than just the sum of a catalogue of parts.

The Word was made flesh and dwelt among us. The blasphemous thought flashed into my mind and captured my imagination. There was something divine about such flesh. Jack could have been a model for an angel. Not even a fallen angel. Everything I knew of him said Jack was firmly on the side of right and light. Lucifer, glorious before the fall.

I came back to myself and found Jack watching my face. He seemed slightly amused, as if he could read my thoughts. He reached his hand out and pulled me upright. I could feel the warmth of his body even though we were barely touching.

"Your turn now?" he asked. His question left me the choice of backing out, but I'm not one to refuse a challenge.

I looked into his eyes and nodded slowly. He lay back on the bed watching me.

Most of the buttons of my pyjama top were already undone, so it was short work to unfasten the remainder and slip out of it.

I shook my hair back off my shoulders and stood there a moment so that Jack could see me. The combination of cold air and erotic activity tightened my nipples into peaks. I heard his soft intake of breath, and my hands began to shake.

I bent, pulled down my pants, kicked them off my ankles and stood up. It was surprisingly hard to stand there quiescent, consenting, while Jack ran his eyes over me. My breathing was ragged with nerves and desire. I tried to read his face.

He twirled a finger. "Turn."

I swivelled round slowly.

It was a child's question I wanted to ask, 'Do you like me?' I clung to my dignity and stayed quiet as I stood facing him once again.

Jack stood up. He reached out, pulling me towards him. "Your body is perfection," he whispered. Slowly he drew me back to the bed.

Nelson decided there was far too much disturbance going on, jumped off the bed and removed himself tactfully to the living room.

Our loving was leisurely. We had to find our way round each other's flesh. Hands, lips, tongues and fingers explored and caressed as we gave and received pleasure.

Later I curled up against Jack as we drifted to sleep. Nelson joined us in the night and lay hard up against my back. I may have been constricted, but I was warm and very happy.

I woke to the smell of coffee drifting in from the kitchen. I started to sit up as Jack came through the door with two steaming mugs. "I think you said you were a coffee person in the morning?" he asked.

I nodded. "Bliss," I said as he handed me a mug.

He was still naked, apparently very comfy in his skin. He slipped back into bed beside me.

We leaned back against the bedhead and sipped our coffee. Nelson returned from whatever foray he had been on and sat on the foot of the bed washing himself. It was a very restful, domestic scene.

Sunlight filtered in through a gap the curtains. It was going to be a beautiful day.

Jack stirred and turned to smile at me. "Pretty good?"

I nodded. "Last night was …" I ran out of vocabulary.

Jack gave a short laugh. "Yes, last night *was*." He paused. "Do you think it was just a fluke? To be so good, I mean?"

His hand disappeared beneath the sheets and started moving over my skin. I almost purred. I felt like a concert piano being played by a maestro.

"Maybe we should practise some more," I gasped. "Then it might get even better."

This time our loving was playful and joyous. We teased and touched and enjoyed with exuberance.

Later I joined him in the shower. I leaned against the wall while he scrubbed my back and gave myself up to pleasure.

Afterwards we went for a walk over the farm on the track that led up the ridge. It was chilly, but the path climbed steadily and our exertions soon warmed us. The sun was still low in the sky. The track zigzagged up the hill and we would be suddenly blinded each time we turned a corner and faced it directly. Happiness invested every sense. The light was clearer, the colours more crisply defined, the sky was bluer.

We stopped at the top and looked down over the Kapiti Coast. In the distance the Waikanae River mouth was a shining silver ribbon where its waters met the sea. Further south we could just make out the buildings of the airport. It would be a beautiful day for flying.

Central in the background, the triangular shape of Kapiti Island was being picked out by the early rays of the sun, its low angle marking the deep valleys and ridges of the bush-cloaked hills. Already the channel between the island and the shore was busy with small leisure and fishing boats making the most of the day, the sea a soft, silver mirror with barely a ripple to mar the surface.

In the foreground the sinuous line of the newly formed motorway wound its way northward.

We sat down on a convenient bank, and I sighed in satisfaction as I looked at the view. "Sometimes I really do feel amazed that I've been lucky enough to be born onto this perfect planet," I said.

Jack smiled. "You wouldn't have lasted too long on any other."

We sat for a while, quiet with our own thoughts.

After a while I turned to him. "This girl you mentioned last night, what was her name?"

"Cheryl."

"How did Cheryl meet Jorge?"

Jack sighed softly. "That's a sad story. Cheryl's school was celebrating Book Week, and one of the teachers, who knew Jorge slightly, thought it would be nice to invite a published author along to talk to the kids."

I gave a gasp. "That's what Jayleen said, although as she isn't bookish she wasn't very interested in him."

Jack shrugged. "So she did. I might ask her some questions. No matter. Apparently the speech was a great success. Jorge was a good speaker, entertaining, happy to take questions and generous with his time. He talked about the science fiction elements of his novels, leaving out the overtly sexual bits. The kids liked him. He said he was always happy to accept questions, and if anyone thought of some later they could email him, or he could usually be found at the Robert Harris café most Friday afternoons. It was as simple as that."

"As simple as that," I echoed. "So kids showed up to see him?"

"Cheryl certainly did. We believe several other girls visited as well. He represented a glamorous profession," said Jack. "And he was apparently genuinely interested in the kids. Many of them didn't get a lot of attention at home."

"I thought there were police checks and things like that done by schools?" I remembered Kate holding forth on this very topic, complaining about the endless vetting involved in attending a school camp as a helper.

"In this case no one thought it was necessary. It was a one-off situation covering a relatively short talk by a person in a controlled environment. The teachers were completely unaware of Jorge's other side, or that he was meeting pupils out of school hours. Now, of course, we're checking on all the girls who were in that classroom. It's difficult work because Cheryl's story is five years old, and those girls have left town, married, changed their names, gone overseas. You name it, they've done it. Thank the lord it's not my job to research this one. Some conscientious PC will be charged with the task, and I don't envy them."

I gazed out at Kapiti. I wasn't so certain about the perfection of my planet any more. I shivered. We had been stationary long enough for the chill to start cutting through. I stood up. "Let's go."

Jack left after lunch. The weather was just warm enough for us to sit outside and munch our soft rolls, pastrami, salad, olives and cheese. As he went to leave, he stood behind me, his hands on my shoulders, and bent to kiss the side of my neck. "I must go," he said.

I leant my head sideways so my cheek caressed his hand. Even such slight contact made my body react. My cheekbone rubbed across his knuckles as I breathed in his natural scent. I felt his fingers tighten on my shoulders in response. I turned and kissed his hand. "Do you want to come round tomorrow night and I'll cook?" I said. "Nothing fancy, mind you."

"Home-cooked food," said Jack appreciatively. "I'll be there with bells on, as my Mum used to say."

I grinned.

He kissed the top of my head lightly and was gone.

Nelson and I looked at each other. He stood up, arched his back and stretched. I smiled at him. "I feel the same," I said.

I like cooking, and while I don't claim to be Masterchef material, I can competently make a tasty meal. Chicken scaloppine with pasta and salad, I decided. Late-season tomatoes still held their rich flavour and would be good for a sauce, and apples and walnuts were in season if we had room for dessert.

I spent a happy afternoon slicing and dicing, preparing the sauce and dessert for the next night's meal.

CHAPTER
EIGHTEEN

THE NEXT MORNING I WATCHED THE Monday commuter traffic in front of me come to yet another halt on the motorway. Jack had picked me up at seven o'clock. "This just reminds me how grateful I am I don't work in the city," I complained.

Beside me Jack grinned. "Did we get out of bed on the grumpy side this morning?"

I made a rude noise, but subsided. It was too early in our relationship for me to reveal just how childish I can be. I'd slept well and should have been refreshed and buoyant. Instead I'd woken up frustrated, and full of sexual energy.

Sex, I've discovered, is much like food. I can go on a diet for a few weeks, no problem, but let the first hint of proper food pass my lips and restraint sweeps away. The same with sex. Jack's presence had reminded my body that it had needs I wasn't taking care of, and it was tipping my mood towards sulky. Fortunately Jack was busy, happy enough to concentrate on driving while I admired the muscles moving in his forearms.

The weather was grey and depressing. How could it change so quickly from the warm sun we'd had the day before to that murky morning? Greig wouldn't be flying today. The cloud was barely high enough to reach minima. I hoped it would clear by tomorrow. Nick would be starting his training, and although there's a lot of theory to learn for an instructor rating, the real fun is translating the theory into practice up in the air.

I was still mulling over the programme for Nick when we pulled up in the Te Papa car park.

Te Papa, or more officially Te Papa Tongarewa, is New Zealand's national museum, and Wellington is extremely proud to have it in its city. The Maori name means 'container of treasures' and it fills that role admirably. There had been reports recently that government wanted to relocate the museum to the more populous city of Auckland. I, for one, would be marching in the streets if they tried it.

I climbed out of the car and waited while Jack walked around to me. "Ready?" he asked. His arm brushed mine, and I felt an electric shock cross between us. I looked up at him with startled eyes. He was looking at his arm as if it had surprised him.

"That was a shocking experience," I murmured.

Jack looked puzzled but was distracted when he was hailed from across the car park.

"Oi, Jack."

I turned to see who had called, and recognised the man I had met on the beach in Greville Harbour.

"Hi, Pete," said Jack. "I see you've got the goods."

Pete nodded.

"Can I introduce you to Claire?"

"We've already met," I said. "The day of the murder. Hi, Pete."

He grinned at me. "Did you come down with Jackie Boy? Careful of him, he's got a reputation."

Jack frowned. "Thanks, Pete."

Pete grinned unashamedly. "I've got to warn the girl," he said primly. "I met her before you did, after all."

I laughed at the silliness.

Jack stalked across the car park with us trailing behind.

Tony Martin was an unlikely academic. He met us at the top of the elevator and escorted us to his office. With his beard, strong, rangy, physique and easy movement he looked like a young Ed Hillary. I thought he would be more at home working in the field than sitting behind a desk.

Pete carefully unwrapped the pendant and put it in front of him. All four of us stared at it.

"We've circulated photographs to every museum, but none have identified it. Nor has there been a complaint laid relating to its theft," explained Jack. "Yet the deceased went to the effort of hiding it in an obscure location. We want to know why. Can you give us any idea at least which part of the country it's from, or something about it to help us focus in the right direction? None of the antiquities dealers recognise it; nor have the universities had anything very helpful to say about it."

Tony pulled a pair of gloves out of a drawer and put them on before picking up the amulet. He held it up to the light and stared into the greenstone. "It's lovely," he said. "Not a cheap Chinese nephrite copy, that's for certain. It's in excellent condition, particularly as I'm assuming it's an antique. Someone has looked after this well."

I gave an involuntary snort, and Tony glanced at me for a brief, assessing moment.

He turned the artefact over and ran his finger along its edges. "It's a beautiful piece, isn't it? And certainly not one I recall seeing before."

Tony looked up. "The family who owned this would be of very high status. They probably wore it for ceremonial occasions and as a sign of their chiefly authority."

He drew out a magnifying glass and stared at the artefact. "You see these holes? The pendant would have been suspended by a flax tie. There may be some microscopic remains caught in there that we can use to date it."

"Date it?" I asked. I didn't think you could date stone, and if there were flax fragments they would be tiny.

"Yes, flax has very robust plant fibres," Tony explained. "It's also got a short growing time, making precise dating results easier. We might manage to scrape together enough material to make it viable. I don't know whether anything else would show up under a microscope. You have no idea where this was kept?"

"Claire found it hidden under a water tank, wrapped up in bubble wrap and stuffed in a plastic canister. Other than that, we have no idea of its history," said Pete.

"Our interest in this relates purely to the homicide we're investigating. It's been suggested the victim found the pendant in an unknown grave on D'Urville Island and that he rifled the site, taking the pendant for his own purposes," said Jack. "We think he wanted to sell it overseas. Is that a possibility, and would that be a sufficient motive for someone to want to murder him?"

Tony shrugged. "Maybe. I'll need to have some colleagues look at it, and if it has come from a grave, that's going to raise all sorts of issues. I'd hate to imagine someone would sell this out of the country." Tony picked up a magnifying glass lying on his desk and examined the holes more closely. "Perhaps we can tease some information out. If we find any flax fibre we could date it and get some idea of its age. The most unusual feature is this carving. As I say, it's a very unusual piece."

"I've always thought Maori carving to be curvy, or in spirals. This is quite starkly geometric," I said. "Is that significant?"

Tony looked down at the pendant. "I've seen similar carvings, mostly on artefacts from further north. This would be the first time I've seen this kind of work so far south, particularly if you say it was found on D'Urville."

"Remember, the hypothesis is that it was hidden away by a homicide victim," said Jack. "Do you think an artefact like this could provide a motive for an attack?"

"To a certain person, quite readily, I should think," replied Tony. "It's a fine piece of work, and probably valuable simply as a sale item, let alone for its spiritual significance to the family that originally owned it. Still, at the same time, the value lies in its history, and it would help to establish the provenance."

"What about the suggestion that the victim thought this had come from a tribe or civilisation predating Maori settlement? Is there any possibility of that?" asked Jack.

Tony shrugged. "That depends on what you're suggesting. As

far as I know, no archaeologist has ever found any evidence in New Zealand to suggest humankind was here before the great migration. There are, needless to say, lots of theories and fairy stories."

I thought Tony looked slightly miffed, as if his professional credentials were being questioned. He stared thoughtfully at the pendant for a minute then looked up at us with a grin. "Of course, if your last question was serious, I can imagine any number of people wanting to murder your victim. It's a highly controversial theory. So inflammatory, in fact, it might get difficult to choose between the suspects!"

"It's just one motive we are exploring," said Jack. "We haven't found the grave, if one exists, although we do have coordinates we are following up on. It may turn out to be irrelevant to the investigation."

"If you do find such a grave, I'd be interested in hearing about it," said Tony.

"Are you coming back to the office, Jack?" asked Pete when we got back to the cars.

Jack shook his head. "I'm returning up the coast again. I've got to take Claire home, and then I've a meeting with Jorge's lawyer."

Pete nodded. "Take care, Claire," he said cheekily as he waved us away.

*   *   *

I poured Jack a drink. "How did the search for the photos go?"

"We didn't find an album," he said, "but we did find a bundle of individual photos, almost all of which were young women. Very young women."

I wrinkled my nose. "Were they sexual in content?"

Jack shook his head. "Not at all. Perfectly ordinary photos of young girls. Not posed or pornographic. Just natural, young, pubescent women. If you had sent them off to get developed – and some of them dated back long enough for that to have been necessary – no one would have questioned them as sleazy."

"Then why …?" I began.

"I don't know. He just liked girls. Liked looking at them, liked touching them, but he wanted them looking like the children they were."

I thought about that. "Actually, that's almost more horrid than if they were pornographic," I said at last. "He must have known what he was doing."

"I'm sure he did. And the jury must have thought so when he was convicted and sent to prison."

"Which obviously didn't cure him," I said.

"It rarely does. Just gets offenders out of the road for a while. Who knows how and when sexuality develops? We accept now that being gay is hardwired into us. Maybe paedophilia is as well. If it didn't involve the predation of a non-consenting minor, maybe we'd see it as just part of the spectrum of human sexuality. One thing is for sure, deviance isn't easy to fix."

Jack had a large envelope of papers which he spilled out onto my table. "I thought you'd be interested in these," he said.

"What are they?"

"We've been doing the forensic work on Jorge's computer. Among all the largely irrelevant stuff we found some notes – and the start of his new novel. I thought you'd like to read it, so I printed a copy for you."

"Thank you," I said. "Is it any good? I mean, his track record as a writer seems a bit dodgy. Even Bill couldn't stand his books."

"I haven't read it myself yet," said Jack, "although I've been reading through his working notes. As Bill said, the novel *is* set on D'Urville, and there *is* a rediscovered grave in the story."

"Which means there probably is one on the island," I said. "OK, I'd like to read it. Even just to know what he said that got Bill all wound up."

"Dinner?" I asked.

"Please. What can I do to help?"

I told Jack about my afternoon's cooking the day before. "Most impressive," he said. "That's the sort of thing my mum does. Are you channelling Martha Stewart?"

"My sister Kate as well," I replied. "In fact, it's because of her shining example that I developed the urge to cook. Make the most of it, I like cooking, but I'm not usually so organised."

We munched hungrily through fresh pasta tossed with my newly made sauce, served with a fresh salad. We finished with walnut and apple shortcake.

"Oh, I nearly forgot to ask you. I've been offered free tickets to the dress rehearsal of *Mamma Mia* next Thursday evening in Wellington. Would you like to come with me? A friend of mine is in the show."

I wondered whether Jack would turn out to be one of those people who detest musicals. There were so many things yet to discover about each other.

"Sounds fun," he said. "The only thing is – I'll be in Wellington all day until the early evening. Are you fine to drive down and meet me in town?"

I smiled. "No worries."

* * *

"Magic," he said. "I feel a new man. It's been a long day and I've been on my feet for most of it."

I washed up while Jack lit the fire. The early morning rain had disappeared, to be replaced by a cold, squally wind that rattled at the door and windows. We drew the curtains against the storm.

"That's the first time I've had to do that this winter," I said, shaking the folds out so the curtain hung well. "I usually hate to shut the light out, but it's going to be a very dark night."

We'd finished dinner and were nibbling cheese slices with our crackers. Jack had brought a bottle of Australian Shiraz, and I was beginning to feel pleasantly warm and relaxed.

"So what happens next?" I asked.

"It was a dark and stormy night," Jack quoted mournfully, before giving me a big grin, "so we'll read, have coffee and a port, and make sure that we lighten up the place by our own efforts."

"Corny." I smiled at him.

"That's me," he said.

"I meant investigation-wise, as you well know," I said sternly.

Jack shrugged. "We'll try to identify as many of the women as we can. Find out whether they were molested by Jorge, and find out whether there is any connection with his death. Frankly, I hope it's due to a nice simple grave-robbing problem. I really can't bear the thought of having some poor mistreated woman forced to take the stand and defend herself on a charge of murder."

"There weren't any young women on the island at the time," I objected. "Well, not if you discount me."

"There was the young woman staying with Jason Harris," Jack reminded me. "Mind you, she didn't look as if she would say boo to a goose, and she was almost hysterical at being forced to stay on an island with a murderer. She doesn't really strike me as having the right profile for violent crime."

*   *   *

Much to my surprise, I found I was enjoying Jorge's book. As Jack had said, the novel centred on D'Urville where a character named Brunell was hunting wildlife in the bush. He was a Great White Hunter type: expert tracker, crack shot and skilled in the ways of the bush. I wondered whether Jorge had read too many Wilbur Smith novels at an impressionable age.

I was sure the characterisation of his hunter wasn't realistic for a New Zealand bushman. Brunell was too well dressed and gentlemanly. I've encountered hunters at the airport because we regularly fly them up into the ranges. In New Zealand they usually wear rough pants, a singlet, Swanndri and solid boots, and model themselves on Barry Crump. They've fairly basic social skills, although I grant they are also probably expert trackers and crack shots. If they aren't strong, silent men by nature, they do their best to become so. I was also repelled by the descriptions of dead animals. I don't find dead deer and pigs compelling, even though I like venison and pork.

But by the third chapter Jorge had his character fall from

a steep ridge as he chased a boar through the bush. Brunnell slipped a long way down the slope, and only stopped because he ended up in a scrubby grove of rangiora, makomako and bush lawyer that caught on his clothes and halted his slide.

He lay for a while recovering, then discovered that his fall had landed him in a screen of scrubby bushes ripped recently from the side of the hill. Unconcerned by his recent spill, he got to his feet and discovered he'd arrived at the site of an old burial. The slip had exposed a skull and the upper part of a torso. Being the man he was, and unconcerned about scholarship or protocol, he investigated the remains of the body. In the loose soil rested a greenstone pendant, which presumably had fallen from the skeleton's neck.

"Hey, listen to this," I said to Jack in some excitement. "Brunell, our hero, has just found a greenstone pendant at a gravesite. He takes it, but refrains from further disturbing the grave. The pendant is old, the fastening around the body's neck long since rotted away. It's getting too dark for him to clearly make out the decorations on the artefact although he can feel carvings with his fingers. But," and here I paused for effect, "Brunell immediately recognises this pendant is many hundreds of years old, and that its presence in this grave clearly establishes that the body belongs to pre-Maori times. Therefore a non-Maori race was in New Zealand before the great fleet arrived."

"It seems one hell of a big leap to reach that conclusion," said Jack. "That must be what annoyed Bill so much. Does he provide any evidence for that theory?"

"No," I said, after reading a bit further. "His argument just seems to be that he has identified the pendant as very old and therefore pre-Maori. It stands to reason, then, that the corpse is either from a pre-Maori race, or else the artefact was obtained from someone who was. QED."

"I think an archaeologist might be unconvinced by that argument," said Jack.

"You think? I would hope so. There must be scores of alternative explanations. They haven't even dated the thing."

"Mind you," said Jack, "it's shaping up to be a fascinating

story. I can see how it would capture the imagination."

"How much more of the manuscript is there?"

"Not much, only another page or two," said Jack.

"Does he make any mention in his notes about where the storyline was going for the rest of the book?"

'It's hard to work out,' said Jack, "because his notes aren't very coherent, and he uses characters' names without giving us a clue of who they are or how they relate to the story." He shuffled through the pile. "I'll give you a few examples: 'Clive hates Robard'; 'International press spread theory'; 'Brunell threatened anonymously, probably Manu' and so on."

"Oh, that's not very helpful," I said. "I doubt if a writer could finish the book based on that."

"I doubt if anyone would bother," said Jack. "He'd barely started it, and he's not regarded as a great literary figure."

"Do you think the 'Brunell threatened' note refers to Bill?" I suggested.

"Who knows?" Jack stood up and shrugged. "That's enough murder and mayhem for one day, I think."

"Can't we make some mayhem of our own?"

He grinned at me. "Oh, I hope so." He poured us both another glass.

"I need to be careful how much of this I drink," I protested. "I've got a new student tomorrow who wants to start his flight instructor training. It would never do to turn up with alcohol on my breath."

Jack smiled and looked at his watch. "You've got enough time to process the alcohol long before tomorrow," he assured me. "I, on the other hand, have to drive home tonight, so I've kept a close eye on what I'm drinking. I'm in Wellington tomorrow working on some evidence forensics have come up with."

"What about the site out on the island?" I asked. "Aren't you interested in what's there?"

"Our only interest as an enquiry is whether the site – which we are just supposing is a grave – actually relates to the homicide. It seems a bit of a long shot. Still, if all else fails, we'll need to get the chopper to D'Urville and do a bit of bush bashing to find those coordinates of yours. Frankly, I'd almost prefer it if you hadn't decoded those numbers."

"I would love to be on a treasure hunt. If you do investigate the site, I don't suppose I could come too? After all, if it weren't for me you wouldn't have the coordinates at all. The police owe me one."

Jack snorted. "You've got to be kidding."

"Seriously," I wheedled. "Could I come?"

"I'd have to slide it past the boss," said Jack. "Depends on the mood he's in."

"Please." I smiled at him.

"It will be steep, slippery, no forward visibility, heaps of bush lawyer to rip the skin and maybe tapu," said Jack seriously.

"I've been tramping before," I assured him, although I privately wondered whether a college tramping trip from ten years ago really counted. At least I still had a pair of decent boots dating back to my schooldays.

"I'm not saying you can't come. That's up to Trevor. All I'm saying is I don't think it's going to be much fun. D'Urville's hills are steep, and looking for a grave is a bit creepy in itself. You've read what Jorge wrote. I don't practise Maori tikanga, but I'm leery of plunging into sites that probably have a whacking great curse on them. I don't care who placed it originally. You wouldn't have found me at the forefront of Tutankhamun's tomb opening either. Look how many of the archaeological staff died after they'd opened the grave."

I grinned. "I think the deaths related to mosquito bites that became infected."

"You may mock," said Jack. "Next thing there'll be a plague of locusts."

"Locusts are fine," I said brashly, "just as long as they're not wetas." I hated the large insects with their spiny legs.

"Wetas don't bother me," he said.

We'd reached the point of the evening when we were sparring for the sake of it. He stood up, reached out his hand and we went to bed.

I came out of the bathroom to find Jack sprawled on the bed

with his eyes shut. I gave a wicked grin to myself and jumped. He gave a quick grunt of surprise as I landed on top of him and held his arms down.

His eyes opened and he watched me warily. "Are you trying to have your way with me, woman?"

"Nah," I said, as I straddled him. "I want you to promise to take me to D'Urville when you go. I won't release you until you do."

"Like that is it?" he chuckled.

"Yup, I want you to take me."

"There's 'take me' and then there's 'take me'," he murmured.

He twisted out of my grip, grabbed my arms and we mock wrestled. For him it must have been like a tiger playing with a small kitten. His strength far exceeded my own, although I used as much effort as I could.

Eventually he rolled me onto my back and tickled me. Gentle as he was, he was impossibly strong, and all my wriggling and squirming made not the slightest impression on him. At last I admitted defeat, largely because I was laughing too hard to continue fighting. We made love, and when he left I was soft with satiation.

"Don't let some idiot student kill you tomorrow," he said as he left. He kissed me sweetly.

I rolled over and went out like a light. Nelson joined me later but I was too deeply asleep to notice.

CHAPTER NINETEEN

"GOOD MORNING," I GREETED NICK. "ARE you ready to rock and roll?"

He nodded although I could see his apprehension. I grinned at him. Taking a student through their instructor course is always fun and automatically involves everyone in the organisation. For the period of their training the student is pretty much on the premises full time every single day. The questions they ask and the skills they have to learn means everyone involved with them ups their game. For those of us long qualified, it's a very efficient way of revising some important basics.

The process is formulaic.

"Lesson one," I announced cheerily. We established early on that Nick couldn't write a straight line of script across a whiteboard to save himself. His work ran uphill, downhill and was illegible. "We all start here," I said sympathetically as I watched him stand back and look at what he'd written.

"I want to be a pilot, not a school teacher," he said in protest.

"If you want to be an instructor, this is instructing 101," I said. "Suppose you have to instruct a student when you haven't got access to computers, overhead projectors or other technology?"

He huffed but moved on to practising drawing aerofoils. I

grinned at the row of breakfast sausage shapes he managed to draw on the board.

"You're sketching our barbecue?" I asked.

He looked at me questioningly.

"Sausages," I said.

He stood back and looked at his work. His shoulders slumped.

"It gets better," I assured him. "It all gradually falls into place."

I took pity on him, and we went out to fly the lesson he had so painstakingly attempted to put on the board. This meant he had to shift from the pilot's left hand seat he was accustomed to, and fly from the instructor's seat on the right for the first time. Nick predictably found this difficult, right and left hands now having to change their duties.

We landed more or less safely an hour later. It wasn't the smoothest landing but it was a creditable first attempt for someone now operating back to front. Nick looked exhausted.

Roger greeted us, took one look at him and laughed. "Hardcastle, you've worn him out already."

I smiled. "He's doing just fine. We came close to death only a couple of times."

Nick smiled wanly. Greig, walking out the door with his next student, patted Nick on the back. "It's always like that. You'll get there," he said helpfully.

"I thought I could fly," said Nick plaintively.

"When you can teach your gran to fly and make her understand the theory as well, then you'll know how to fly," said Roger.

Maria put the jug on and we had a tea break. Afterwards I started into the theory of the Principles of Flight. Roger sat in as well. It was very collegial. Nick perked up a little when faced with a lesson on basic physics, which he had done at college, and the day ended well.

After he had left, Roger asked, "What do you make of him?"

"Well," I said carefully, "he's played a damn sight too much Flight Sim, which means he's got a very good understanding of some parts of aviation but complete ignorance of other aspects. I think he'll be OK, though. He grizzled a bit, but I think it was mainly for show. He wasn't going to quit when he found he was making a fool of himself on the right side of the plane. He wanted to sort it out for himself."

"Good," said Roger. "Keep at him."

I nodded. I was tired myself. It had taken a lot of concentration and focus to get Nick through the day.

* * *

The library sent me a text to let me know my reserve book had arrived. I collected it, and that night after dinner I put my iPod on, banked up the fire and, with Adele's percussive rhythms as background noise, I sat down to read.

When I put the book down two hours later my brain was buzzing with theories. This had to be the source of Jorge's confident identification of the pendant. I'd wondered about his certainty that it belonged to the Waitaha people and culture. It was a big leap from finding a pendant to stating it was an antique from a lost mythological people.

My library book made a compelling case for their existence and if Jorge were reading it when he started writing his new novel I could see it might influence him considerably. When he found the pendant, a simple act of wish fulfilment could lead him to claim its unique history.

I moved to the computer and googled Waitaha. It took about two minutes to find that the theory of their early settlement of New Zealand had been thoroughly debunked by modern historians, which would explain why I hadn't been taught this version of history at school.

"Spoilsports," I grumbled. I'd rather liked the concept of a lost mysterious tribe adding a layer of exotic drama to our history. It had all the ingredients for a great yarn, and I rather regretted that I would never read Jorge's completed novel.

Of course academics are always uncovering forgotten history. They'd thought the takahe was extinct until it was rediscovered in a remote valley. Maybe one day someone would discover the Waitaha were more than just a legend.

I was intrigued by the concept and lay awake for some time wondering what the true facts were.

CHAPTER
TWENTY

NICK WAS BECOMING MORE CONFIDENT IN the right-hand seat of the aircraft and no longer threatened to kill us each time he landed. We were making progress through the curriculum.

Greig and Nick had struck up a friendship. They'd invited me to join them at the pub after work, but I'd declined, happy to leave them to be lads together.

"What do you think?" asked Roger, as we watched them leave.

"If it helps Greig break away from a certain Jolene person, then bring it on," I said.

"Her name isn't Jolene," said Roger smiling, "but yes, I agree. I doubt if Greig will be with us for long. He's too ambitious. As soon as he gets his hours up, he'll be off to the airlines as fast as he can go. With any luck he'll have dumped that girl by then, because she won't be an asset in his career."

I was busy tidying up the waiting room so it was ready for the next morning. I lifted my head and looked at Roger. "Actually, I wondered the other night whether that process had begun. We were at the trivia night down at the pub, and Jayleen reacted rather too enthusiastically when I introduced her to our detective."

Roger looked blank.

"Jack Body," I said impatiently.

"Oh, him."

'Oh, him' indeed, I thought. My body was still thrumming with everything Jack could do to me.

Roger thought about what I'd said. "How's your own love life, Hardcastle?"

"Fine," I replied shortly as I stacked and tidied magazines. I wasn't going to have a discussion about it with Roger, however nosey he was.

"I just asked because Sam looked a bit wistful last time he dropped by."

Ah, Sam. I should never have encouraged him in the first place. I'd known we weren't a good match. Now I felt guilty, as if in some obscure way I'd treated him badly, which I knew I hadn't. I sighed. "Sam's a colleague, Roger, that's all," I said firmly, shoving a chair back into place. "There's nothing else between us, and we've agreed to leave it like that."

"What went wrong?"

I looked round at the room. Everything neat and tidy again.

"What do they say? You can't please everybody, so you'd better please yourself?"

Roger looked at me shrewdly. "Let me hazard a guess. You found you had bigger balls than he has," he suggested.

I glared at Roger. "That's crass. We were just incompatible."

"You make me happy I'm not young anymore," he said. "I don't have those problems."

I thought of his groupie ladies. "Yeah, right," I said, grinning at him. "Tell that to your fan club."

* * *

Greig and I were busy. Students were taught, Nick's skills improved, and we had no alarms or interruptions relating to crime. There'd been no further thefts of Avgas from the airfield to worry us, and there was no longer any reference to Jorge's death in any of the media. For the rest of the world the whole event might never have occurred.

I spent the afternoon helping Nick with his studies. It's not enough to parrot the material. The budding flying instructor needs to be able to understand it well enough to explain it in simple terms to someone who knows nothing of the subject. We were dealing with propeller theory, never my favourite subject because it is both simple and highly complex. Greig came in for a while between his flights, so it became a shared learning experience.

I would swear I learned from students every time I taught them something. Some question, some phrase or action would trigger in me a deeper understanding or greater skill level. If you ever want to be good at a skill, teach it to someone else.

Greig had a new student who was on his second lesson, so Nick was roped in to provide the ground briefing while Greig and I listened in. I was impressed with Nick. He had a pleasant manner, wasn't afraid of questions, nor of asking his own when he wasn't certain.

Greig took the student off for the practical flight part of his lesson, and I debriefed Nick. There were various tricks and techniques that all instructors learn which made the lesson more visual and interesting, and I worked with him on ways to leaven his presentation.

"Overall, not bad," I commented at the end. "Were you nervous?"

"Scared shitless," he admitted. "It's one thing to learn the lesson, quite another to deliver it."

After lunch we went flying. The lessons in the air were coming easier to Nick, and I could now ask him to teach me several skills and he would mostly get the lesson right and in its entirety. I was well satisfied by the time we taxied back to base.

* * *

Nick would be one of the good ones after he'd completed the course. I wondered whether Roger had spoken to him about him sticking around once he was qualified, and about the possibility of him getting a little freelance work with us. It's one thing to have a shiny new instructor rating, quite another to get the opportunity to use it. At best, a new instructor has to earn their way, doing a lot of hard yakka to prove themselves before they get the opportunity to teach a lesson they actually get paid for. If all went as usual, there would be a lot of aircraft-washing and hangar-sweeping in Nick's short-term future. But Roger was usually generous to students who paid to qualify at his school – as long as his established instructors didn't suffer.

I didn't envy Roger his job. It must be a constant juggling act keeping the organisation on an even keel. All pilots by default are ambitious to accumulate flying hours and experience.

I'd told Roger I was pleased with his progress. "What are your plans for Nick after his exam?" I asked.

"Early days," said Roger non-committally. "He'll need to talk to me and ask for a place if he wants it. I'm not going to offer him one on a plate. And don't you go prompting him either," he said. "He needs to learn to ask for what he wants, or he'll miss out."

*　　*　　*

That Thursday evening I drove to Wellington to meet Jack in Courtenay Place. I'd driven past the jammed, north-bound commuter traffic, grateful once again that I worked on the Kapiti Coast.

We met at the Bangalore Polo Club. I loved the faded faux-Anglo-Indian décor and the food was always reliably good.

Pete was sharing a drink with Jack. He nodded as I arrived.

Jack stood up to greet me. "Busy week?" he asked.

"Very," I said.

He drew me into his arms and kissed me.

Pete smiled at us both indulgently. "Oh, just look at the two little love birds."

Jack shot him an evil look. I grinned.

"What about you two?" I asked a few minutes later. "How's the week been?"

"Interviewing young women who were in the same class as

Cheryl," Jack said. "It hasn't been a pleasant experience, and it's not over yet. We still haven't managed to track down half of them. Those interfered with by Jorge mostly wanted to forget the experience and weren't very happy with us raising the subject. The rest, of course, had no idea what we were talking about. So it's been a frustrating week."

Pete finished his drink and stood up. "Have a pleasant evening," he said, and bent and kissed my cheek. As I was fairly certain the gesture was designed to get a rise out of Jack, I accepted it with serenity. Jack simply ignored his friend.

We ordered our meal. We were quiet while we ate, and I realised how comfy I had become with Jack. It was easy to talk together or share silences. Neither seemed awkward. I smiled at him. He lifted his head and smiled back.

Lucky me, I thought.

Mamma Mia was on at the St James Theatre. It was colourful, fast paced and fun. If this was the standard at the dress rehearsal, I could only imagine how it would be further in to the season. If there were any fluffs or mistakes, I didn't see them. I was aware of Jack sitting beside me enjoying the antics on stage. Another first in our relationship, I realised. It's a delicate business exploring each other's tastes. Music, food, books. There are so many things to disagree about in a relationship.

And then the decisions. Should one person compromise to accommodate the other? I had been all too aware of how often I'd caved in when I'd lived with David. He'd a godlike assumption that his choices were the correct ones and that I would comply.

Jen was happy and rather overexcited. She joined us for a drink after the show. I introduced her to Jack and watched her inevitable reaction to his physical attributes. Jack complimented Jen on her performance, which won him a dazzling smile. I grinned to myself. I would trust Jen with both my man and my bank balance. She was utterly straight in her dealings but an incorrigible flirt. I assumed it was part of her dramatic persona and it was strangely asexual, but she couldn't help turning her charm on whoever she was speaking to, be it a small child, or an older person of either gender. I'd watched hardened theatre directors crumble under its effect. David had succumbed instantly, and then irrationally disliked Jen for his automatic response.

Jack appeared impervious. We sipped our drinks and discussed the show.

"There were a few boo-boos," confessed Jen. "It's always a tense moment when you've got a real live audience. Sometimes dress rehearsals seem more nerve wracking than opening night. Still, I think we're all proud of the show we're in and it's going to be good."

"It's a real feel-good piece," I said. "Make 'em laugh, make 'em cry, sort of thing. It's a silly story, but you can't help but go away at the end feeling upbeat."

"You can't beat a good ABBA number," commented Jack. "I grew up with my mum singing their songs, so I know all the words. Even when someone told her they were gay icons, Mum just laughed and carried on singing the songs."

It was late when we arrived back at my house, but not so late that we couldn't find the time and energy for an amorous episode in the bedroom, after which I was glowing with languorous satisfaction. I kissed Jack goodbye and returned to bed, positively purring with pleasure. Now I knew how Nelson felt when he caught a mouse.

A pleasant side effect of good sexual activity is the excellent night's sleep which inevitably ensues. I slept blissfully, without interruption, until the alarm clock went at seven, and I woke feeling positive and energetic.

I even managed to maintain my positive attitude at work over the next couple of days.

* * *

I was already at work and brewing myself my early morning fix of coffee when my phone rang. "Hi," I said.

"Hi," said Jack. "You said you wanted to come with us to look for the grave? We're planning on going down next Monday. It's not high priority because we're still focussed on the girls. But if nothing else develops, we'll check out your coordinates. Are you still keen, because you can join Pete and me if you want."

"That would be awesome," I said. I was grinning as I put the phone down.

"Sup?" asked Greig, glancing across at me.

"I'm going to play Lara Croft and tomb raider," I replied.

My good humour coloured the day until I fielded a phone call. It was a clipped, educated, older man's voice.

"It's Saturday morning and your planes are making too much noise. Kindly stop flying over my place. We've lived here three months now, and every weekend we hear this racket and have to put up with it. It's gone on long enough and we're fed up."

I rolled my eyes and set my voice to saccharine sweet. "Good morning, sir. I'm sorry the aircraft are disturbing you, but it is the weekend and our recreational flyers are enjoying their hobby. It's a lovely day to be up in the air."

"Then stop flying over my place."

"I'm sorry, sir, but it wouldn't be possible for us to avoid flying over a particular house. As I'm sure you know, Paraparaumu has had an airport here since, I think, the 1930s. It's a community asset and much envied by those towns that don't have one." I didn't bother to point out we were only one of several flying establishments on the field. The aero club was just next door and had aircraft up as well, Heliworx had their choppers working and the gliding club hadn't yet started for the day. Once they were in action, their tow plane would be flying in and out every few minutes.

"Well, at least make them fly in the opposite direction. They're taking off right over my back garden."

I grinned evilly. This guy was a complete dipstick.

"Unfortunately, sir, our ability to fly is dictated by the laws of physics. We have to take off and land into the direction of whatever the prevailing wind is each day. It is nature that dictates our flight path. We simply cannot change the direction of the circuit. Alas, the laws of physics are immutable."

By now Greig had come in and was listening with a big grin on his face.

"I'll report you to the CAA."

"Well, that of course is your right, sir, but you must bear in mind that the airport has been here for nearly a century, and you've only been here for three months. We can't change operational procedure just for one person. I'm sure the real estate agent must have pointed out the airport to you? The open space it provides in the middle of a town is much valued by local residents."

The caller slammed the phone down. I straightened up.

"Do you want to kick something?" asked Greig helpfully. "You were starting to sound a bit acidic."

I made some foul mutterings under my breath. We all have hobbies and interests, and I'd never understood people who wanted to spoil a perfectly legitimate form of entertainment for others out of sheer, selfish bloody-mindedness.

We'd already lost our low flying zone further up the coast because some officious sod had complained about aircraft flying too low near his property. I've no doubt the complainant had long since left the area – probably for a retirement village, I thought viciously. But for those of us trying to train pilots in safety skills, we had lost forever the valuable ability to teach our students something they might need in an emergency. In a life-or-death situation, which should win – one selfish man's whinge, or a pilot's life?

It's the same with people who bought property hard up against a stadium, then complained that the noise of sport or rock concerts was too loud, or those who lived next to a children's playground and complained that kids actually make a noise when they are enjoying themselves. The airport already had a curfew limiting the hours it could operate so that neighbouring residences weren't affected.

A pox on that mean-minded caller!

"He wants to report us to the CAA," I said.

Greig shrugged. "Good luck with that. Idiots." He walked off with his next student.

The public are *not* always right and idiocy is not attractive. It took me a while to simmer down, and the day was only redeemed when I remembered I was going on the trip to D'Urville with

Jack.

*   *   *

Jack picked me up at six o'clock on Monday morning and we drove down to meet Pete at Wellington airport. I'd shoved lunch and wet-weather gear into a daypack and my feet were heavily weighted in my tramping boots. I was as excited as a small kid. I felt a proprietorial ownership of the coordinates, and after reading Jorge's notes I couldn't wait to see the site for myself.

It wasn't an ideal day for such a venture. There was a threat of rain in the air and low cloud hung about the top of the Sounds. The coordinates took us to Mt Woore, and we landed above the site, on the ridge further up the hill. It was the only clear space for the chopper to get down and drop us off. The bush was thick, so we had to jump out and make our own way down.

As we left, the pilot was eyeing up the cloud cover. The mist was building on the hills, and he'd had to do a bit of manoeuvring to get us to the site. I was always impressed with what chopper guys could do. A fixed wing pilot wouldn't be going anywhere near those hills in the prevailing conditions. We agreed that if the mist rolled in further, the pilot would drop down to the beach and wait for us there. We'd have to bush-bash our way down to meet him.

Jack had the coordinates loaded on his phone. We were way outside any chance of phone coverage, but at least the GPS function worked for as long as we could access some satellites. I'd brought an aviation chart with me and Pete had a Lands and Survey map. With Jack leading, we forced our way down the ridge towards the site the coordinates indicated.

The bush was thick and obviously hadn't been disturbed in a long time. It wasn't a bright sunny day anyway and beneath the canopy of the trees the cover cut visibility to the level of twilight, so it was depressingly gloomy. As sole representative of the female gender, I was determined to keep up with the guys, so I focused on a spot between Pete's shoulder blades, and scrambled down the hill behind him, making sure I kept him in sight.

At last the coordinates led us to the site of a recent slip. We'd had quite a bit of rain a few weeks back, which must have loosened the soil. A large karaka tree had toppled, bringing the surrounding canopy down with it and opening a clearing in the thick bush. Part of the hillside had slipped away, and beneath the tree the ground had crumbled, revealing a cavity. The rubble at the foot of the slip showed that the ground had been disturbed.

"This is definitely the spot," said Jack, studying his phone.

"And someone's been here before us," said Pete, indicating a clear footprint impressed in the clay.

We stood for a moment looking around. There didn't appear to be anything that resembled a grave, if Bill's theory was correct and that was what we were looking for. There seemed nothing significant about this spot.

I looked at the fallen karaka. "If a tree falls in a forest and there's no one there to see …" I began, before breaking off with a gasp as I realised the stone I was staring at was the top of a skull, and I'd come close to standing on it.

"Well, this certainly wasn't what I expected," said Jack as he bent down to gently clear the soil away.

The body hadn't been laid out flat but was buried in an upright position. You could only see the very top of the skeleton, down – now that Jack had brushed away the loose dirt – as far as the upper ribcage, which was why it had been hard to see. The rest was still buried.

"However did Jorge discover this?" I asked.

"I'd say he lost his footing on the scree above, fell, slid down the slope, and purely by accident fell into the site," said Jack. "He could have been a couple of metres either side of the cavity and never noticed it."

"So Bill was right," I said. "He was certain all along that Jorge had found a grave. Jorge also gives a similar sort of description about how he discovered the site in his novel."

Pete had pulled his phone from his pocket and was busy taking photographs. I saw him focus on the footprint in the mud before turning to the grave itself.

"If the pendant was originally round the skeleton's neck, it would have been pure chance that Jorge saw it," said Jack. "It must have been lying beside the body because there's no sign that he dug around the bones."

"So what happens next?" I asked. "Do you have to dig the body out for evidence?"

I wasn't keen on the idea. I'd been interested in a treasure hunt, but it seemed disrespectful to be staring at the remains of what had once been a human being. The people who'd buried him had chosen such a remote site to grant him his privacy. It seemed wrong to expose him.

"No, thank god," said Jack. "I wouldn't disturb it if my life depended on it. We report it to the Maori liaison officer who can pass it on to the appropriate tribal authorities and archaeological people. That's as far as our interest goes. In terms of evidence or motive connected to Jorge's death, I'm afraid it doesn't add a lot to the mix, apart from establishing that he almost certainly fossicked in a grave site, which is illegal in itself." He gave a bit of a shudder.

Pete moved round the grave taking more photographs.

I looked up. A heavy mist and rain had come in while we'd been studying the grave.

Pete put his phone away, and by common consent we moved a little away from the grave to a couple of fallen logs. I emptied my pack and pulled on all the wet-weather gear I'd brought with me. We sat there in sodden misery waiting while Jack tried to radio the pilot.

I felt the change, as subtle and indefinable as a difference in air pressure, or the precursor to a shower of rain. The hair on my arms began to lift as I looked round, but I saw nothing.

Thirty seconds later I saw Pete's head jerk up as he too became aware of it. I saw his head move round, and then his eyes met mine.

"What is it?" I whispered.

"Buggered if I know," he said, "but there's something wrong."

I had the uncomfortable feeling we were being watched.

The wind got up and tossed the bushes around angrily. I could hear it moaning through the upper reaches of the trees. I looked at Pete and knew we were both thinking about the grave we were sitting so close to. The bush no longer felt like an exciting, adventurous place to be. I was regretting the impulse which had led me to treasure hunt up in these hills.

Then the mist thickened. Within minutes it was so thick the three of us could barely see each other. The upper levels of the hills were completely covered in cloud, and now it had reached us. It became cold and dark and frightening. I was shivering from a nasty combination of cold and nerves.

Jack was fiddling with the radio and hadn't yet noticed the change in the atmosphere. Reception was lousy, and it seemed ages before he made radio contact with the pilot.

"There's no visibility up here," he said. "If it's this thick here, it's probably worse up above where you dropped us off."

He listened to the pilot's reply.

"OK, I agree. We'll have to climb down the ridge. Yep, we'll meet you at the airstrip." Jack looked down the slope. "It should be fairly straightforward. We just have to follow the ridge down."

There was some more chatter from the pilot.

"No, I don't know how long it will take us," replied Jack. "The weather isn't going to make things easier. OK, we'll see you there."

He disconnected the radio and looked at me and Pete. "It's all downhill from here," he joked.

He must have registered the tension in our faces because he gave a slight frown, and I saw his mouth open to speak. Then, as I watched, he become aware of what was around us. "Shit, what's going on?" he asked.

Pete shrugged.

It was spooky, but I couldn't help but feel the bush was talking; that there were ancient stories being told in the stands of trees and eerie figures reaching through the mist for us. I had no doubt at all there was a curse protecting those poor remains and that we were currently the focus of it. Every story I'd ever heard regarding tapu, or about angry ghosts, was beginning to seem far too real.

Something moved in the bush and I jumped out of my skin. I gave a shamefaced laugh. "It was probably just a possum."

Jack's hand reached over and tightened on mine. "If Jorge went fossicking on his own around that body and was prepared to tamper with it, he was a braver man than me," he murmured.

I looked across at Pete. He was pale, and I swear his eyes were rolling in his head. At least I wasn't the only one affected by the atmosphere. I couldn't wait to get out down the hill and back to the chopper.

"Let's get the hell out of here," said Jack.

We were all grateful to be moving.

Even if we hadn't had the wind up us from having found the skeleton and from the eerie atmosphere, it would have been a difficult descent. Conditions were wet, cold and nasty. The ground was incredibly greasy and unstable. You'd have thought sliding down a hillside would be easy, but it seemed to take us hours, and we had to manoeuvre round steep bluffs and impenetrable thickets that pushed us away from the direct route down.

Jack led the way, guided by the GPS; Pete followed and I brought up the rear.

It was a horrible trip. I had waterproof gear on, but the dampness clung to my trousers and seemed to have penetrated my bones, making every step a misery. Each time I stopped looking at the ground and lifted my head to see ahead, water dripped into my eyes.

To add to the misery, the eerie feeling of being watched remained. If anything, it intensified. I fancied I could hear the sound of feet moving behind me in the bush, and involuntarily kept looking over my shoulder as we made our way downwards. I saw movement flickering in my peripheral vision, but when I turned to look, there was nothing there. There were noises right at the edge of my hearing and I couldn't distinguish them. I was terrified I'd lose sight of the men and be stuck on the hill by myself, even though I was certain they'd never leave me behind.

The maps weren't a great deal of help. I hadn't thought to pack mine in a plastic bag, so it got soaked. Pete's was on waterproof paper, but the bush was too thick for us to get much visual confirmation of where we were, so we just kept doggedly heading downwards wherever we could.

Several times we had to pick our way round fresh slips. Thickets of makomako, supplejack, and rangiora blocked our route and caused us to detour. The hillside was so steep I had to hold on to branches and swing myself down to the next handhold through supplejack, nettles and bush lawyer which tore at my hands and clothes. I stopped in one place and looked almost vertically down the hill below me. It was like climbing down a skyscraper, and I had to pluck up all my courage to force myself to pick my way down. All the time, I fancied I could hear the shuffling of shadowy feet behind me, driving me forward in frightened desperation.

I'm a sceptic, I reminded myself. I'm not superstitious and I don't believe in ghosts. My rational mind was struggling to deal with this experience, but reason was proving to be no protection against the terror which chased us down the hill.

My knees, braced to support me, began to quiver with sheer exhaustion. At one point the scree gave way under my feet and I fell on my bum and slid. Pete grabbed me before I went too far.

"OK?" he asked, as he hauled me up.

I nodded breathlessly. I was too terrified to stop and talk. I hadn't hurt anything seriously, although the wind had been knocked out of me and my numb hands had been grazed.

I've never been so pleased to see anything as I was when we finally found a tree marked with a metal tramping tag and were able to follow the route down to the bay.

Abruptly we came out below the cloud layer.

Visibility improved, and the unnatural, claustrophobic pressure of whatever had followed us lifted away. I heard birdsong and drew a deep breath of clean air.

Jack, Pete and I looked at each other and exchanged shamefaced grins.

"That was horrible," I said. "I was really freaked out. I swear something was following us."

"Makes two of us," mumbled Pete. "Let's not talk about it here, but just get the hell out of it."

Jack nodded. "I'm glad to be out in the open again."

It was easier terrain now, and in a short time we came out of the bush and saw the helicopter below us on the airstrip.

"Are you guys OK?" asked the pilot as we came up to the chopper.

I registered the note of concern in his voice and wondered what we looked like. We must have been a right sight, wild-eyed and covered with scrapes and bruises.

"It was quite a trip," replied Jack.

We buckled ourselves into our harnesses, and I watched as we swung up off the beach and headed back towards Wellington. For the whole journey the cloud kept us low over the water. I looked down at the churning waves beneath us and felt grateful to be back in the air.

My legs were still shaking, but I was safe, warm and almost giddy with relief. I saw Pete had his eyes closed. I looked across at Jack who gave me a reassuring smile.

"You know," I said eventually, "our experience mirrors what Jorge wrote in that script you gave me. Maybe we were just influenced by what he wrote. Did you read it yourself? I thought he added the spooky stuff to make a good story. His character, Brunell, was genuinely scared."

"So was I," said Jack. "It's good to know I wasn't the only one. No, I haven't read his manuscript, nor, I think, has Pete, so that wasn't the cause of our reaction. I swear I'll be more respectful of tapu from now on. It explains why Jorge hid the pendant. He wouldn't have wanted to keep it round his house, attracting whatever that horror was we met up on the hill."

"When we set off this morning I was hoping to find a treasure chest, or something really interesting," I said. "But I suppose that's it?"

"It was quite interesting enough, thank you," said Jack firmly. "But you're right, any police involvement in the gravesite is pretty much finished with. I suppose desecrating a grave might be a motive for murder if you were a fanatic, but it's a bit of a stretch. The only person concerned about the grave being disturbed was Bill. He's still a likely candidate, because he was in the right place at the right time. He could have killed Jorge, and his actions at Jorge's house were pretty dodgy. But his only motive seems to be offence at a breach of cultural courtesy and a grave robbery, which is a crime in itself. Is that enough to drive a man to kill?" He shrugged.

"So that's as far as the pendant link goes?"

"Probably," said Jack. "The site, and eventually the pendant itself, will be handed over to local iwi to decide what to do, and may end up in the hands of archaeology boffins."

"What happens next?" I asked.

"Next is back to the miserable slog of following up on the kids whose photos we found in Jorge's effects."

We waved goodbye to Pete, and Jack and I drove back to Paraparaumu. We were both tired so we grabbed takeaways to eat and went home. Later I used my own brand of magic to lift the horrors of the spirit world from me and my lover.

After Jack left I lay awake for a while. We were rapidly reaching the point where it was going to be more convenient for Jack to keep a toothbrush and a change of clothes at my place. I wondered about that. I had come to like living alone. Jack was fun to be with, and a more than satisfactory lover, but I didn't think I wanted to live with him. At least not yet.

CHAPTER
TWENTY ONE

KATE CALLED. SHE HEDGED AROUND THE
subject, then, "Who's Jack?" she asked at last.

"How did you hear about Jack?" I countered in surprise.
"No, never mind. Someone told you."

"One of the school mums I know has a sister in the police.
I met her the other day and she said you and this Jack person
looked very cosy when she turned up one night to arrest that
burglar who broke in to your place."

I chuckled to myself. I loved living on the Kapiti Coast, but
everyone knew your business. It was a large, small village. I
gave her a quick rundown.

"Is it serious?" she asked.

"It's much too early to tell," I said. "But he was there when I
needed him, and he's special."

"Invite him to join us for tea this Sunday," she said.

I hadn't expected that and wondered whether it would be too
soon in the relationship Jack and I were building.

"I'll ask him," I said eventually. "I'll let you know, OK?" I
wasn't going to commit to arrangements without talking to Jack
first. This was one of what you might call the 'I'll show you
mine if you'll show me yours' moments where we got to meet

each other's friends and families. I wondered if Jack would even be prepared to do so, although he'd been happy to meet Jen.

Relationships don't automatically mean your partner has to get on with your family. David hadn't liked Kate and Martin much. He'd thought Kate, a stay-at-home mum, was lazy and unfulfilled, and regarded Martin's status as inferior to his own. I thought Martin had considered him a prat but had been too polite to say so.

*　*　*

Greig agreed to take Nick night flying that evening for me. Nick had to get his hours up, and he wasn't current. I like flying at night but decided that dinner with Jack was an even better option.

We drove up to Waikanae to the Prah Ta Pang for some Cambodian food.

"My sister Kate has invited you to join us tomorrow for tea," I said. "She phoned up this morning. Someone has told her I'm seeing you. Now of course she wants to meet you."

"I'd be very happy to accept her invitation," said Jack.

"She's got children and a husband," I warned.

"I can survive a husband and children. Or are you saying you don't want me to meet them?" Jack asked, a slightly puzzled look on his face.

"Oh, no. I just didn't want you to feel pressured into seeing them if you didn't want to." I explained my 'I'll show you, you'll show me' theory.

Jack grinned. "On that note, I think we'd better go home and explore the possibilities. As far as meeting your family, though, that would be cool. One of these days you're going to have to meet my lot, and then you'll have good reason to be worried."

*　*　*

I don't know why I had been so anxious. Jack fitted in with Kate and Martin right away. For a kick-off, he was a natural with the girls, which won Kate's approval. Then he and Martin hit it off.

Jack had been looking at their bookshelf. "Who's the chess player?" he asked.

"I am," said Martin. "Do you play?"

"Yes," said Jack. "I warn you I'm not brilliant, but I like a good game, and I'd love a new opponent."

They set the board up.

"It's been ages since I did this," said Martin.

The girls were fascinated by the pieces, particularly by the horse-shaped knights.

"Why are they called knights?" asked Sophie.

"Because the knights used to ride horses into battle," Jack told her. "Then the one here with the crown is the king, but the most important piece is the one beside him, which also has a crown. That's the queen and she can go anywhere."

Kate poked her head round the door from the kitchen and gave her husband an affectionate look. "We'll have lost them now for the next few hours," she said.

I gave her a hand to do the dishes and clean up. "That was a great meal, Kate, thank you. Have you forgiven me for not telling you about him?"

"I guess so," she said with a smile. "I like your Jack. He's charming." She dropped her voice, "and very good-looking."

"I know. It's quite disconcerting going out with him, seeing the reaction of other women. As soon as he encounters a woman I watch them go into a trance as they gaze at him. It takes some waitresses minutes to get over it. I've got used to receiving slower service."

"He doesn't seem vain, though," observed Kate.

"Not so far, at any rate," I said. "I'm not sure if he really appreciates just how beautiful he is. If he were a work of art, a collector would pay a fortune for him."

We carried on wiping the benches; then it was bedtime for the girls, to which they objected. They had decided I was famous because I'd been in the papers. It sounded to me as if they'd made mileage out of this at school, scoring kudos by association.

I glanced at Kate.

"Don't tell anyone," I whispered to them, "but they have to fill up the paper somehow. That's why I appeared in it. Not because I'm really famous."

They digested that.

"That's not true," said Sophie. "We talked about it at school, and I said you were a heroine."

In spite of myself I blushed. Praise from peers is nice; praise from an eight-year-old is exceptional. "Well, thank you, Sophie," I said. "That was very nice of you. I'll try not to let you down."

Charlotte cuddled up to me. "Was there a bad man who could have hurt you?"

"No, darling. No one wanted to hurt me."

Kate and I eventually got them to bed. They'd gone to Martin and Jack to demand their normal kiss from their father. They'd automatically turned to Jack. I wondered how he'd handle it. One of the things I've always admired about Kate and Martin's parenting is the confidence their children feel when dealing with new people. They knew Jack had come with Aunty Claire, and that was all the introduction they needed.

Easily he reached forward and kissed each child gently on her forehead. "Sleep tight, little wahine," he had said. "Dream of the new world in the morning."

"There's a man who's used to being round children," said Kate as she bundled her offspring into bed.

I wondered about that. Jack had mentioned he had a large family but hadn't yet gone into specifics. Yet more fertile ground for the two of us to explore.

Kate and I took our place in the living room. The chess game was obviously all-consuming, with neither contestant ready to quit.

"He seems a good man," Kate commented. We were keeping our voices low so as not to disturb our intellectual opponents.

I nodded. "As I say, it's early days. No pressure. Let's accept each day for what it is."

Kate's face clouded on that thought, and she reverted to Jorge's untimely demise. "I still can't get over how dangerous your job can be."

"Hush, Kate," I chided. "We've been through all that. I can't help the fact that Jorge was killed, but there was no danger to me. That's all we need say about it."

Kate nodded. "OK," she smiled. "I'll let it go. What's the situation with finding out who did it? How far have the police got with solving it?"

"I don't know," I said. "I try not to interrogate Jack, although he does tell me some stuff. The most likely suspect is Bill, who has already admitted discovering the body before I got there and who has a nasty tendency towards illegal activities when they suit him; but then there's Joe the caretaker, who may have some motive I'm not aware of yet and whose movements are unaccounted for. Matt has children who would be in the age group Jorge fancied, but I haven't heard of any trouble there. Matt had another friend whose name I don't remember but I think he had an alibi that afternoon, and then there's Jason, who has a difficult girlfriend. Take your pick. I don't know what the police think, but any one of them could have done the deed. Just why, and maybe more importantly, how, is the question. I don't think the police have even found the murder weapon, which might be critical. Still, there's a lot of sea at Greville Harbour. My theory is the weapon is lying forty fathoms deep."

"It's not," said Jack.

I jumped.

Jack apparently could hear what we were saying, and it wasn't distracting him from the game of chess at all, while Martin, whose move it was, focused fiercely on the board.

"The divers checked the seabed. If there had been anything there, they would have found it," Jack pronounced. "They grid-searched it; there was no room for error. Forensics then reported finding traces of wood, salt and sand in the wound. So early indicators suggest driftwood as a possible murder weapon."

"Was he killed because of that pendant thing you found?" asked Kate. "Didn't you say it was valuable and that he had written about how he found it?"

Jack nodded. "Jorge robbed a grave and then hid the evidence so he couldn't be caught with illicit treasure. The night of Matt's party he got a little pissed and started talking about things he shouldn't have mentioned. Bill, as we know, cottoned on to what he was saying; put two and two together and probably made six. Hence his attack on Claire. Is it a sufficient motive for murder? Who knows?"

Martin moved his piece and Jack snapped back to focusing on the game.

"You're a nicely aggressive player," he commented.

Martin glowed with pleasure. "I'd have said the same about you."

Kate and I looked at each other. Apparently this was a compliment in the chess world.

"What about women?" she asked. "Does the suspect have to be a man?"

"We haven't ruled it out," said Jack. "But then again, there are only a very limited number of possibilities. Joe's wife, Matt's wife, and the girl staying with Jason Harris. Our money at first was on Claire, although she seems to have managed to prove she was somewhere else at the time."

Kate looked slightly shocked.

"Oi," I said. "I thought you took me off the suspect list ages ago."

Jack grinned and concentrated on the game.

"They're nice people, your family," he commented later.

"They certainly seemed to like you." I was relieved. There'd been no reason of course why I should have worried. Jack could fit in almost anywhere and get on with anyone. But with unhappy memories of David still lingering, it was nice to think we could enjoy family occasions together in the future.

I yawned. I was very tired. Excitement takes it out of a girl. The joy of having Mondays off: I could sleep in the next morning. I shifted Nelson so I could slip into bed. Jack joined me, and Nelson tactfully left to check out his dinner bowl.

* * *

Jack left some time later. The nights were getting colder, and I missed the heat reservoir of his body beside me. Nelson wasn't quite as good at keeping me warm.

I lay in bed planning a leisurely day. I could hear the sound of rain falling on the window as I went to sleep. If it was still pouring in the morning I would have a legitimate excuse for complete indolence.

The rain carried on all night. I brought my coffee back to bed and looked for something to read. I had finished a book yesterday and was in that annoying phase of still being so involved in its storyline that I was unable to commit to a new novel, although I had several waiting to be read. At last I gave up trying and picked up my tablet. I played Solitaire, then studied the Words with Friends games that Jen and I were playing. I was still ahead, which pleased me.

I checked out my emails, bank balance, the news, Facebook and Twitter before accepting I was thoroughly bored. So much for a leisurely lie-in. I got up and padded to the kitchen for another cup of coffee. I was getting spoilt having Jack around. The house felt empty this morning without him.

What I needed was some vigorous exercise, but I wasn't going walking up the hills in this weather. I considered my options. I could go to the gym, to the swimming pool or clean the house. I compromised by doing none of them; instead I felt the urge to cook.

Kate's domesticity the previous night had inspired me. After a week of excitement it was very comforting to create a homely nest for myself. Kate cooked a lot of dishes in advance and froze them so as never to be caught unprepared by unexpected guests. I decided to emulate her. Some hours later I was the proud owner of vegetable soup and a fresh loaf of home-made bread.

I served myself up some soup and sat down by the window to eat it. Woman's work, I thought. Hundreds of generations of my forebears had spent their days in honest labour performing similar tasks. It was the life Kate had chosen for herself.

My thoughts wandered to Joe's wife on D'Urville. She must spend her days like this. I didn't imagine she'd gone out on the hills with her husband, fencing, dagging and crutching – or whatever sheep farmers did, back in the days when the harbour had been their farm. From my observations, women on farms worked as hard as their husbands, but role stereotypes and gender demarcation were still strong. It would be a lonely life for a woman to be stuck out on a farm in the Sounds. Even now that the Department of Conservation had turned the harbour into a reserve, the area was very isolated. I imagined supplies probably only came in once a week, if that. Maybe once a month.

What did Jack say she had been doing on the day of the murder? Gardening. A task that meant she had seen none of the comings and goings of the pilots past her house at the far end of the lagoon, nor Bill descending the ridge that ran down on the northern side of the farmhouse. Which also meant no one had seen her either.

Violent murder wasn't usually a woman's crime, but if it were to be the case in Jorge's death, I'd be putting my money on Joe's wife before I considered Jason's crying girlfriend.

*   *   *

"It's karaoke night. Do you want to join us at the pub?" asked Greig. "Nick and Sam are coming out with us as well."

I declined the invitation, although I like karaoke. "No thanks, I've got a date tonight. Look after Nick and don't lead him into paths of unrighteousness. He's got a way to go yet. But he's a good guy. How does Jayleen find him?" If Jayleen was jealous about the amount of time Greig spent with Nick there would be ructions.

"Oh, she likes him," said Greig. "We all get on well together." I wondered whether this was a good or bad thing, then shrugged my shoulders. Not my concern, I reminded myself.

*   *   *

We ate at Rangoli in Kapiti Road. I love Indian food but try to eat it in moderation because it does terrible things to my waistline. We were halfway into our mains when Jack looked at me thoughtfully.

"You know you said 'you'll show me yours and I'll show you mine'?" Jack tore a piece from his naan.

I looked at him in surprise until I remembered the context. "Of course. You mean your family?"

Jack nodded. "My youngest sister is coming down to stay with me for a few days soon. She's seventeen and finishes college later this year, so she's deciding where she wants to study next year. She's interested in Maori studies and wants to check out the Maori University in Otaki. Would you be prepared to meet her?"

"I'd love to," I said. "You survived my family, after all."

He grinned. "You have a nice family. Awhina, however, can be a handful."

"Forewarned is forearmed," I said optimistically. "Awhina. Is that her name? It's pretty."

"She's the baby of the family. I'm the oldest, then there's Mark, Rachel, Marama and Awhina."

"I look forward to seeing you be a big brother then."

Two days later he phoned to tell me Awhina was travelling down that weekend and invited me to meet her for dinner that Saturday evening. I hoped I would make as good an impression on her as Jack had made on my family.

Roger came out to talk to me as I was putting the planes away. "Here, Hardcastle. I want a word."

I pushed the aircraft into its spot in the hangar and turned to him.

"We've just got a job come through. A group of stockbrokers need to be flown out to Awaroa next week. They're joining a conference at the lodge. The majority are getting there by water taxi, but these three want to be flown in."

"OK?" I knew it wouldn't involve me. I hadn't been to Awaroa, and Roger would never send me into a strip I'd not flown into before with him.

"I'm flying down there tomorrow to check it out. It's been

some years since I flew in there myself, so do you want to come? You could try a couple of landings yourself."

"Hell, yeah," I said in excitement. There's nothing like a spot of free flying, and learning my way into a new strip would be fun. "That would be great."

The economics of aviation being what they are, there isn't a lot of fat in the budget for joyriding. Roger was careful each flight we made earned its keep. Even ferrying an aircraft to Wellington to get its avionics overhauled could be made into a training exercise for a student so they paid for the flight. I assumed Roger made a profit from his business, but it would be a small one. Fuel, maintenance, landing fees and compliance costs were huge. Opportunities for a free training flight didn't come along that often.

A thought struck me. "What about Nick?"

"Greig can take care of him for a day," said Roger. "It will do them both good."

"Done," I said happily.

Greig had been listening, and I wondered if he would be resentful, but he thought flying with Nick would be a bit of fun.

"Don't let him get away with being sloppy," I said.

Greig gave me a scornful look. "As if," he sniffed. I thought it would turn into a macho competition between them, shrugged and decided to let them sort it out themselves.

CHAPTER
TWENTY TWO

ROGER AND I FLEW OUT THE next morning. It was
perfect weather for flying. Light winds, clear blue sky
and a chill in the air. Our little plane hummed along out
into Cook Strait. We flew over D'Urville Island at altitude. I
studied Mt Woore. It seemed bizarre now to think how terrified
I'd been there, and unsettling to look down on it after we'd been
intimately involved with the place. My arms still bore grazes
from clambering around in the bush.

"I wonder how they're getting on down there," I said. "It
must be odd trying to get back to normal after all the excitement
they've had."

"There's only Joe and his wife left," he replied. "Matt's lot
won't be back until the school holidays, and the people in the
other bach rarely go there anyway. It'll just be Joe working
there. I doubt if he'll have any campers or other visitors over
the winter."

We headed out across the water.

Awaroa is situated in the Abel Tasman National Park on the
north-west tip of Tasman Bay. We crossed the large bay, and as
we approached land, Roger swung the plane towards the south
for a while until we skirted a headland, then turned north again.

"Our approach is up through this gully," he said.

There were clearly established protocols at airports about approach and the circuit, or pattern to fly around the field in preparation for landing. Strips were different. Every strip had a combination of geography, altitude and local weather that was idiosyncratic. It was often impossible to get a straight-line approach because the landing area was tucked in a valley or some pesky hill got in the way of the track and had to be manoeuvred around. Hence the value of being shown approaches by an experienced pilot.

Roger pointed out landmarks and the appropriate altitudes and speeds required at each one. I hardly had time to notice the beauty of the bay as I focused on his instructions.

He flew two circuits and landings before handing the plane to me. "Just keep your speed under control," he said. "Fly the numbers. That's all you have to do."

I copied his approach and made it safely down onto the strip.

Roger ostentatiously crossed himself. "Thank you, God," he said.

I laughed. "Don't you go all Irish and RC on me. I know for a fact that you're no more Roman Catholic than I am, and I'm flying one more circuit yet."

"That's why I was praying."

I rolled my eyes at him as we taxied back to start our take-off run.

By the end I was well satisfied with my work and certain I would be able to land at Awaroa if I ever needed to, which was another notch on my belt.

We turned for home, and Roger left me to pilot the aircraft back to Paraparaumu.

In a short while I turned to say something to him but saw he had slipped off into a doze.

I smiled. It was easy to forget his age, he always seemed so vital. But Roger would be ten years older than my dad who was also known to drop off for a nana nap in his armchair.

"Good flight?" asked Maria.

"She nearly killed me a couple of times," Roger said. "It's a mercy I'm still with you."

"That's a downright lie," I said indignantly. "Let me tell you he was so relaxed about my flying, he went to sleep all the way back."

"Nonsense; I was too frightened to keep my eyes open."

Maria chuckled. "So you both had a good time."

"Yeah. It's beautiful across there. I could fancy attending a conference in those surroundings, although I think I'd be looking out the window at the view all the time."

Roger bustled off to the hangar. He might have the odd catnap, but he was a man who liked to keep busy.

Greig and Nick were out flying, so I settled down to paperwork.

We met outside the restaurant and Jack introduced Awhina to me. I smiled at her. "Hi, it's nice to meet you."

"Hi," she replied, without returning the smile. I sensed tension in her and wondered if she was shy.

We covertly studied each other. She was tall, at least a couple of centimetres taller than me, and she carried herself athletically, suggesting she played a lot of sport. She was dressed entirely in black, which gave her a goth vibe. Black leggings, black boots, black velvet mini. A carved bone manaia hung round her neck.

The waitress at Kilim welcomed Jack enthusiastically. I doubt if she noticed either Awhina or me as she showed us to our table.

I sat opposite Jack and his sister. They were an attractive pair. I thought I could see familial similarities, not just in their height, but in the shape of their finely moulded nose and lips.

"Jack says you've come down to look at the Wananga in Otaki?" I asked.

"It's one of the options I'm considering," she said. Her voice was low, husky and attractive although the tone she used towards me wasn't at all friendly.

"What do you want to major in?"

"Dunno."

I didn't feel I was making much headway, so I just nodded and turned to include Jack. "You wouldn't believe the idiot conversation I had last weekend." I was laughing as I told them about the caller who wanted me to change the direction the aircraft flew. Spiced with humour, it made a good tale to dine out on.

Jack grinned appreciatively. "Ah, the joys of working with the public. Try being in the police. If we don't arrest people we are useless and incompetent. If we do, then we automatically become bullies and bad guys. You can't win."

"Learn from us, Awhina," I said, hoping to include her in the conversation. "Avoid a job dealing with people if at all possible. There are days when I think being a funeral director and dealing with dead bodies looks appealing. At least they can't talk back."

She nodded but avoided making eye contact. I supposed she was jealous of my friendship with her brother.

The food arrived, providing a diversion.

"Has Jack told you about the burial site on D'Urville?" I asked Awhina.

She nodded again. I gave up trying to start a conversation with her. This one was going to be hard work.

"I meant to tell you about a book I borrowed from the library," I said to Jack. "It was the one Jorge had on his desk when I went into his bach the day of the murder. With all the excitement of the helicopter trip the other day, I forgot to mention it."

"Interesting?" asked Jack.

"Fascinating. It was written last century, in the 1930s I think. It claims there's real archaeological evidence that Maori were not the first settlers in New Zealand at all, but that a couple of centuries before they arrived, a people known as the Waitaha came to the country. It also claimed that a couple of burial sites discovered on the Kapiti Coast were clearly pre-Maori. When the author spoke to local Maori at the time the book was written, they actually disowned these graves as belonging to 'others', although they claimed other burial sites as belonging to their own ancestors. Then there were sketches of skulls which looked slightly different to what we could call normal, photos and sketches of implements, and – which interested me most – a sketch of a bone pendant very like the greenstone one I found."

Jack considered this. "So that was why, when Jorge found the grave on D'Urville, he made the decision straight away that it was a Waitaha grave, not Maori?"

"I assume so. It must have influenced him."

Awhina shifted in her seat but said nothing.

"Reading that book made him jump to that conclusion. It doesn't mean he's right, of course. I'd never heard of the Waitaha before," I said.

"I have," said Jack. "I don't know a lot, but I understood they were a tribe, no different to any other in the great migration of canoes, that spread down from the north and eventually settled in a large portion of the South Island. They had a reputation for being a peaceful people."

"Had you heard that they came to New Zealand before the rest of the big canoes?"

Jack shrugged. "I hadn't heard that one, but there are lots of old Maori myths and legends. Who knows?"

"Bullshit." The remark was so explosive that both Jack and I turned and stared at Awhina.

She saw us looking at her. "It's absolutely bloody typical. You whitey Pakeha just can't leave us Maori alone. Every time, you want to knock us back, and it's always over cultural things." She focused on me. "Why can't you just accept that we came to New Zealand first? Over the years I've heard all the crap I can take: Maori are a lost tribe of Israel; we came from Egypt; we were originally Celts; that the Chinese came to New Zealand before the Maori. Well it's all crap. Why can't Pakeha acknowledge that we Maori were perfectly able to get to New Zealand by ourselves, using our own skills? We don't need to be anyone else. We are the tangata whenua, and we got to New Zealand first. You Pakeha want to steal our stories and take our culture."

"Whoa," said Jack. "It's just a theory, Awhina. No need to get on your high horse."

She ignored his intervention. "Yes, but you believe it, don't you?" she asked me. "It's fucking bloody racist of you. Just typical of you white supremacists, believing they're the only ones who can achieve things. It's colonialism all over again."

"Now that's not true," started Jack, but I cut over him.

"What a load of crap," I said angrily. "I'm not racist, thank you very much. That's a foul thing to say. It's not true and it's really insulting. All I've said is that a book, written nearly a hundred years ago, clearly influenced the thinking and writing of a man who's just been murdered. That's all. It's an interesting suggestion. And I'm damned if I can see why that's racist or why you should want to attack me. I would have thought you'd have been fascinated by it yourself and not so bloody bigoted that you can't explore alternative ideas."

"It happens all the time," said Awhina angrily. "Pakeha steal our culture and our stories, just like they used to steal our land – and on the same immoral basis. It's cultural theft and you're part of it." She glared at me to reinforce her statement.

"That's enough, Awhina," said Jack sharply.

She subsided, but I could feel the attitude pouring off her. So much for hoping Jack's family would take to me.

I took a deep breath and tried an olive branch. "What I was going to add is that I googled the Waitaha and found references to the book I was talking about. But I also found a quote from the late Michael King which basically said the whole story was nonsense. He was our best-known historian, and that was his opinion."

Awhina sniffed – actually sniffed – at that. I didn't think anyone other than characters in books sniffed in disdain, but this glowering teenager was really giving me the treatment. So much for the olive branch.

"Of course," I added, with some malice, "lots of eminent scholars said that *The Iliad* and *The Odyssey* were just myths and legends until Schliemann persisted and discovered the actual historical site of Troy. The same may well happen here. Maybe Jorge's site really will provide us with a breakthrough and show that there were other races here before the Maori arrived. Wouldn't that be fascinating?"

Jack gave me a seriously irritated look that said surely I was adult enough not to deliberately provoke the girl? I glared back. I wasn't the one with a delinquent sister.

The rest of the meal was spent in a rather awkward silence.

Jack tried a couple of conversational gambits but was stymied by his sister's clear hostility and my own perverse reaction. I was upset Awhina hadn't taken to me straight away. My family had warmed to Jack immediately. Was it too much to expect his family would like me? I was even more upset to realise that, childishly, I didn't want to share Jack at all, not even with his sister, which rather sank me to her level.

Mercifully the meal came to an end and we walked back to the cars. Jack pulled me to one side. "Sorry," he said stiffly. "I didn't expect Awhina to react like that."

I shrugged him off. "It's OK. Nothing you can do anything about. Not your fault she's obnoxious. I hope it's just a phase she's going through and she gets over it soon." I didn't bother to sound conciliatory.

I knew I sounded pettish, but I was shocked and hurt by the accusation of racism. I've got lots of prejudices, some of which I'm even proud of. I maintain that another term for prejudice is 'having standards', and I have serious prejudices about the unmannerly, the uneducated and those who inflict their BO upon me in small aircraft. In fact, my prejudices were a testament to the values my Mum and Dad installed in me. Maybe we never truly outgrow our childhood.

Race discrimination, however, has never been a prejudice of mine. I'm mongrel bred myself and proud of it. I would despise anyone stupid enough to judge people by either gender or race. I was furiously angry with Awhina and sadly aware that, ridiculous as it was, I was also jealous this girl was going to cost me my lover for the weekend.

Jack looked at me without smiling. "I'll be in touch."

* * *

I usually love Sunday mornings. Sunday is the start of my weekend; the day I can lie in bed until ten o'clock, eat and drink too much without worrying about flying and, of course, more recently, spend time with Jack. Unfortunately, Jack was not going to be part of this particular weekend so suddenly I had far too much time on my hands.

I told myself that I refused to be pathetic and sit around missing him, so I settled into a day of domestic discipline. Cleaning, washing and ironing. I had noticed my standards were slipping in the pleasant debauchery of an itinerant lover. Today I was all stern resolve. My house would become my very clean castle. Nelson, who doesn't approve of this level of disturbance, took himself off to find a quieter corner outside.

Several hours later I emerged from a flurry of chores with the warm certainty that a long line of female ancestors would have approved of my industry. Plants had been watered, skirting boards dusted and I had sorted out my wardrobe. I don't know why there is something so satisfying about packing away one season's clothes and hauling out another's, but I have always found it to be therapeutic. I put into storage all my spaghetti-strapped tops and dresses, folded away any floaty skirts and pulled out, in their stead, merino tops, winter jackets and heavier trousers. Come rain or snow, I was now equipped to deal with winter.

It still left me with a long, empty evening stretching ahead. I considered phoning Kate and cancelling my usual visit but then realised I'd be left with nothing to do but sulk, self-medicate on wine, feel sorry for myself and go to bed early with Nelson. I couldn't even phone Jen for a chat. She would be busy getting ready for the evening performance. I tried Lisa but her phone went directly to voicemail.

"Is Jack coming?" was Kate's first question.

"No, he's got his sister staying with him. He'll have his hands full looking after her I should think."

"Oh? How old is she?"

"Seventeen."

Kate looked puzzled so I forestalled her next question. "She's come down from the Waikato to visit him and check out the Maori University in Otaki. And boy, does she travel with baggage." I told her about the awkward meal the night before.

"She sounds very different to Jack. I mean, he doesn't seem

to have any issues at all. Do you think the rest of his family are like her?"

"I don't know," I said miserably. "But I've certainly got off to a bad start with Awhina. I didn't mean to provoke her, but she seemed determined to prove I was a colonial oppressor."

"How did you handle it?"

I ignored her. "Would you like a drink? I've brought a nice Shiraz."

"Did you behave badly?"

I knew Kate wouldn't let it go. She's far too like our mother, and years of being a parent herself have made her acutely aware of childish evasions.

"No, I didn't behave badly, all things considered. But I also didn't behave particularly magnanimously either," I muttered.

"Oh Claire! He's such a nice man. Don't blow this one away."

"Thanks for the sisterly solidarity," I snapped.

"Well, I know you," said my sister candidly. "You speak before you think, and you let your emotions carry you away sometimes."

I opened my mouth.

"Don't tell me you're a pilot and a steely-eyed professional, or whatever you're going to throw at me. You're still the little sister I could wind up dead easily when we were kids just by pulling your strings. You haven't changed that much, you know."

"You're talking years ago, that's not fair, and anyway you were a cow trying to get me into trouble all the time."

"Do you remember when we had that fight, and you put your foot through the wall?" Kate giggled.

"I didn't mean to," I protested. "It was an accident. My foot pushed against it while we were wrestling."

"More like a cat fight, the way I remember it."

We looked at each other, and I gave a rueful grin. "We must have been a right handful for poor Mum."

"I remind myself of that when I deal with my own kids," sighed Kate. "Anyway, the point is, you shouldn't have allowed Jack's kid sister to rile you."

"She's not a kid, Kate. She's seventeen. She knew what she

was doing."

"She was probably scared stiff about meeting you. Jack will have told her that you're his friend and she'll have worked out he's sleeping with you. You're years older than her, you're in a respected profession and you're attractive. She probably figured you'd take her brother away from her and didn't feel she could compete, so she got antsy. Am I right?"

"Maybe," I replied. I'd recognised that irrational jealousy had pushed my own buttons.

"What did Jack say?"

"He sort of apologised for her. I said it wasn't his fault he had a cow of a sister."

Kate stared at me. "Oh my god, Claire. You didn't?"

"Well, not quite," I said.

"She's his sister. You can't go around criticising her. Of course he'd have to stand up for her. I'd stand up for you if someone criticised you, even if I thought you're making a tit of yourself."

"You have an unkind way with words, Kate."

"Maybe." She took a breath. "But I haven't told you anything you hadn't already worked out for yourself, have I?"

I nodded reluctantly.

"Pour me some of that wine then, would you."

I poured us both a slug, while Kate busied herself getting dishes out of the oven.

"So where does that leave you and Jack?" she asked after a few minutes.

"I don't know," I said sadly. "He said he'd be in touch, but I don't know when. That's where it got left. He hasn't called me today."

"Let's hope little sister goes home soon, and you can get things back on track. Help me get the plates on the table?"

When I sat down to dinner between Sophie and Catherine I had been made to understand that my sister viewed the three of us as equally childish.

I texted Jen when I got home to see if she had time for a cup of coffee the next day.

I love my sister, and she has a privileged place my life, but

I felt a desperate need for girl-talk with Jen. Families can be claustrophobic, and Kate's honesty felt unnecessarily critical.

I can do late lunch? 1.30 at Felix? she texted back.

Jen was wearing black again. I wondered why – when their clothes were pretty much identical – Jen wore hers with chic style, whereas the effect of the same gear on Awhina had been dark and heavy.

Thank heaven for friends. They share with you, let you dump your problems on them, laugh with you and cry with you. We sipped our cappuccinos.

"I'm not surprised she riled you," Jen commented at last, blessedly free of any recrimination. "Calling you a racist is a bit over the top."

"I should have been able to deflect the comment or laugh it off; instead I allowed her to get under my skin and needle me. It just caught me by surprise," I admitted.

"Well, if you held back from actually smacking her, I think you did well," said Jen. "Where does that leave things with Jack?"

"I don't know. I hope I haven't stuffed it up."

"That would be tragic," Jen agreed. "He's way too much of a hunk to be allowed to get away. Now, I've got news for you. Did I mention Michael to you last time?"

I shook my head. "You said there was a guy you'd been going geocaching with, but nothing else. Is this the same guy?"

"Yep. He's one of the dancers in the show. All muscles, graceful moves and a nerdy interest in GPS coordinates. Anyway, it's taken a while, but we finally went out on a real date last week, and it was great."

I grinned at her animated face. "Good one. I knew you'd land your man eventually."

Jen shrugged. "It's probably just a show romance, and we were so slow getting going that the show closes in two weeks' time. Who knows what we'll all be doing after that? But he's nice, and it's fun while it lasts."

"What does he do the rest of the time?"

"He's with a modern dance troupe. They're based in Wellington but tour the regions during the summer months."

"Time will tell," I said sagely, thinking I could say the same about my state of play with Jack.

We walked across the road back to my car, and I hugged her before I climbed in. "Thanks for letting me dump on you."

"You're welcome," she said. "I always know you'll return the favour when I need it. What are friends for?"

I smiled as I drove away. What indeed are friends for? Then I thought of Jack and the friendship I hoped I hadn't thrown away.

*   *   *

Tuesday morning and I was back at work. Still no call or message from Jack. I didn't know if he'd managed to send Awhina home yet. It wouldn't be easy being in the middle of a murder enquiry and have the responsibility of looking out for a bolshie teenager.

I found I was checking my phone every five minutes, a weakness I despised in myself. I toyed with the idea of calling Jack, but felt awkward after the petty attitude I'd displayed. I didn't know what his reaction would be and it stopped me each time I went to dial.

Nick and I spent the morning in the classroom. He was becoming increasingly proficient with the theory and could now write a presentable briefing on the whiteboard. I teased him a little about his early attempts and he grinned.

"Yeah, well I had to give you a challenge."

"It was enough of a challenge surviving your early attempts of flying from the right-hand seat," I replied. I smiled inwardly. He'd come a long way from the self-effacing young man of a few weeks back. He'd do well as an instructor, having a nice manner about him, good aviation skills and enough attitude now to take no nonsense from either a student or an instructor. I was pleased with him.

"Have you totalled up your hours and checked you're close to the requirements?" I asked. There are minimum flight requirements that a candidate must meet before being eligible for a flight exam.

"I don't want to book you in for your test and find you don't qualify."

"I'll get round to it," he assured me. "I think I'm pretty much on course."

"Well make sure you do. You don't want to get to the day before the exam and find you're five hours short. It's an easy thing to happen."

I was walking across the tarmac with Nick when I saw Roger lead his Awaroa-bound clients out to the aircraft. I waved to them cheerfully. "Have a good flight," I smiled.

One of the men looked familiar, and I turned to look at him again as we passed. He was young and thin. I couldn't place him.

Nick and I carried on with our lesson. We'd reached the stage where I would make deliberate mistakes, he would have to fix them and then explain to me what had gone wrong, why, and how to correct the issue. He was doing well, becoming more positive as his confidence increased, and he proved to have a good sense of humour. He'd survived the teasing new pilots get, and was prepared to give as good as he got. His friendship with Greig had been beneficial for both of them.

I didn't think about Roger's passengers until we'd landed and taxied back to base and then the nagging sense of familiarity returned. Anyone who deals with the public and sees a lot of people is familiar with this – was the person an old client? Did you meet them at a party? Should you know their name?

It tugged at me, and after I'd sent Nick off to self-study some theory, I pulled out Roger's flight plan and checked the names of the passengers.

"What are you looking for?" asked Maria.

"Dunno. Just that one of those guys looked familiar and I can't place him. Here we are: Lee Caldwell, Roger Hampton, Jason Harris. Why does Jason Harris sound familiar?"

"I don't know the name," said Maria. "He's not one of our students."

"No," I said slowly, as I remembered where I'd heard it. "He was the young guy staying at the house next to Jorge's on D'Urville. I only saw him the once. Joe told me his name."

"So he's a stockbroker," said Maria.

"Or a forex type. How did Roger come to get this charter?" I asked.

"He said one of the men is a friend of Matt's and he recommended us, which was nice of him. Word-of-mouth business is always good."

I was thinking about the coincidence which had caused Jason Harris to walk into our office, then laughed at myself. That was it, simply a coincidence, and life was full of them.

After lunch Nick and I went up in the air and flew again. The art of giving a lesson in the air was coming easier to Nick. I could now ask him to teach me several different manoeuvres and he would mostly get the patter right. I was well satisfied when we taxied back to base.

I asked after Jason Harris when Roger came in from his flight.

"The quiet guy? He was the one you saw the day you found Jorge?" asked Roger. "It's a bit of a coincidence him ending up here, but I suppose it's not that surprising. Wellington's a very small town and everyone knows everyone else. We don't have six degrees of separation here, we have about two. As it happened, Matt put them on to us, and I imagine the number of financial folk in town is fairly limited. They probably meet at conferences all the time."

"What did he say?"

"He just sat in the back of the plane and looked out the window."

"So he didn't say anything about D'Urville?"

"Nothing at all. I don't think I heard him speak. I thought he was a bit feeble actually and wondered if he was feeling airsick, he looked so washed out and pale."

"Probably the effect of your flying," I said uncharitably.

"Wash your mouth out, girlie," he ordered.

Actually, Roger didn't mind being teased as long as we didn't cross the line.

I came back from taxiing a plane needing maintenance across to the Aerotech hangar, to find the office unexpectedly crowded.

Several people had gathered round the front counter and I was surprised to see Rick, the security guard, there with his son Cam. He'd accompanied his father to work occasionally during school holidays, as many children do, so we were used to seeing him round.

"Hi, Cam," I said.

He was, or would be, an attractive boy of about sixteen, currently afflicted with pimples, which marred his otherwise pleasant face. Cam, I noticed, wasn't looking very happy.

"You'd better hear this, Hardcastle," said Roger. "Rick's solved the mystery of who stole the Avgas from the aero club."

"Well, as I was saying," Rick continued, "the fences were all fine, and there were no problems with the locks. We couldn't fathom how anyone had got in to the secure area to nick fuel from the planes. Then yesterday my wife overheard Cam and a friend talking."

He gave his son an unfriendly glance. "Cam took the security keys off my ring one day when I was off duty and used them to access the field that night. I wasn't working, so I didn't notice them missing. He returned them the next morning so I never knew they'd gone."

I gave a small gasp. Poor Rick, I thought.

Cam had turned scarlet and was staring at his feet.

Roger looked at him sternly. "Why on earth would you do such a thing?" he asked. "Not only was it theft, which I'm perfectly certain you know is wrong, but you've compromised your father whose job it is to keep the airfield secure. What have you got to say for yourself?"

"I'm really sorry." The words were almost inaudible.

Roger had no time for that nonsense. "Speak up, and look at me!" he demanded. "Why did you do it?"

Cam turned an even deeper shade of red but was courageous enough to lift his head to face Roger.

"We wanted it for our car. Aviation fuel makes it go faster. I'm very sorry. We didn't think."

Roger made a rude noise. "You disgust me and you've shamed your father. You knew perfectly well it was the wrong thing to do."

There was a moment or two of silence while we digested the information.

"What happens next, Rick?" asked Maria.

"We've already been to the Air New Zealand terminal and the aero club. You're the last place on the field. Now we're going to the police station so Cam can turn himself in. I've reported it to my company. They're considering their options, but they've indicated there is a high probability I'll be fired over the breach in security. I'm still working for the next couple of weeks, but that's only because they haven't got anyone else to replace me."

Cam had dropped his head again so his features were largely hidden. From what I could see of his sad, twisted mouth I rather thought he was crying. I felt a surge of irritated compassion for his misery.

"I'm sorry, Rick," said Roger. "That's tough. If I can put a word in to support you, I'd be happy to do so."

"Thanks," said Rick heavily. "I appreciate it. I'm really sorry that it's my son who has caused this trouble. I don't know where Jenny and I went wrong as parents. I can't imagine how he would have got the idea that lying and stealing are OK things to do."

"I feel terribly sorry for them," said Maria after the miserable pair had left.

"Well, I feel sorry for Rick," said Roger. "He's right, though. Chances are he'll lose his job over this. He shouldn't have left the keys where anyone could access them."

"Maybe," said Maria, "but it does seem very tough."

"What do you think the police will do?" I asked.

Roger shrugged. "It depends. Air New Zealand won't be at all happy about the threat to their security, whatever the reason. They may try to throw the book at Cam. I suppose it will be in his favour if he confesses to the police, although it's obvious that he wouldn't have done so if his mother hadn't caught him out."

"At least one mystery is solved," said Maria. "I didn't like knowing that someone had managed to break into a secure area. There are so many nutters around these days, it makes you wary. It's a sort of relief to find out it was just a couple of kids."

Roger shook his head. "Just a pair of boy racers nicking Avgas to make their souped-up car go faster. God help us all. What a mess. I feel sorry for Cam in a way. In my day his dad would have given him a hiding, and it would all be over with. Instead of which he's likely to end up with a criminal record, which is not a good way to start his life. What is he – sixteen or so? It's a great shame because he's really just a kid."

We were all subdued for the rest of the day. The pleasure Nick's progress had given me that morning evaporated in the mess Cam's actions had caused. It would be a bitter lesson if his actions brought not only his own punishment but his father's dismissal from his job.

*   *   *

By the time we left the airport that evening, the weather had turned foul. I dropped into the library to return my book and was soaked by the time I'd made it back to the car.

Lying in bed that evening I listened to the rain on the windows and thought about how easy I'd found it to describe Cam as a silly kid, when I'd loaded Awhina, barely a year older, with the full weight of my adult scorn and intolerance. I felt ashamed and ungenerous.

Another day went by with no communication from Jack. It was beginning to look increasingly probable that I had blown what we had. I felt wretched and knew I only had myself to blame.

It was Roger's day off and being a weekday the office was quiet. The rain continued to pelt down outside, flattening both the light and our moods.

Nick and I worked on his theory, then joined Greig out in the hangar to clean some planes. I vacuumed while the other two washed and polished the aircraft. It seemed an unusually long, slow day. At the end of it I was grateful to get home, pour myself a glass of wine and stare blankly at the TV.

My mobile rang and I grabbed it, realised it wasn't Jack, and swore silently. "Hello."

"Hardcastle?"

"Hi, Roger," I said resignedly. At least this wasn't first thing in the morning, which was an improvement on his usual interruption.

"We've got a problem," he said. Well, I've heard that before, I thought.

"Some idiot driver ploughed into me this morning. No, not my fault," he carried on, having heard my gasp of breath.

"I'm OK. Well, no, I'm not completely OK. He's broken my ankle, the bastard, and I can't fly for a few weeks."

"Oh crap, I'm so sorry, Roger. Thank God you're alive. What do you mean, ploughed into you? What happened?"

The facts were simple. At the intersection of Kapiti Road and MacLean Street the driver of the offending vehicle had failed to look for oncoming traffic and sailed across the road straight into Roger's car. His vehicle was a write-off, but surprisingly and perhaps even miraculously, Roger wasn't. Even so, his ankle was broken and was now in plaster. He was grounded until the leg healed.

"Shit," I said.

"Double shit, and raise you one," he replied. "The thing is, I've had a call from Awaroa. One of the passengers needs to get out urgently tomorrow. They wanted to be picked up this evening until I pointed out it was too late."

"But you only just dropped them over there yesterday," I protested.

"I know, but there's a family tragedy or some such drama. You're the only one left standing, Hardcastle. Tomorrow you're across there picking him up."

I thought fast. "OK," I said. "I can do that if the weather clears."

CHAPTER
TWENTY THREE

I LAY IN BED THAT NIGHT TRYING to recall everything I'd learned on the flight Roger and I had done together. I knew the theory – Roger had taught me the route and cautioned me against obvious dangers – but I needed to mentally fly the approach so I was confident when the moment came to do it for real.

"What are you doing here?" I asked Roger in surprise when I saw him struggling on his crutches the next morning.

"I thought you were supposed to be at home, keeping your leg up and rested."

"Can it, Hardcastle," he said shortly. "I'm here because this business is mine, and someone's got to bloody well run it, so quit with your comments."

He was in a foul mood. Inaction, discomfort and frustration had turned him mean and nasty. I felt sorry for his wife who would be bearing the brunt of his misery and wondered if she had encouraged Roger to get out of the house.

"Can't he just go home?" asked Greig plaintively. We'd only been at work an hour, and already Roger had snarled at me, then torn strips off Grieg for not having the maintenance records complete.

For Greig and I, our usual escape route into the air was impossible. The rain had been bucketing down all night, and it was currently hard to see across the airfield. If it carried on this hard after our long, dry summer, there would be floods and slips all over the region. The forecast was for it to clear after ten. If it didn't there would be no way I could get across Cook Strait to Awaroa.

We had sought shelter in the hangar, ostensibly to wash oil and fuel stains off the floor. Running outside through the rain to reach the hangar was preferable to remaining within range of Roger's withering sarcasm. No one and nothing was going to please him today.

"I feel guilty leaving Maria inside," I said. "She looked a bit desperate as she saw we were doing a runner."

"Each man or woman for themselves," said Greig. "The way the old man is carrying on, we'll either murder him or he'll have us in tears before the end of the day."

I agreed. Roger is a lovely, warm, generous man and it's a privilege to work for him. But frustration had worked a Jekyll-and-Hyde transformation, and the sarcastic, bullying monster he'd turned into today was best avoided.

I looked at the sky which was lightening. With any luck, if the cloud lifted, I would be up in the sky and away to Awaroa, out of Roger's reach, very soon.

We scrubbed the floor and cleaned out the oil tray for an hour until we judged it safe to return inside.

"You go first," urged Greig. "You can be the recce party and let me know if it's safe. You're a girl; he won't be as nasty to you as he would be to me."

"Yeah, right," I said as caustically as I could manage.

*　　*　　*

Mercifully the weather was kind and the forecast accurate for once – overcast, with more rain threatening, but no obvious wind concerns, for which I was grateful. Wind can be a critical factor when flying into the tight confines of a small strip. I've flown approaches into D'Urville where wind shear has sucked me out of the sky. Alternatively there've been days where lift from an updraft is so strong I've needed full flap, no power, the aircraft nose pointing down, and I've still barely managed to descend onto the strip.

I landed at Awaroa and taxied to the pull-up area. I was a little early, having left Paraparaumu at least fifteen minutes before I needed to so as to ensure a stress-free flight. I climbed out of the aircraft, and as a matter of habit found the wooden dipstick and climbed up to check the fuel in the tanks in the wings. All was good. Awaroa was a beautiful place, but not much of it was visible from the actual airstrip. I would need to be airborne again before I could fully appreciate its beauty. I checked the wind – a light westerly. Perfect for a clean take-off. I smiled and waited for my client.

Sod's Law, of course, but my passenger was none other than Jason Harris. He looked terrible, with red-rimmed eyes and sallow, unhealthy skin. He'd lost weight since I'd seen him on D'Urville. I wondered whether he was ill, and hoped he wasn't going to be sick in the plane. I briefly introduced myself, got him into his life jacket, explained its use and strapped him into the passenger seat. We would be a light load taking off, which was to our advantage.

It was a short take-off roll – the weather was cold and the wind positive – and we were airborne. I looked down at the bay. "It's lovely, isn't it?" I said.

Jason gave a sullen nod, but refused any comment.

"Did you have a good couple of days?" I asked. I respected a person's right to silence, but Jason irritated me, so I was pushing him a wee bit.

"It's OK," he said. "Nice enough, I suppose."

"Nicer than D'Urville Island?" I asked.

His head shot round so fast I'm surprised he didn't put his neck out. "D'Urville?"

"Yes, the island," I said. "Didn't I hear you were there recently for a holiday?" I didn't bother to explain I'd seen him there. His reaction was weird enough.

"Oh, yes, OK. For a few days," he conceded.

Jason was never going to be one of the world's conversationalists. I gave up and concentrated on flying a direct route home. I was enjoying the flight, and my passenger was safe, secure and about to be delivered in one piece. You could ask no more of me. I let the miles float past underneath the empennage. We were approaching D'Urville Island's northern end. From where we were, Greville Harbour was hidden behind the intervening hills.

"I know who you are," Jason said suddenly. "You're the pilot who was on D'Urville that day. They said you found the body."

"Yes," I said, shortly. I was no longer interested in talking to him.

"What did you see?" he asked. "Did you see who killed that man?" There was a tight urgency to his question which surprised me. After all, if Joe's statement was to be believed, Jason and his girlfriend had only arrived on the island the morning of the murder.

"Jorge?" I asked. "No, of course not. I just happened to be the one to report his body to the police. That's all." I couldn't even claim to have been the one who discovered the body. Not now I knew Bill had been there before me.

"Do the police suspect you?"

Well, I hadn't expected that one. "I don't believe so," I replied coldly. "But of course you'd have to ask them yourself if you want an answer."

"Well, you were the one who discovered the body," he said relentlessly. I swear that for the first time he appeared to have colour in his cheeks. He continued, "And you were the only one there at the time. Surely they must wonder about you?"

"I'm sure they wonder at me, for many reasons," I said, as politely as I could manage, "but so far they haven't tried to pin the blame for the murder on me."

We flew on in silence. I glanced sideways at Jason and saw he was looking distressed again. He had sweat beading on his forehead, his skin was the colour of porridge and his hands were clenching and unclenching in his lap. Well, he'd been briefed where the sick bags were. I gave a mental shrug and ignored him.

There was something unbalanced about him that gave me the creeps. If it weren't for the fact that I knew he'd barely arrived himself on D'Urville the day of Jorge's death, I'd have wondered whether he was the murderer. As it was, he probably hadn't been on the island long enough to even meet Jorge, let alone have time to quarrel with him. I mulled the idea over as the miles flew past underneath us. I'd be glad to get back to base and be rid of him.

We were close to the southern tip of Kapiti Island when he made his move. Without warning, he grabbed the controls with both hands and turned the aircraft sharply so we were heading directly towards the seaward cliffs of the island.

"Hey, cut that out!" I shouted, trying to straighten the yoke up. "What the hell are you doing?"

He'd taken me completely by surprise. I tried to wrest control of the aircraft back, but he had a solid grip on the handles, and it was beyond my strength to turn them. Most aircraft have dual controls, which is a great asset when instructing a student – the instructor can take control if needed. In all my years of flying passengers around, I had never encountered one who interfered deliberately with the steering. Most people look at the controls in mild panic and keep their hands well clear in case they do something dangerous.

We were approaching the island at a fast clip, and my struggles to out-wrestle Jason weren't working. I reached forward and flicked the transponder to 7500. I knew the emergency code for unlawful interference would garner attention from any station monitoring our blip on a radar screen, even if they couldn't do a lot to help me.

"What are you doing?" shouted Jason. "Don't touch anything. I'm going to finish it all right now." I understood his dilemma. If he took his hand off the yoke to change the squawk frequency back, he'd weaken his grip and probably allow me to regain control. Eventually he shrugged. I assumed he'd no idea what

I'd done and was probably discounting it as irrelevant. I tried to make a radio call, but he kept twisting the column out of my grasp so I couldn't press the transmit button.

The cliffs were getting uncomfortably close. I could see every detail of the rocky, inhospitable face, and we were running out of clear space over the sea. It was now or never. Without trying to turn the yoke again, I grabbed control column with both hands and shoved forward as hard as I could. Jason hadn't expected the move so wasn't braced against it as I pushed my full weight forward on the yoke. The nose of the little plane dropped like a stone, and Jason, startled by the sudden weightlessness of the resulting zero gravity, took his hands off the controls to make a panic-stricken grab for the roof. I saw his knees fly up, as his feet floated off the floor.

"Shit," he said as he scrabbled for a grip. The effect of weightlessness was only there for a second or two but had given me the break I needed.

I straightened the aircraft up, got her flying straight and level again, and turned back towards Paraparaumu. I was incandescent with fury.

"You keep your filthy, fucking hands off my plane," I snarled at the shaken Jason. I saw his hand reach towards the yoke again and remembered the heavy wooden dipstick was in the pocket beside me. I brought it smashing down over his knuckles.

"Keep your hands on your lap where I can see them," I said again over his agonised shriek.

I pressed the radio button. "Paraparam Flight Service, this is Papa Romeo Hotel squawking 7500," I said.

Sam's startled voice came over the waves. "Papa Romeo Hotel, confirming 7500. Copy."

"My passenger attempted to hijack the aircraft. I have regained control. Will be landing Paraparaumu in five minutes."

"Police will be contacted."

"Joining downwind for 34."

We landed safely enough, although I never remembered anything after that radio call. The fight had gone out of Jason, and he sat hunched in his seat.

I pulled up outside our building, shut the plane down and got out without talking to him. I stood on the apron, alive, safe and back in my proper environment, but I was shaking with rage and reaction. I saw shocked faces peering from the office window, and already people were on the veranda waiting for me. Rick and Dan, the security men, stepped down and began the walk to the plane, intent on securing Jason.

"He's all yours, guys," I said as I left him to their care.

My work was done. From somewhere further up the airfield came the background sound of a helicopter coming in to land at the Heliworx terminal. Two aircraft down on our line a fixed wing engine fired up, prior to its pilot completing his pre-flight checks. I could hear the beat of the propeller.

Everything was normal. Except me. I couldn't control my breathing, my mind was in spasm, my vision clouded, and I had a rage of berserker proportions. My body overrode my brain and I stormed into the office. "Fucking bastard just tried to kill me!" I announced as I strode past Roger and Maria. I barely saw Greig who had been leaning in the doorway as I shoved past him. I was beside myself with the frantic energy of my reaction. All was well. I was safe, I reminded myself. Safe, sound and home. I could relax, breathe. It was time for a return to normalcy.

I'd taken one more stride when I heard Roger give a mighty shout. "Oh, no!"

I turned back. Jason had eluded the security guys. As they stepped forward to grab him he'd veered away down the line of aircraft towards the plane that had just started up. Rick gave a horrified cry and rushed to intercept him. From some metres out Rick flung himself towards Jason in a desperate tackle, but missed and went sprawling on the tarmac. Jason didn't even turn to look. Instead, and without any hesitation, he opened his arms wide and deliberately stepped forward into the circle of the propeller.

The result was appallingly brutal and quick. The spinning prop grabbed Jason and pulled him into itself. A hideous spray of bright blood spiralled up into the air and fell to wrap around the body of the plane. Window, wings and fuselage were covered in Jason's gore. Mangled flesh fell to the ground. His death must have been instantaneous.

I heard a scream. It might have been from me, or any other of the onlookers.

The bloodied plane lurched sideways and then silence as the pilot inside cut the engine. They would have been helpless to prevent the disaster. Even if they'd realised what was about to happen, they'd never have been able to manoeuvre the plane away. Aircraft can't reverse.

There was sudden movement as Greig charged through the door and ran onto the apron. Recalled to duty, I followed him out onto the tarmac then stood uselessly, staring at the carnage. Greig reached the plane, grabbed the door open and helped the pilot out. Still no one else moved. I watched as the pilot climbed out, staggered away from the aircraft, bent over and spewed over the tarmac. Greig held his shoulders as the vomit added to the mess on the ground and mingled with parts of Jason and a good deal of his blood.

I looked at one lump of flesh and suddenly identified it as a hand, the one I had hit so viciously barely half an hour earlier.

I managed to shut myself in a cubicle just in time before I vomited up my breakfast and dinner from the night before. I stood bent over for a long while, clutching the sides of the toilet bowl, my insides churning.

Eventually I stood up on shaking legs, flushed the toilet and went to wash my mouth out at the sink. The sheer intensity of my emotion frightened me. I recognised it as chiefly anger, but that didn't explain my sobbing. A reaction to fear of course; reaction to the threat on my life; outrage that someone would try to destroy a perfectly good aircraft just to commit suicide and the whole culminating in the unbelievable horror of Jason's death. The scene had imprinted itself in my brain.

After some long minutes I took a deep breath and braced myself to go back outside.

There were people everywhere. My radio calls earlier had been broadcast over the local airways, so every flying organisation on the field knew there had been trouble, and a number of their staff had come over to see what was happening and offer help. A couple of our students, including Nick, were standing staring. Sam had come rushing down from the tower, and the police had arrived.

Roger was trying to take control of the situation but looked rather less authoritative than usual with his foot wrapped in bright pink plaster. He welcomed the police with palpable relief.

I felt sorry for the cops. They had come in response to an attempted hijack and now had to deal with Jason's dramatic suicide. Their constable took one look outside the windows at the carnage on the tarmac and called for reinforcements.

Greig was comforting the person who'd been in the aircraft Jason had used as a suicide tool. The man raised his head, and I realised the poor sod was Tom. I went towards them.

Greig saw me first. "Are you OK?" he asked.

I nodded and reached out to grip Tom's shoulder. "How about you?"

His eyes filled with tears as he looked at me. "I'm sorry," he said. "I just couldn't move out of the way. I didn't know what to do."

"Of course you couldn't have done anything," said Greig. "There was no way you could have avoided him. Even if it were possible, he'd have followed you. It was his choice. Not your fault at all."

I hugged Tom fiercely, willing with all my might that this awful thing hadn't happened to him.

"Greig's right," I said. "There was nothing you could do. Jason wanted to die. He'd already had a go at killing both of us when I was in the plane."

What had happened to a simpler age when people just used aircraft because they wanted to fly? Now they're weapons in the hands of lunatics.

I heard my name called. I recognised the policeman. He had been at the station when I'd gone in to sign my statement about Jorge. I nodded to him. "Hi," I said.

"Can you tell me what happened, please?"

I ran through the attempted hijack. I could hear horrified gasps from behind me as I told him the details.

"You are certain he intended to fly the plane into the cliff when you were with him?"

"Absolutely certain," I said. "Aside from the fact he was pointing the aircraft directly at the rocks, he said he wanted to 'finish it all right now'. He used all his strength to prevent me regaining control."

"So, how *did* you get control?" The officer sounded dubious. "I wouldn't have thought there's much space in one of those little planes for you to put up a fight."

I explained how I'd bumped the plane forward and the resultant loss of gravity. I watched the officer writing it down verbatim but was certain he didn't understand what I was telling him. I shrugged. I didn't care. I was still in a fog.

The ambulance arrived, and more police. Roger, Greig, Tom and I were taken into separate briefing rooms for interrogation. The police sergeant I dealt with was courteous, but I was questioned for hours about the sequence of events: what I knew of Jason, about my position in Roger's business, how it ran, and what safety steps we had in place.

"So you got out of the aircraft, walked to the office here and left your passenger still in the plane unsupervised?"

"Well, yes. But …"

"Is it normal procedure to leave passengers out there, alone on the tarmac?"

"No, of course it's not. It's a security area. But Jason had just tried to kill me. I wanted to put some distance between us. And the security men were right there."

"You said they were coming down the steps? That would be how many metres away from the parked aircraft?"

"Twenty or so. I don't know, you'd have to measure it."

I was getting a very nasty idea of where this was going. Before long, I'd be charged with negligence resulting in the death of a passenger. It took a real struggle to contain my anger, settle my nerves and carry on answering the questions politely. I managed because the woman interviewing me was in uniform. I, too, wear a uniform and have to deal with the idiots collectively known as 'the public'. I felt an obscure sympathy for the officer and kept my answers civil. But by the time she finished I was shaking, convinced I'd be arrested at any moment.

I emerged after signing the statement. The waiting room was still full of curious people, and I desperately wanted to be alone, preferably somewhere I could burst into tears without an audience.

I looked out the window for an escape route, but it was impossible. On the apron outside was a posse of officials. I identified a couple of friends from the Civil Aviation Air Accident Unit who would be investigating the incident. They were talking with police and taking photos.

Jason's mangled remains had been removed, and Rick was using the fire hose to spray the plane and the tarmac.

At last the onlookers departed, and just core personnel were left. Maria fetched hot coffee for all of us.

Roger propelled himself on his crutches from behind the counter and sat down beside me. "You OK, Hardcastle?" For once he wasn't teasing. He searched my face for an answer. "I know a lot has happened since your crisis in the air, but it must have been a hell of a shock when he grabbed control of the plane."

I felt my eyes tearing up and hoped to God I wouldn't cry in front of him. "I'm fine," I assured him. "I'm settling down now they've taken Jason away. I'm even having trouble believing it all occurred. I mean, what are the odds? It was so quick in the air when it happened, and then I was so ballistically angry. I swear if the plane door had been open, I'd have shoved him out." Fine words, of course, but I felt my bottom lip quiver.

Roger looked at my face rather shrewdly, but let it be. One thing I'll say for Roger, he has a great sense of tact. "Well you handled it OK. We'll do a full debrief later, and you'll have to fill out an incident report for the CAA. In the meantime, do you want me to organise a counsellor for you? Someone you can talk this through with?"

I was so surprised I gave a little gasp of laughter.

"You may snort, Hardcastle, but the victim support person has already been round here looking for clients."

"Jesus. No, I don't think I want counselling. Not unless we all need one after this afternoon's horror. It's Tom I feel sorry for, poor sod. I've got you guys and can talk the attempted hijack through, as you put it, with you or Greig or anyone else I can bore in the weeks ahead. This isn't going to put me off flying, although I do wonder whether we ought to talk about how instructors protect themselves in these situations."

He nodded. "We will. I think pilot protection needs to be at the top of our list for discussion during our next staff meeting." He sighed. "OK, no counsellor, but let me know if you change your mind. I must say, Hardcastle, trouble seems to be following you round these days like a bad smell."

"How's the ankle?" I asked, firmly changing the subject.

"Painful. Annoying. I'm supposed to sit with my leg up for the next couple of weeks."

"Then why aren't you doing so?" I asked. "I don't imagine you're supposed to be at work at all."

"I got bored. Wendy kept fussing over me and bringing cups of tea. It drove me insane, so I made her bring me down here this morning. At least I can work behind the desk, and it's just as well I was here during your latest adventure. You're going to need a full-time minder if you carry on like this. Go home, Hardcastle, take the rest of the day off and get that boyfriend of yours round to put a smile back on your face."

Really, Roger was impossible.

I had a cunning thought. "I'll go home if you will," I offered. "You can go and put your leg up, and I'll sit and watch daytime TV."

He snorted.

"It's a fair deal," I said.

"No, it's not, it's attempted blackmail," he said, "and I should probably fire you for it."

We glared at each other, then he laughed. "You're a stubborn, difficult woman, Hardcastle, but you aren't going to bully me. Stay here then if you feel OK. Oh, and the *Kapiti Observer* came in for the story. I gave them the basics, but they wanted a photo of you. I said I didn't know how long your interview with the cop would take. So they gave up and went away."

"Thank you," I said with real fervour. The last thing I needed was to be associated with a hyped-up hijacking drama. It would do nothing for my reputation in aviation, nor in the community. I shuddered to think of Kate's reaction. It was a reminder that I'd have to phone her soon.

*   *   *

By common consent we gathered for a drink in the office once we'd kicked the voyeurs out and closed for business for the day. Sam had joined us.

"I must say, Claire, today has been the most exciting day in the tower since I started in Flight Control. There I was, having to call police, CAA and airport security and alert them to a hijacking at Paraparaumu. My only regret is there wasn't an Air New Zealand flight due in at the time that I'd have had to divert. I felt for a moment like I was in the control room at La Guardia."

Blessed are the simple-minded, I thought ungraciously, and then recognised that Sam was trying to lighten our mood.

"Thank heavens it's all over," said Maria. "I feel sorry for Jason, I suppose, but at least in the end he only damaged himself and didn't take anyone else with him."

"Makes you realise what hell it must have been for everyone in New York when the twin towers went down," said Roger.

We all paused for a moment's silence. Nothing in aviation had ever been the same since 9/11.

Mercifully Greig broke the solemnity before it got maudlin. "Do you think anyone was at the top of Kapiti Island watching as Claire's plane headed straight for them?"

Nick cracked a laugh. "They'd have been scared shitless if there was."

"That would be unfortunate," murmured Roger. "There are no facilities at the top of that island."

I rolled my eyes. It was good to be back in the silly world

of bickering and corny jokes. We'd deal with the after-effects of the drama in our own time, separately and collectively. When the chips were down all professional pilots were part of a fraternity. It was an unspoken bond between aviators, and we were enormously supportive of each other.

We'd come through this.

CHAPTER
TWENTY FOUR

I STOPPED OFF AT THE SUPERMARKET ON my way home and wandered round the shelves. There was a mist through my brain and the products I stared at didn't seem real. I knew I needed supplies but couldn't quite focus on the specifics. I ended up buying cat food, wine, milk, bread, butter and some vegetables. I paid for them at the checkout, knowing I was missing stuff but incapable of remembering what.

Kate phoned as I was putting the groceries in the car. I was conscious of a deep reluctance to talk about what had occurred, and I nearly chickened out of answering the call but then thought it best to get it over with.

"Claire, I just heard about it on the news. My god, how awful. Are you OK?"

"Yeah, I'm fine. I was going to phone you," I said before she berated me.

"What happened?"

I told Kate the basics, assured her I was fine and managed to get her off the phone by promising I'd call the next day. I felt exhausted. I could barely cope with my own emotions at that moment. I simply couldn't handle Kate's expressions of shock and fear.

I reached home and unpacked. There was a terrible unbridgeable distance between me and everything I was doing. Then Nelson came in, pleased to see me. I gathered him up in my arms, crushing him to me in desperation.

I might have died today, and then who would have cared for Nelson? He would have been an orphan. I couldn't bear it. What would Nelson do? Who would have fed him, looked after him? Would he have missed me if I hadn't come back? I wallowed in the bathos.

I hugged Nelson even tighter, and the potential melodrama of his fate tipped me over the edge, finally allowing my tightly wound emotions to release. I started crying. Tears of fear, relief, loneliness, horror and crushing guilt poured down my face as I clutched Nelson ever tighter. My lips trembled, my nose ran, and I had to use my sleeve.

There were tissues in the bedroom, but I couldn't move to reach them.

I'd refused help or counselling – I was still certain I didn't need them – but now, riding the wave of reaction, I was torn apart. I wondered if I had precipitated Jason's meltdown by my comments in the plane. I knew the irritation I'd felt towards him in the aircraft would haunt me. Then I'd been guilty of walking away from him once we'd landed.

There were so many 'ifs' involved: if I'd been kinder when I picked Jason up; if I'd stayed with him in the plane. Such a little word; such terrible repercussions.

The policewoman hadn't directly accused me of negligence, but she'd implied it. I'd failed to live up to the high standards I aimed for. Today had shown just how limited a human being I was. All this on top of having failed with Awhina.

Deep, wracking sobs shook through my shivering body. I was ice cold, as if I'd never be warm again.

Jack came barrelling up the drive and found me a short time later, still clutching Nelson. Nelson, who had tolerated my emotions because he's a nice cat, was very relieved to be freed, and Jack took his place. He held me close and rocked me like an infant.

"I didn't think you were coming back," I sobbed.

"Huh?" he asked. "Oh baby, I've been away up country. I had to take Awhina back to Hamilton, and then the murder case has blown right open. I'm sorry I didn't call, but it's been crazy."

"What's happened in the case?" I managed through my tears.

"Nothing you need worry about at the moment," he said. "Tonight it's all about you and helping get you through this."

"I'm OK, really I am," I protested as the tears ran down my cheeks and I hiccupped on my grief. I clung to his body and its warmth as if it was a life preserver.

"Of course you are," he said agreeably. "But I'm not OK. I heard about the crisis at the airport on the police frequency. It wasn't nice news to hear."

I held on to him. "I'm sorry," I said. "Roger said today that crises seem to follow me like a bad smell."

"He's right," said Jack. "They do seem to, and although I like an exciting girlfriend, I'm looking forward to life settling down a bit."

"I'm sorry," I said again.

"I was teasing, sweetheart," he said. "You are wonderful. I can't believe the shit you've dealt with over the last few weeks, and you still come up smiling."

"I'm not smiling at the moment," I sobbed.

"You will," he assured me, which of course produced a shaky smile. He passed me a wad of tissues which I grabbed from him and scrubbed my cheeks.

The crisis passed eventually and I was able to blow my nose and dry my eyes.

"Thank you," I said finally. I couldn't meet his gaze. I felt shame scald me. Jack was always being kind to me and I'd been a bitch to his sister.

He reached over, and lifted my chin with his finger. "Look at me," he said.

Reluctantly I lifted my head. "Thank you," I said again, a little more coherently this time.

Jack looked at me steadily. "It was my pleasure," he said softly. "Think nothing of it."

I wanted to make sure he really understood my gratitude. "No, I really mean thank you. I thought I was fine, but I wasn't."

"It can take people that way," he said.

Freed from my clutches, he stood up and poured both of us a glass of wine, then I heard him enter my bathroom and start running a bath. "Get in there," he ordered.

I made a rather feeble attempt at standing autonomously. Jack gave a quiet laugh, picked me up like a child and carried me through to the bathroom, where he pulled my clothes off. I turned to see he had poured bubble bath into the tub, so it was foaming like a scene from a 1950s Hollywood epic.

I twisted my hair up in a knot and stepped into the water. It was so hot it took my breath away, but just as I was about to complain, my flesh adapted and I lay back in the water and allowed my troubles to float away on a cloud of bubbles.

Sometime later I surfaced and looked up to see Jack stripping his clothes off. I admired the sight through drowsy eyes, before he climbed into the bath behind me. Fortunately the cottage I rent is old fashioned, with an equivalently large, old-fashioned bath tub.

He pulled my body against his, and I leaned back against his shoulder and let the world float still further away. Later still he grabbed a flannel and began to soap my back. His fingers worked the knots and tensions out of my neck and shoulders.

"Aaah," I breathed as his fingers kneaded me back to wakefulness. I twisted in the bath and kissed him. It was a long, deep kiss and shortly thereafter we had made it, if still slightly damp, as far as the bed.

Is there something about tragedy that makes humans have sex?

There was release and relief; kindness, forgiveness, affection and absolution. A dialogue our bodies understood but our words were incapable of expressing. I looked into Jack's eyes and saw a kindness and understanding I didn't deserve. At the end there was the blessing of sleep.

"What do you want for dinner?" he called from the kitchen a

couple of hours later. I stretched slowly and considered the idea. Suddenly I realised I was terribly hungry. I hadn't eaten since I'd returned from Awaroa, and I'd lost anything I'd had before that in the ladies' loo. The couple of glasses of wine had killed my appetite earlier, but now it was back with a vengeance. I needed calories. Now.

I said as much to Jack.

"Come on then," he said. "Get some clothes on. What you need is good solid food, and I recommend steak, chips and all the trimmings."

He drove me to the Fisherman's Table where we did indeed have steak and all the trimmings. I worked my way through the entire salad display and devoured my steak with an enthusiasm worthy of a caveman.

"Can you stay tonight?" I asked when we got home. I hoped I didn't sound too needy.

"I'm not going anywhere," he assured me.

I lay in his arms until sleep took me.

Later in the night I woke, and the horror of the day before engulfed me in a mudslide of grief and horror. I moaned softly in a frantic effort to release the pain, and Jack stirred, gathered me in against him and stroked my back until I settled again.

I went back to sleep and woke when the alarm went at seven to find him watching me.

I was unnerved. I don't like feeling defenceless. Then I considered the stupidity of that thought. Jack had seen me at my most vulnerable the night before and he'd helped me through it all. I relaxed and smiled at him.

He bent his head and kissed me. "Better now?"

I nodded. "All better."

* * *

I wasn't completely *All Better* of course. But I was twenty-four hours removed from the day, and Jack had helped me through the worst of it. Even so, and without deliberate thought, I found myself stop by the glass doors and stare at the tarmac. Rick and Dan had done a good job of cleaning up. There were no obvious signs of the tragedy, and yet the stain was still there in my own mind.

I wasn't the only one. I saw Greig and Maria separately pause and do the same thing, and wondered how long it would take to forget, for us to be able to cross that patch of the apron without remembering horror.

We had a stream of visitors dropping in to express their shock. Soon the walls of the waiting room were lined with vases and jars of floral tributes dropped off by students, other pilots on the airfield and some of the CAA people who flew with us. We were rapidly running out of containers to put the flowers in. Others had brought chocolates or wine as a gesture of sympathy and solidarity. Our office was beginning to look like a shrine.

I walked down the row and read the cards. Few people would have known who Jason was, so he was rarely mentioned, although I came across a large display from Matt and his family, which did name him.

Why had Jason been so desperate to kill himself?

* * *

It was a lovely late autumn day, yet I had no desire to fly. For once it was almost a relief to pull the manuals out and go to work on them.

Roger was in a better mood. The crises of the day before had reenergised him. He was a man who thrived on excitement and stresses that would kill someone half his age. He called me over to him. "Hardcastle, I want to talk to you."

I looked at him in surprise.

"I want to talk about yesterday, when you said you were OK, and you weren't. You looked shocking, and I just wanted to tell you that it's fine to cry when things go wrong. No one would have thought less of you. Tom, poor lad, had a tear or two. I know you like to be tough, but there was no need. Sometimes it's better to let emotions out."

Oh, shit. So now I had Roger trying to be a psychiatrist. That's all I needed.

"I was fine," I said, "and crying's not something I'm going to do in public if I can help it. Maybe it's OK for a guy to tear up. I don't know. Those politicians seem to think it makes them look sincere when they get weepy. But it's different if you're a woman. It's never safe for a woman to cry at her job or in public." I saw his head move in protest. "Never," I said harshly. "We just look weak, emotional, and it's like handing a weapon to everyone who sees you do it. It's something people remember forever and will hold against you."

"You're wrong, Hardcastle. Just be told, will you, and accept for once in your life you're wrong. You don't have to be so bloody defensive all the time," he said.

"No, I'm not," I said firmly, "but I know what I'm talking about." I walked back to my desk.

"For fuck's sake," I heard him mutter, but I didn't turn.

I saw him glance over at me when I sat down quietly with my paperwork.

He watched me work for a while, then said, "Take young Nick up and get him to give you a lesson. It'll be good for both of you."

I opened my mouth to protest, and he overrode me. "That's an order, Hardcastle. I can't have you neglecting Nick, however sorry you feel for yourself." The complete injustice of that remark stung, as I'm sure he had intended.

"Come on, Nick," I said. "It seems Roger wants us gone," and I flounced out to the hangar.

Roger was right of course. It did do me good. In spite of my proud words I had been badly shaken and probably wasn't fit to fly on my own, but I had confidence in Nick. We spent a pleasant hour or so practising his lessons. He was getting really good, and eventually, when I'd demonstrated how to teach max-rate turns, I realised the worst was over and I had settled down. Nick had long lost any shyness around me and was full of questions about the flight with Jason. I demonstrated the effects of bumping an aircraft's nose down, and he laughed as his knees floated up towards his chin.

"Cool," he said appreciatively. Then more seriously, "That's a pretty useful manoeuvre to have if you end up in a difficult situation with a student."

"I suppose so. It's not one I recommend teaching to a PPL, though," I cautioned. "They'd likely rip the wings off the plane if it gets out of control."

When we got back I found Margaret Campbell, the chief flying instructor from the aero club, sitting in the lounge having a cup of coffee with Roger. I liked Margaret. She was a lean, fit woman in her fifties, with a no-nonsense haircut and a brisk manner. She was a very capable pilot, and the aero club were lucky to have someone of her calibre at their helm.

"I've been hearing all about the hijack," she told me. "You coped very well. All credit to you."

"I'm afraid it was more gut instinct and fury that guided my actions," I said. "I couldn't bear to let that evil little gremlin destroy my plane."

"There speaks a true pilot," she laughed. "Well done, whatever the reason."

"Rick came and spoke to you yesterday?" asked Roger.

"Yes, poor man," she answered. "What a mess. And I'm sorry for Cam, too, idiot though he may be. He's always been a nice kid, but he's really stuffed things up this time. They say young men's brains don't mature until they are in their mid-twenties, and Cam would be a case in point."

I looked pointedly at Nick and Greig. "You're probably right."

Greig quirked an eyebrow at me and grinned. "That statement will cost you later," he said.

"Rick did a good job yesterday," said Roger. "He tried to prevent Jason's suicide and nearly managed to grab him in time. Then he was a great help in the clean-up afterwards. He was a tower of strength, which was all the more remarkable given the personal stress he must be under. I hope his company decide to keep him on."

I phoned Tom to see how he was doing. I'd felt terribly sorry for him the day before.

"I'm fine," he said. "Well, OK anyway. You know how it is."
I admired his staunchness.

"Yes, I do know how it is. But at least here we're all together, sharing the misery, so to speak. I worry that you are out there on your own with no one to talk to."

"Oh, the guys at work have been good," said Tom. "I'm sort of a celebrity at the moment for them, and they're helping me through it and letting me talk."

"That's good. I just didn't want this to put you off flying, or something awful."

Tom gave a little laugh. "No, it won't stop me flying. But you never covered a situation like this with me when you were training me for my licence, Claire."

"You reckon we need to rewrite the syllabus?" I smiled a little. "Let's hope such a horrible thing never happens again."

"Agreed. I'll see you at the weekend. I'll definitely be in for a flight."

"If you want company, any one of us would be happy to join you for free," I said. "I was grateful I had a student to fly with the first time back in the air, so don't be too proud to ask."

"I won't," he said.

I hung up feeling a little better about him.

"Is he OK?" asked Roger who'd been listening in.

"He will be," I said. "He wants to go flying at the weekend, so that's positive."

"The sooner he gets back on the horse, the better it will be," agreed Roger.

Jack phoned mid-morning to invite me to dinner. I accepted; although I wasn't fooled for a minute. He'd been checking up on me, without making it obvious. I smiled to myself then realised Roger was watching me shrewdly. "All OK?" he asked.

"Thank you," I said. But I was still smiling.

The reassuring routine of my work folded itself round me. There was Nick to teach, paperwork to fill out, including my incident report for CAA. Parts of that document were multiple-choice boxes to tick, and I puzzled over some of the questions.

No one appeared to have considered a suicidal lunatic grabbing the plane, so I had to improvise some of my answers. Greig spent some time in the classroom with me and Nick, working on theory and on Nick's presentations.

There was a sense we were all urgently trying to be peaceful and normal, and that by acting it out together we were at least achieving a simulacrum of calm.

Wendy, Roger's wife, came in to pick up Roger and take him to have his cast checked at the fracture clinic. "Is he still being impossible?" she asked.

I grinned at her. "Much better since he's had yesterday's excitement to deal with. It's perked him up no end. I take it lying on the sofa at home with his foot up didn't work?"

"Not even for ten minutes. He accused me of trying to emasculate him, and smother him with cups of tea."

I chuckled. I liked Wendy. She was a calmly assertive woman in her sixties, and I reckon she'd got Roger's measure. She rarely attended aviation functions, and we didn't often see her round the office. She and Roger must have been married for decades and most of the time seem to go their own separate ways, so I imagine being thrust into the roles of nurse and patient must have been trying for both of them.

Maria went into town to drop off mail and pick up supplies for the kitchen. Greig was out flying, and Nick tucked away in the briefing room writing up his notes. I was alone in the office.

I heard the swing doors bang and looked up to see a young woman enter carrying a bunch of flowers. Another tribute I'd have to find a container for. We were down to using old paint tins now. "Hi," I said. "Can I help you?"

She walked to the front desk and I saw she was very young.

"Is this the place it happened?" she asked.

"You mean yesterday? Yes," I said, wondering what her purpose was. The flowers suggested she was a mourner, but she wasn't one of our students, or any pilot I knew.

She stared at me. "Where did he die?"

No one had asked that question before. The tributes we'd received had been to comfort the staff. None had been to mourn Jason. I looked closely at her. Her face had the swollen, waterlogged look of someone who'd been crying for hours. This was a girl in deep grief, with red eyes and an unhealthy flush on her cheeks.

"Do you mean Jason?" I asked as gently as I could.

She nodded.

I led her to the glass doors and pointed outside. "He died out there," I said.

"Can I go outside and see?"

I nodded, opened the door and escorted her onto the tarmac of the apron. I showed her where Jason had fallen. Involuntarily I glanced round to see if there were any grisly remains left, but thankfully Rick had done a great job cleaning up. Even so, I felt like tiptoeing over the place as if it were hallowed ground. "It was here," I said.

She knelt on the hard tarmac and laid the flowers down. I could see her shoulders shaking with sobs as she bent her head. She knelt for a long while. I wondered if she was praying.

At last I couldn't bear the sight and sound of her grief any more. I crouched beside her, put my arm round her shoulders and held her. Her body gave a great shudder. "I'm so sorry," I whispered.

"I loved him so much," she sobbed. "Then I drove him away. Now I can never say sorry. He's gone." This produced a fresh spasm of crying.

I held her and tried to make soothing noises. "Come on," I said when the worst had passed. "Come inside. I'll make you a cup of tea or coffee."

I helped her stand and supported her back into the office. I grabbed a box of tissues on the way through to the kitchen and handed them to her. She leaned against the kitchen cupboards as she dried her eyes and blew her nose.

"Coffee?" I asked.

She nodded.

I made the brew.

"You're his girlfriend, aren't you? I saw you on D'Urville Island," I said.

Her eyes widened as she turned and looked at me properly for the first time.

"I didn't meet you," she said flatly.

"I'm Claire. I was the pilot who found the body that day. We never met properly. I think you were upset when I saw you."

She nodded slowly. "I'm Josie."

I drew her over to the kitchen table and sat down with her. I considered whether it was fair to ask her for information, but there were questions I wanted answering.

"I was with Jason yesterday," I said. "I flew him back from Awaroa. Do you know what went wrong? Why he was so desperate?"

She shuddered. "Oh, shit," she said softly. Her lips wobbled with misery as she looked at me. "It was all my fault," she began. "I broke up with him because of something I'd done. I couldn't bear his distress, you see? It made my own guilt and pain unbearable. I said we'd better not see each other again, and put everything behind us. Forget everything." Her eyes watered again. She grabbed another bunch of tissues and scrubbed at her face while I tried to process what she'd said.

"So Jason was distraught because you'd broken up with him?"

"That. And other things."

"I thought I'd heard that you quarrelled with him that day on D'Urville Island because you wanted to get married?"

She shook her head but said nothing.

"What happened that day you went to the island?" I asked eventually.

There was a long silence. "The boat dropped us off," she began. "We walked to the bach and dumped our bags and settled in. We'd brought bread and cheeses and stuff with us, so we had lunch. Jason was happy to be there again. He said it was ages since he'd been on the island." She started crying. "He was so happy," she repeated.

"Then what happened?" I prompted.

"We went to bed. To celebrate being alone and on holiday."

There was more, soft, heart-breaking, crying.

"You told the police that you and Jason spent the afternoon quarrelling. That wasn't right?"

"No," she sobbed. "We made it up for the cops. We never quarrelled, we loved each other."

"Here, have some more tissues." I passed the box across the table. She blew her nose. "I know this is hard for you, but you should have told them the truth," I said. "What happened next?"

"We got up."

"What time was that?" I found myself slipping into Jack's interrogative technique.

"I don't know. Around three o'clock, maybe."

"What did you do then?"

"Went out to gather driftwood for the fire. We were going to have a barbecue. I'd brought potatoes to cook in the ashes."

I nodded encouragingly. "So you gathered firewood. What happened then?"

"We were coming back from the beach through the dunes. Jason was carrying the wood and I was still fossicking for more. Then I saw him."

"Who did you see?"

"Mr Jorgensen."

"You knew Jorge?" I asked.

She nodded. "I recognised him straight away."

I had a sick feeling that I knew where this was going. "Did he recognise you?"

"He stopped and started to say hello, like you would a stranger, then he recognised me."

"What happened then?"

"He said, 'It's little Marie, isn't it?' and smiled. 'All grown up now I see. What are you doing here?'

I didn't know what to say. I was so shocked that he could be there. I hadn't told Jason about what had happened with him, nor about my old name or anything."

"You changed your name?"

She nodded. "When I left school."

I wondered why but didn't want to interrupt her narrative to ask. "Then what happened?"

"Jorge leered at me. 'If you're not doing anything we could take up where we left off. You're a bit old now, but that's OK.' I hated him so much."

She blew her nose. I watched her give a resigned shrug.

"When I first met him I thought he just wanted to help me with my writing. I wanted to be an author and he said he could show me how to write better. I can't tell you how great that made me feel. Shit, I was so young and so stupid." She stopped for a long minute before continuing. "I thought he was being kind and was really interested in my talent." She gave a sort of snort that turned into a sob.

"Then he told me I'd never be a real author until I could write about sex, and to do that, I'd have to know how to do it. 'I'll show you properly,' he said, 'better than some silly schoolboy who won't know what he's doing.' I knew it was wrong, but I didn't know how to stop. He'd got into my mind. And then, it wasn't enough for him to use me, he wanted to humiliate me as well. He wanted me to use posh words for what we did. He told me he was educating me. We didn't fuck, we had sexual congress, or coition. He didn't demand a blow job, he made me fellate him. It was like a game to him, forcing me to use that language." She burst into tears again.

My stomach roiled as I thought of the word games which, in a different context, I too had played with Jorge. He was a monster.

Eventually Josie steadied herself, gave a small sob and continued. "Jason had come up from behind the sand dunes. He was across the other side of the dip Jorge was in, so Jorge had to turn his head to see him. When he did, Jorge laughed. It wasn't a pretty sound. 'I see it all now. You've got another boyfriend, have you? Have you told him about the things we did?' I was frozen with horror at what was happening. I couldn't say anything.

"Jason looked at us both. 'What do you mean?' he asked Jorge. Jorge turned round to him. 'I had her first, boy, long before she was yours. Does she go down on her knees for you as well? She's good at it. You should get her to show you.' He was foul and cruel, and he knew my pain. I could see him feeding on it, taking pleasure from it, and then he laughed again."

The girl broke down entirely then. I could hardly bear to listen as she sobbed and cried. I would have done anything to salve her pain, to soften her grief. My eyes filled, and useless tears of sympathy ran down my own face.

She cried for a long time. Eventually she blew her nose and straightened her back.

"When he laughed, I lost it. He'd caused me so much pain, separated me from my family, made me feel worthless, shameful and wicked for years. All those things. It was only because of Jason that I was starting to come right again. And Jorge was trying to destroy that. I had a lump of driftwood in my hand. His back was to me as he taunted Jason. I didn't think, I just swung the stick. I hadn't planned to kill him. I just wanted to stop him laughing. I hit him, and then he did stop."

"Oh fuck," I whispered.

I got up from my place and wrapped my arms round her. I could feel her tightly wound body shaking in my arms.

"You poor, poor girl." I shook my head, trying to understand how one man's evil predation had led to the ruin of so many lives. I hoped Jorge rotted in a particularly nasty hell.

She calmed her crying eventually.

"Jason helped me," she said. "He took me back to our bach and was very kind. He said it wasn't my fault. He wanted me to be straight with the police and tell them exactly what had happened and why, but I couldn't do it. I've tried for years to get over what Jorge did to me and put it behind me. I'd buried the secret so deeply that sometimes I'd been able to pretend it had never happened. I couldn't go through it all again and make it public. I just couldn't. In the end we made up a story we hoped would convince the cops that we knew nothing about Jorge's death. Jason burned the piece of wood in our fire and we got off the island as soon as the police let us go."

I released her from my embrace and stood up. "What happened then?"

"Nothing was the same between us," she said. "I had to tell

Jason everything that had happened with Jorge, and I could see the difference in his eyes when he looked at me. He didn't say anything, but I knew he saw a murderess each time he looked my way. And then there was the sex. Everything Jason and I had done together had been clean and true and lovely, but now that he knew I'd done it all before with a pervert, it was different. It was horrible and twisted."

She fell quiet. I watched her pull herself together, blow her nose, wipe her face and stand up. She turned and faced me. "In the end, I couldn't stand it. I told Jason it was all over between us. I knew he'd hated lying to the police. His grief was tearing me apart. So I left him. He begged me not to go, but I had to get away. His niceness and decency were claustrophobic. I knew I didn't deserve him. And now I've killed him too."

It was a sad, sad story, I thought. "You'll have to tell the police, you know," I said gently. "I'm sure they'll be sympathetic."

She nodded. "I'd already decided that. It was why I called Jason when he was down in Awaroa. I thought he ought to know, because he'd lied for me. I said I was going to hand myself in. He said he'd come back to support me, but I told him I didn't want him. I didn't ever want to see him again."

"You turned him down?" I asked, surprised.

"I didn't want to deal with his emotions as well as my own. I told him again I didn't need him. I didn't expect him to come back from Awaroa." Her voice caught on a sob. "But I did need him, and I did want him. I loved him more than ever and I never told him. Now it's too late."

I was lacerated by her grief. Her despair and wretchedness were sickeningly horrible to see, and I had no comfort to give her.

Abruptly she stood and turned her face from me. I understood I was rejected. As she walked out, I followed her to the swing doors.

Concern for her gripped at me. "Are you sure you're OK to drive?" I asked. "I can give you a lift, or call someone if you need me to."

She turned. "I'm not going far." Her tone was hostile, and I realised she already regretted our conversation.

I watched her get into the car and drive away. Did she realise, I wondered, that Jason's death allowed her to pin the killing on him? In the absence of other witnesses it was perfectly possible, and no one would be the wiser. Perhaps Jason had understood and had intended his death to be his final gift to her. I was wrung out with pity for them both.

* * *

It was four o'clock when the phone rang. I saw Maria pick it up.

"Oh, hello. Yes, I'll get him for you. Roger!" she called. "It's Matt on the phone for you."

Roger picked up. "Hi, Matt, what can we do for you? Really? No, we hadn't heard."

Roger waved his hand at Maria with his hand over the mouthpiece. "Quick," he said to her, "find the local news page on the computer. They've arrested a suspect in Jorge's murder case. A young woman."

Maria switched on the screen of the office computer, and I began to search Google on my phone.

Roger was still talking. "What? No, Hardcastle is still here. It's not her, at least."

"Here it is," said Maria.

"Thanks, Matt, I'll call you back later," said Roger, hanging up. We shifted to look at the screen, but I was getting a better view on my phone, so I carried on reading.

It was a simple police statement to the effect that a suspect had handed themselves in to the police, and was being held for further questioning in relation to Jorge's murder. No charges had yet been laid. A news briefing would be held at seven that evening.

"What made Matt say it was a young woman?" asked Maria. "There's nothing here to indicate that."

I'd been scrolling down through other articles. "Not in the police statement, it doesn't, but this report mentions they've been interviewing a woman. The implication is pretty clear that she's the one they've arrested. Jack did say last night that they had a breakthrough on the case."

"He didn't give you any details?" asked Roger.

"He was too busy being a shoulder for me to cry on," I said shamefaced. "I never got round to asking him."

Roger grunted. I waited for a crass comment. "Just as well he was there then," he said, and left it at that.

My phone pinged, and I saw it was a text from Jack. *Sorry, can't do dinner after all. You'll see why on the news. I'll come round later. XX.*

I wrinkled my nose at that. If they were in the final stages of solving the case, I imagined Jack would be very busy indeed. I lifted my head to find the others looking at me.

"News?" asked Roger.

"No, just Jack deferring our plans for the evening. Obviously they're all flat out at the moment."

"How many women were on D'Urville Island the afternoon Jorge was killed?" asked Maria.

"Other than me? Matt's wife, Jane. But she was sitting on the beach in full view of her family and friends at the time. That leaves Joe's wife, and Jason's girlfriend."

"And some crisis brought Jason back from Awaroa early. It's only reasonable that something must have precipitated his terrible actions," observed Roger. "He looked terrible when he was my passenger, and you said he was even worse when you picked him up yesterday. My money's on the girlfriend."

"Poor girl," said Maria quietly. "If you're right, then something terrible must have driven her to do it."

I kept quiet. All I could feel was a terrible grief for her.

"If it was her, then it's likely to be another tragedy in the making," said Roger.

"Why can't it be simple?" complained Greig, who'd been quietly listening. "I like it when the story is straight forward. Good guy killed by bad guy. Baddie found and arrested. Everyone lives happily ever after."

"Except for the murdered good guy," I pointed out.

Greig rolled his eyes at me. "But we know Jorge wasn't

an entirely good guy. By the same logic, the young girlfriend probably isn't a really bad guy. It's very muddled."

"If she did it, of course," reminded Maria.

I switched the TV on when I got home and watched the news conference.

Detective Inspector Trevor Mallet was his usual suave, foxy self. He was a man who looked good on camera, the light falling on jaw and cheekbones gave his face a gravitas and authority which reflected well on the police force he represented.

I saw Pete standing behind his boss but was frustrated to be unable to pick out Jack. I saw a glimpse of a hand, or the turn of a head I recognised, but Jack had his head angled away, as if he was shy in front of the camera. It came to me that Jack was never shy. If he was avoiding the camera it was deliberate. I would have to ask him his reasons.

After clearing his throat, DI Mallet looked directly into the camera as he confirmed progress in the case of Operation Seawind. "A woman, aged 18, will appear in Wellington District Court on Friday in relation to the death of Jorge Jorgensen," he said. "She has been granted interim name suppression and is held in custody, without bail, awaiting a mental health assessment before her appearance in court."

The cameras panned over the bent heads of the journalists, busy scribbling notes, before returning to DI Mallet.

"The Operation Seawind homicide investigation team has made good progress, including receiving back results from recent forensic tests," he continued. "Today represents a significant step, but there is still a lot of work to be done as our team works towards finding answers for Mr Jorgensen's family. The homicide team's focus is on ensuring we complete a robust and thorough investigation to support the court process going forward."

DI Mallet went on to thank members of the public who had come forward with information to assist in their enquiries, but would provide no further details.

Subsequently the news presenter reminded us that the body

of 42-year-old author Jorge Jorgensen had been found in sand dunes on the beach at Greville Harbour on Tuesday 22nd of March.

There was a definite frisson as the press absorbed the age and gender of the accused. If Jorge had been bashed over the head by an aggrieved gang member, there wouldn't have been much to the story. Murder by a young, possibly delicate, young woman however, with the backstory implicit in those details, lent the statement legs, and the reporters clamoured for answers.

"Did the accused know the deceased?" asked one journalist.

"Yes. We believe they knew each other," replied Mallet.

"Do the police know what the charge will be?"

"That's still to be determined. We're waiting on reports which will determine the nature of the charge or charges."

There were inevitable questions about Jorge's criminal past and whether it was connected to his murder. DI Mallet dealt with each question smoothly, but at the end I thought there had been little extra information shared.

I switched the TV off and settled down to wait for Jack.

So Josie hadn't tried to pin the blame on Jason. I wondered how she was doing. If she were given a choice of fight or flight, I'd picked her as one who would always choose to run. Now she had nowhere left to flee. The pointless misery of it all dragged at me.

Jack was very late. I snuggled down on the sofa beneath a blanket and dozed on and off while I waited. Neither Jack nor I'd had much sleep the night before.

It was past eleven when his car drew up and I opened the door for him. He looked exhausted. I shut the door and turned to him. "Difficult day?"

He nodded. "You could say that. A long and very difficult day."

I put my arms around him and leaned into him. After a few seconds he wrapped his around me and rested his head on mine. We clung together for some long moments in silence. I could almost feel the palpable misery seeping through him.

"Is it Jason's girlfriend?"

I felt his nod of assent, although he said nothing.

So she must have left the airport and gone straight to the police.

"I need to tell you that Josie came into the office here today with some flowers for Jason. She was in tears and terribly upset. She told me what had happened. She implied she was going to turn herself in."

"She told you she killed Jorge?"

I nodded. "It's what you were afraid of, wasn't it? That she had been one of Jorge's victims?"

He gave a body-shuddering sigh and separated from me.

"Come and sit down," he said. "I'll tell you what happened when she came in."

"Do you want a drink?" I asked. "Wine, or would you prefer tea or coffee?"

"No, it's too late for those. Just a glass of water would be good."

I poured it then sat down beside him. He reached out for me, and I settled into the crook of his arm.

"We'd had her on the suspect list from the beginning because she was the only woman on the island of the right age to have been in the group of girls that attended school in the same class as Cheryl. But we couldn't find anything to link her to the college. Also, although she was hysterical the day of the murder, she didn't strike us as the sort of woman who would be strong enough to take someone down."

I remembered the slight, tearful girl I'd seen at the mystery house, and agreed. I'd thought the same. "So what changed?" I asked.

"We found out that her name isn't Josie Antrim, the name she'd given the police. Previously her name was Marie-Josephine Moritelli, which was how she was listed on the college roll. She changed her name two years ago, a fact she hadn't even shared with Jason."

"And she changed it because …?"

"When she left school, she cut loose from her friends and family. She changed her name and has been working under the new one ever since."

"When she came in today we started with the basics. Why had she changed her name? Why she hadn't mentioned this to the police, and so on. She tried to evade questions about any prior involvement with Jorge, but in the end she admitted that she had visited him when she was a child, and that he had used her for sexual purposes."

"She told me," I said. "Bastard."

"Yes, he was," said Jack, pulling me in closer to his shoulder. "Josie comes from a good, law-abiding, middle-class family who'd given her a protected childhood. She was good at school, academically inclined, and wanted to be a writer when she grew up."

"Which I suppose was why she was drawn to Jorge?" I groaned, imagining the eager young girl she must have been.

"Yes. All she wanted was to discuss her writing with him. He used that interest to gain her trust then started the abuse. She knew what was happening wasn't right but didn't know what to do about it or who to tell. She was afraid it was all her fault. I've seen her college reports and they follow a pattern common to abused children. From being a popular, outgoing girl she changed to being surly and inhibited. Her school grades suffered and so did the relationship with her family. She had altered so dramatically that they hardly recognised their daughter. When the relationship with Jorge finished, Josie left college as soon as she was able and cut all ties to her past. Friends, family, the lot."

"Poor girl," I said. "No one suspected what was happening?"

"It seems not. Her family thought she was just going through a difficult adolescent phase. The college, who you might have thought would have staff trained to pick up on these problems, noticed nothing. Remember, Josie wasn't the only one. There were other girls as well."

Jack eased me off his shoulder, stood up and refilled his glass of water at the sink. He leaned on the bench as he continued his story. "Of course, police have to ask these questions, particularly in a homicide case, but the humiliation and degradation for the woman is profound. Josie was crying throughout the whole ordeal. We felt like torturers as we prodded and pried into all the pain she'd kept bottled up, poor girl. It was horrible."

"What happened in the end?"

"We asked if she wanted a lawyer, but she waived that right."

"She'd told Jason she was going to hand herself in. That was why he wanted to come back from the conference so urgently, even though she said she didn't want to see him," I said.

"You'll know the guts of it then. She hit Jorge hard enough to kill him outright. Then she had to explain everything to Jason."

"God, no wonder Jason looked so terrible," I murmured.

"She told us he was a pacifist and didn't believe in violence. It was part of why she loved him so much. To protect her, he'd lied to the police, but it went against the grain for him. Then of course she left him."

I looked at Jack and saw the shadow on him. He was a decent man, forced to uncover the evil that other men did, then deal with the aftermath. I stood and drew him to his feet, holding my arms close round him as I led him to the bedroom.

For the first time since we'd become lovers, Jack and I didn't have sex that night. We lay together, holding each other for comfort, too numb with pity and misery to seek our own pleasure.

*   *   *

"What happens next?" I asked in the morning.

"Josie will be assessed by a psychiatrist as to her mental state. As you can imagine, she's not in a very good space at the moment. After that, it will be for the courts to decide."

I thought about the girl and how she was faring. Her sudden coldness as we'd parted the day before gave me pause. Too late she'd discovered that running away had cost her Jason.

"What about you?" I asked, to change the subject.

"Paperwork," said Jack. "We've got a confession, and it's backed up by forensic evidence, but we have to dot every 'i' and cross every 't' to make sure our evidence stands up to the scrutiny of the courts."

"I hope she gets off," I said abruptly. "She's the victim in all this. Thanks to Jorge she lost her childhood. Now she's lost Jason as well, and from what she said, he was pivotal to her recovery from Jorge."

"How do you cope?" I'd asked him this before, but now there was a new urgency to my question.

Jack pulled me into his arms and held me. "I remember each and every life has a value. Even that of bad guys, like Jorge. That's what the police are there to enforce. Jorge was killed, so someone has to explain how and why it happened. Now the facts are known, it's the job of a jury, a judge and the law to determine how to balance the rights and wrongs of it all. It's too much for any one man or woman, and I'm grateful I don't have to make those decisions."

I leaned against him, letting his decency and humanity soothe me. It felt good to know that in a horrid and evil world, there were men like Jack who worked on the side of the angels.

CHAPTER
TWENTY FIVE

INEVITABLY THE MAIN TOPIC OF DISCUSSION at work was Josie's arrest.

"The news report didn't tell us anything we didn't already know," complained Greig.

"Not that it's strictly our business at all," reminded Roger.

"I do feel slightly proprietorial because I found Jorge," I said. "But, knowing what we do now, I think he got off lightly. I regret I felt sorry for him. I should have spat on his corpse while I had the chance" I said viciously.

Greig looked startled. "That's a bit ferocious, Claire."

Roger grunted. "I can't stand child molesters either."

I hadn't passed on anything Jack or Josie had told me. I assumed it was confidential, and the evidence would come out soon enough. I thought of Josie, imagining her incarcerated, mourning Jason, frightened and caught helplessly in the judicial system. I grieved for her. She was only eighteen.

It was a relief to get up in the air with Nick and put him through a gruelling review of everything I'd taught him. He was sweating by the time we landed and looked at me with hurt eyes.

"What?" I asked rudely once he'd parked the aircraft.

"Nothing," he said. "Just that it felt like cruel and unusual punishment."

I gave a rueful laugh and relented. "Sorry, I know it was brutal, but you will be grateful when you get to your exam. You need to know you can over perform, so that even if you have an attack of nerves during the flight test, you'll still have a safety margin."

"I suppose," he said doubtfully.

"Trust me, I'm right," I said.

He gave me a look that said he didn't believe me.

"I'll buy you a drink when you pass."

That elicited a reluctant grin.

*   *   *

I stood at the desk filling out the paperwork for the flight and looked up as the swing doors opened. "Hi, Rick," I said.

"Is Roger about?"

I called him from his office and watched him swing on his crutches out to the front desk.

"I wanted to say thank you," Rick said to him. "My employers have said I can keep my job. Seems they were pleased with my actions when that young chap killed himself. Also they said you'd phoned them and put in a word for me. I'm really grateful."

Roger waved it away. "That's great news to hear. It was the least I could do. You've been a good worker all the time I've known you. I don't know I'd have the same confidence in a new guy."

"Well, thank you anyway."

"What's going to happen to Cam?" I asked.

"It looks as if no one is going to take it further," said Rick, "which is a great relief for his mum and me. The cops tore strips off him but let him go with a warning. They decided not to charge him. He was scared silly of course. Somehow I think he will be a very different boy after this experience."

"They all grow up some time," said Roger. "I could tell you blood-curdling stories about my own boys when they were that age. Now they're upstanding citizens with wives and children of their own. Time fixes most problems."

I carried Roger's words with me. Time had indeed sorted out the mess I'd been in with David. Now Jack was in my life, and I couldn't imagine my world without him. I could only hope time would work its healing for Josie as well, and things would get better for her. It must seem a terribly bleak world for her at that moment.

Jack phoned to make a time to meet that evening.

He appeared more relaxed. "Yes," he replied to my comment. "The worst of Operation Seawind is over, which is a relief for us all."

I nodded and sipped my wine.

"Claire," he said cautiously.

I looked up at him.

"Do you have any annual leave owing to you?"

"Probably," I said. "I haven't really bothered with leave over the last couple of years. My social life has been so dire, I haven't needed any. Why?"

"With this case over, I'm going to take a couple of weeks leave. Go on holiday and have a relaxing break. Would you like to come with me? We could go somewhere nice together. On the way we could go through Kihikihi and visit my folks."

I stared at him in shock. I regret my first coherent thought was, *oh shit.*

"I'll show you mine if you show me yours," he murmured teasingly.

"That's quite an invitation," I said after a pause. "And the idea of a holiday sounds great, although I won't be free until after Nick sits his exam." I paused and fiddled with the cutlery. "Are you sure your folks want to meet me?"

"Of course," he said in surprise. "Why ever wouldn't they?"

"Are they like Awhina?" I blurted.

Jack looked puzzled, then his eyes widened as he understood what I was asking, and a deep rumble of laughter escaped him. "No, Claire, my darling. My folks are nothing like Awhina, if by that you mean her bolshie attitude. The rest of my family is tame in comparison. They'd love to meet you. My mother is driving me crazy with her discreet questions. The only way she'll shut up is if I produce you in evidence. They know you're special to me."

I thought of Kate's nosiness about Jack and admitted defeat. Fairness cut both ways, and I had, after all, been curious about what Jack's people were like.

"Then I'd be privileged," I said and was rewarded with Jack's warmest smile.

EPILOGUE

Six months later.

I HAD FLOWN DOWN TO BLENHEIM AND landed at Omaka. I was there for the flight check which instructors are required to have each year. Marty had been my examiner for the last few checks, and we'd agreed to meet at the Aero Club which had obligingly lent him their briefing room for a couple of hours. I'd arrived early and, trying to settle pre-test nerves, was killing time by flicking through the magazines on the table.

I ruffled through the pile, and pulled out a recent copy of the *Marlborough Express*. I flicked through pages of local news, skipping the various advertisements for fishing and farming equipment. Suddenly my eyes focussed on a small story tucked away on page five.

Ancient Remains reinterred on D'Urville Island, read the headline.

Yesterday morning a small group representing Ngati Toa, DOC, Police, Heritage New Zealand and local Iwi assembled deep in the bush of D'Urville Island (Rangitoto Ki Te Tonga) to rebury bones exposed by a recent landslip. The remains are believed to be pre-European, and may be as much as seven hundred years old. In a short ceremony, Kaumatua conducted karakia (prayer) and tauparapara (incantations) before the remains were reburied close to the original grave site.

Ngati Toa spokesperson, Bill Kahu, thanked those involved and expressed his satisfaction and relief at the safe return of the body to its hidden resting place, in the bush.

Please continue reading for a bonus excerpt from Penelope Haines's next instalment in the *Claire Hardcastle* series –

STRAIGHT AND LEVEL

CHAPTER

ONE

❝ NO," I SAID.

Roger, my boss, typically chose to ignore my protest. "Like it or lump it, but you're coming to this meeting, Hardcastle. It's a good sales opportunity for us and I'm not doing it on my own."

"But ..."

Roger stopped me with a look. I knew it was childish, but I had no interest in wasting a couple of hours at a cocktail party. I wouldn't even get to be dressed up and glamorous; I'd be in uniform. Although I was proud enough to wear it for work, I wasn't so keen when every other woman there would be fashionably dressed and I'd be in a white shirt, tie, epaulettes, navy trousers and sensible shoes.

The Kapiti Coast Chamber of Commerce was hosting the function at the reception rooms of the Southward Car Museum, and the car park was full when Roger and I arrived. Business owners from throughout the Kapiti Coast were attending and it was, as Roger had said, a good sales opportunity for Paraparaumu Aviation. I knew I was being trotted out as a show pony – not just because I was very visible in my uniform, but because I'd also featured in the local press a few months before after an incident at the airport. Roger wanted to get as much mileage as possible out of the publicity.

I loved my job, and was fond of my boss, but I was a pilot, not a salesperson. I followed in Roger's wake as we walked up the steps. I didn't kick a single one, which I thought showed considerable restraint, given how sulky I felt. He paused in the doorway. "You go left," he said. "I'll work the right," and he urged me on my way with a slight push.

I had learned to work a room from my ex, who had fancied himself a rising star in New Zealand's accounting firmament. David canvassed people at the parties to which we were invited with the mindset of a campaign manager launching a political candidate. I'd forgotten how artificial I found such enforced socialising and glared at Roger as he abandoned me.

A waiter offered a tray of drinks. My hand hesitated over the glass of bubbly and moved on towards the orange juice. I sighed. I'd have loved to have some Dutch courage to help me out, but Lisa, my best friend, had bullied me and Jen, my other best friend, into signing up for Dry July.

"It will be great for both our health and our figures," Lisa, whippet thin with not an extra gram of fat on her person, had enthused.

Jen and I had rolled our eyes at her, neither of us considering health or beauty sufficient reason to embark on sobriety.

"And it's for charity," she'd added desperately. "Think of the good that we can do."

After that, Jen and I caved. It seemed churlish to insist on our right to a glass of wine in the evenings when we could alleviate poverty, find a cure for cancer and end up looking like Kate Moss into the bargain.

We were a fortnight through the month, and so far, I'd stuck to my pledge, although tonight I regretted it bitterly. I sipped my OJ and made my way towards the nearest group of people. As I approached they parted and admitted me.

Studies have shown pilots are the most respected and trusted people on the planet. We outrank doctors, lawyers, priests, dentists and, by a large margin, politicians. Thanks to my uniform, I was clearly identifiable as a member of that most desirable of professions and tonight this worked in my favour. Every group I approached opened up to let me in. I smiled, answered obvious and repetitive questions about my job and dutifully tried to sell the possibilities of aviation to them.

I may have had no aspirations as a salesperson, but I've got a wonderful job and, like most pilots, could talk about flying for hours. There's an old joke: *How do you tell who's the pilot in the crowd? . . . They'll tell you!* which pretty much summed it up. Consequently, for Paraparaumu Aviation's sake, I did my best to please and charm.

"Yes, of course you can fly; it's accessible to anyone. I'd love to take you up and share my world with you. You should give it a go."

"Yes, a voucher for a Tiger Moth flight would make a wonderful present for your dad. I'm sure he'd love it," and so on.

I kept an eye on Roger as I worked my way through the crowd. With any luck, we'd bump into each other soon and I'd force an end to our evening.

I was three-quarters of the way around the room and had joined a fresh group of people. Names I didn't bother trying to remember were exchanged. I was excruciatingly bored and frantic to go home. I kept casting pleading looks in Roger's direction.

Then I encountered *him*. He wasn't particularly tall, short, fat or thin. He was neither handsome nor significantly plain. There was a slightly quirky cast to his features which could, in another man, have been unattractive, but here had been enlivened by the very obvious intelligent humour in his eyes. His hair was a startling snowy white, at odds with his vigorous physical presence. Although his skin showed a normal degree of middle-age sag, both his face and physique were attractive. He wore the years well. I put him in his late-forties, well-groomed and well suited. In every facet he was a model of a typically successful businessman.

It was his unshielded vitality which stopped me. I suddenly focused as I automatically extended my hand.

"Jim Mason," he introduced himself.

"Claire Hardcastle," I replied as he shook my hand.

I wondered what he did for a living. The others in our group had faded into a nondescript blur. One was the owner of a local supermarket – was it Pak'nSave, or Countdown? I had no idea which. The other couple owned a lighting business. Again, I hadn't made the effort to remember their names, or their businesses. All of them were mere extras to Jim Mason's leading-man performance.

"I read about you in the local paper," he said.

"They have to fill the pages with something." I didn't want to discuss the events that had led to my brief notoriety.

He looked amused. "Then we have something in common. I, too, dislike being discussed in the media. But if I recall, you emerged as the heroine of the piece?"

"They say you can't always believe what you read in the news."

The supermarket guy had entered the conversation, jockeying for some attention. The slur in his voice suggested he wasn't participating in Dry July. I wasn't sure if his statement was meant to be taken on its own merits or whether he intended some slight to me. Whatever the case, it earned him a frown from Jim.

"I'm sure the article stated nothing less than the obvious when it acclaimed Ms Hardcastle," he said, shortly.

The lighting guy and his wife immediately nodded their heads in agreement.

That's Mr Supermarket put in his place, I thought, as I watched him flush and back off. I was impressed Jim's opinion was so highly regarded and wondered again who he was.

Jack would know, I thought. I missed my sometime lover, not least because, as a detective senior sergeant in the police force, he tended to know all the local personalities and would undoubtedly have been able to tell me who or what Jim Mason was.

Unfortunately, Jack was currently unavailable, being on secondment for a month in the Solomon Islands, providing specialist training in criminal investigations to the Royal Solomon Islands Police Force. He'd been gone a fortnight, and I was missing him like crazy.

Others joined the group, and conversation flowed back and forth. Most of the people there knew each other. Even as I smiled and answered the usual questions about being a female pilot, I was aware Jim's attention was focused on me.

It wasn't easy to ignore. He had a powerful presence and enormous charisma. A ladies' man, I decided. It was hard to mistake that twinkle in the eye, or the overwhelming sense of sexual awareness that surrounded him.

Mr and Mrs Lighting said their goodbyes.

"Lovely to meet you," said Jim. He held the wife's hand a nanosecond too long. "I've no doubt we'll meet again. Kapiti is such a small place." He oozed pheromones over the poor woman.

The woman simpered girlishly as she drew her hand away. I could see she was captured by Jim's attention. "I hope so," she gushed, before her husband led her away from danger.

Mr Mason was definitely a player. He was too old for me to worry about being a notch on his belt, but he certainly intrigued me.

"Hardcastle?"

I turned to find Roger had come up behind me.

"How are you going?"

"Good," I said. "May I introduce you? Have you met Jim Mason?"

"No," said Roger.

The men shook hands. It would be interesting to see what Roger, no mean ladies' man himself, would make of Jim. So far he appeared impervious to the man's charisma.

"Ready to go?" he asked, after he'd run through the niceties. I nodded.

We said our farewells and made our way to the door. We passed from the foyer through the first set of doors into the vestibule.

At the outer doors I stopped and looked out. "Oh, crap." Since we'd been inside, the weather had turned. It was now bitterly cold and rain was teeming down.

Roger was all right. He at least had a jacket, but I had no coat with me. He took in the situation. "Stay here, Hardcastle," he commanded. "I'll go and get the car."

"Thanks," I said, grateful for some old-fashioned gallantry for once.

Roger ran across the driveway. For a man well into his sixties he was surprisingly athletic, particularly considering he'd broken an ankle not more than three months ago. I watched as he disappeared across the large car park. We'd arrived later than most of the attendees, so his vehicle was miles away on the far side.

I retreated into the warmth of the foyer. A classic old sports car was displayed on a podium. Cars, ancient or modern, meant little to me, but I admired its high gloss and the complicated arrangement of pipes attached to its engine.

Across the room a young man also waited. He was young and slight. Rain had glued his curly blond hair to his forehead, framing the chiselled cheekbones of his narrow face. He was so thin the lines of his long neck and a prominent Adam's apple were clearly visible above his T-shirt. Damp jeans clung to his skinny legs, and his jacket looked worn. Hanging around his neck was a beautifully carved bone pendant.

I nodded at him. "Two refugees from the storm," I murmured.

He had a particularly sweet smile as he acknowledged my greeting and looked me over.

"Are you a pilot?" he asked. "Were you at the meeting upstairs?"

I nodded. "My boss thought it would be a great idea if I showed up in uniform. I think he hoped it would sell aviation to the business community."

He grinned, his eyes laughing at me. "The things we do …"

I nodded wryly. "The things we do, indeed."

His smile was warm and friendly.

"What about you?" I asked. "Were you upstairs?"

"No," he said. "I'm just a journalist working on a story about one of the guests here. There's a protest planned in connection with his company and I want to get a few comments at the end of the shindig."

"That's a beautiful pendant," I said, nodding at the carving which hung around his neck.

He looked down and touched it.

"It's antique," he said. "It was presented to me a couple of months ago in recognition of work I'd done preserving local ecosystems. I was very honoured to receive it; It's a valuable taonga. They even carved my initials into the back of it so no one can nick it from me." He gave a slight, deprecating laugh.

"It's lovely," I said, admiring its sinuous curves.

The outer doors opened again, and a number of people entered the vestibule together. As a collection, they didn't match the dress code or social spectrum of those at the reception upstairs. This was a varied group: elderly; mixed race; some clearly Maori, others Caucasian and other ethnicities; both genders; and several young people whom I assumed, given their slight scruffiness, were students. Many carried placards. These would be the anticipated protesters, I realised.

My companion gave me a faint smile of farewell as he walked through the doors to join them.

I waited a few more moments, watching for the lights of Roger's car.

"Fuck," I heard, and turned to see Jim Mason standing behind me. He saw me looking and smiled. "Sheltering from the rain?"

I nodded.

"Are you going to be all right? I'd offer you room under my umbrella, but I think I'm about to run the gauntlet." He lifted his chin to indicate the group in the lobby.

"Yes, thanks. Roger's gone to get the car. He won't be long. Perhaps I should ask you if you're going to be OK. Is that reception committee for you?"

I was now thoroughly curious.

He snorted. "I'd guess so," he said. "Bloody idiots. It's all stuff and nonsense."

He shrugged then turned his twinkly eyes on me. "Well, if you're all right, good night then. I hope to meet you again," he said, giving me a final megawatt smile before stepping out through the doors into the lobby.

He was immediately surrounded. The doors effectively cut off all sound, so I couldn't hear any comments, but I read the placards: Keep Your Hands Off Our Land; No to Development; Profiteering Bastard.

So Mr Mason was a property developer? I had no fixed position on this profession, but he'd obviously annoyed at least some of the locals.

I watched him say something to the hecklers, and after a moment the protesters backed away, letting him through, apparently content to wave their placards and leave it at that. Jim appeared relaxed and good-humoured. I thought he had it all well under control. Whatever he'd said had defused the situation.

He'd just reached the outer doors of the vestibule and was about to pass through, when one of the protesters abruptly broke ranks, stepped forward and blocked him.

It was like watching a silent movie. I was frustrated I couldn't hear what was said, but the young man was clearly passionate about his cause. He tried to grab Jim by his coat sleeves and, when Jim stepped back, followed him, jabbing his forefinger into Jim's chest as he made his points.

I suddenly realised it was the man I'd spoken to in the lobby.

In an instant Jim's demeanour changed. He stepped forward and said something short and sharp to his accoster. Even from behind the glass I could see the menace expressed in his body language. It caused the journalist to back off, obviously intimidated.

"Fuck." The voice from behind startled me, and I had a deja-vu moment.

I turned, and found two other men also watching the action in the lobby.

"He'll be fine" the one reassured the other. "He can look after himself."

"That fucking faggot of a journo needs to be dealt to. He's bloody trouble, sticking his nose in where it's not wanted." The speaker was young, tall, slender, and wearing a leather jacket. I wasn't sure whether his aggression was due to an objection to the journalist's sexuality or his profession. Either way I disliked his attitude.

The other man, was older and smaller, dressed in a non-descript jacket and trousers. "Don't be stupid," he replied.

He'd registered I was watching, and gave me a slight placatory smile as he shut his companion up.

I swung back to watch Jim who was studying the group aligned against him. I assume he said something scornful. The expression on his face was withering and his opponents looked thoroughly cowed.

Just before he turned to stride through the doors, Jim looked up and realised I was still standing on the far side of the glass.

I saw the slight shock on his face before he recovered, gave me another twinkly smile and walked out into the night.

The lights of a car swung around the drive and drew up in front of the doors. I recognised it and went into the vestibule, making my way through the group of protesters which had now gathered supportively around their spokesperson. In the fluorescent light of the lobby his face looked white and shocked.

DEAR READER,

Thank you for reading *Death on D'Urville*. I hope you enjoyed it.

I was fortunate to spend several years working as a light aircraft pilot and instructor, flying out of Paraparaumu Airport. It was inevitable that I would one day use that beautiful and dynamic environment as a background in my novels.

The character of Claire herself is an amalgam of women pilots I met during that time. As a breed they are sassy, courageous and confident women. I hope this series pays tribute to them. Although gender equality has meant an increasing number of women choosing aviation as a career, they make up only a small proportion of the overall number of pilots, a fact I still find surprising.

I realised early on that there were simply too many stories and adventures centred round aviation for me to contain them all in one novel, so a series was born.

As an author and teller of stories, I love feedback from my readers. You are the reason I write, so tell me what you liked, what you loved and what you hated. I'd love to hear from you.

You can write to me at penelope@penelopehaines.com.

Finally, I need to ask a favour of you. If you're so inclined, I'd appreciate a review of *Death on D'Urville*. Loved it, hated it – I'd just enjoy your feedback. As you may know, reviews can be tough to come by. If you have the time, please leave a review on Amazon.com or Goodreads.com. You, the reader, now have the power to make or break the book.

Thank you so much for reading *Death on D'Urville* and for spending time with me.

Penelope

ACKNOWLEDGEMENTS

It takes help from a large number of people to put a book together. To each of you who helped me write Death on D'Urville, some in small ways, others hugely, my heartfelt thanks.

First in line are the wonderful team in my office – Kelly Pettitt and Ruth Holman – who were pressed into service as beta readers. I owe an inestimable debt to Kelly in particular for her frank but constructive criticism during the various revisions of the original draft and for her meticulously detailed notes. Kelly is also responsible for the cover artwork, the photograph of me inside the back cover and was a godsend as my personal IT division every time I ran into problems with the computer or with formatting.

Sergeant Graham Gubb at Police National Headquarters kindly answered my many questions about police procedure. If, in spite of his assistance, there are any errors, they are entirely my own.

Sue Reidy and Tina Shaw provided invaluable criticism, guidance and encouragement during the revision process, patient and helpful in the advice they offered. I also owe thanks to Debbie Watson for early proofreading. Finally, my deepest thanks to Adrienne Morris who edited and proofread the final manuscript.

My gratitude to my husband Cavan who sustained me, helped in a thousand ways and never fails to encourage me.

My thanks to Reilly for spending the long hours with me and wagging encouragement; Pascal who lay on my lap as I typed away at the keyboard; and Cash, on whose broad back I cantered away from the frustrations inherent in the creative process.

ABOUT THE AUTHOR

Penelope came to New Zealand as an eleven-year-old after a childhood spent in India and Pakistan. As an only child, reading was her hobby – she read everything that came her way, a habit which has continued throughout her life.

On leaving school she trained as a nurse, without fully considering that a brisk default attitude of 'pull yourself together and stop whining' might not be an ideal prerequisite for the industry. Conceding, at last, that nurturing was not her dominant characteristic, she changed career path and after graduating with a BA (Hons) in English Literature, moved into management consultancy, which better suited her personality type.

After some years of family life she worked as a commercial pilot and flight instructor, spending her days ferrying clients into strips in the Marlborough Sounds and discouraging students from killing her as she taught them to fly.

Penelope lives with her husband, dog, cat and horse in Otaki, New Zealand.

Death on D'Urville was the first novel in her *Claire Hardcastle* series.

Straight and Level takes place some three months after *Death on D'Urville*.

Stall Turns, the third in the series, continues to follow Claire's adventures.

Her previous novels are *The Lost One* and *Helen Had a Sister.*

All novels are available in various formats from Amazon. com.

Paperback editions can be purchased within New Zealand from Paper Plus, Unity Books and other reputable book stores and suppliers. Alternatively, they can be ordered from Penelope's website - www.penelopehaines.com, and you can visit Penelope on Facebook @penelopehainesbooks.

Made in the USA
Middletown, DE
23 December 2020